THE MERIWETHER MURDER

"Do you smell something?" Pepper asked, halting on the porch steps.

I sniffed. She was right. Mixed with the scent of dust from the house and the reek of river mud that permeated the air was another odor, something pungent. I walked across the porch to open the door and poked my head inside.

"It's gasoline," I said.

Before Pepper could answer a rush of hot air slapped me backward as the fumes ignited.

The flash lasted only a split second, but in that instant an image of the back room etched itself in my mind—cabinets, shelves, counters, an overturned trash can, and the body of a man.

Other Alan Graham Mysteries by
Malcolm Shuman
from Avon Twilight

BURIAL GROUND

THE
MERIWETHER MURDER

AN ALAN GRAHAM MYSTERY

MALCOLM SHUMAN

THE NEW ENGLAND
STEAMSHIP COMPANY
OF MASSACHUSETTS

TWILIGHT

AVON BOOKS, INC.
1350 Avenue of the Americas
New York, New York 10019

Copyright © 1998 by Malcolm K. Shuman
Inside cover author photo by Thomas A. Wintz, Jr.
Published by arrangement with the author
Library of Congress Catalog Card Number: 98-93124
ISBN: 0-380-79424-1
www.avonbooks.com/twilight

First Avon Twilight Printing: November 1998

AVON TWILIGHT TRADEMARK REG. U.S. PAT. OFF. AND IN OTHER COUNTRIES, MARCA REGISTRADA, HECHO EN U.S.A.

Printed in the U.S.A.

WCD 10 9 8 7 6 5 4 3 2

*This is for Patricia Ann Roberts,
with affection.*

ACKNOWLEDGMENTS

The author is indebted to a number of people. These include the authors of previous works on Meriwether Lewis and the mystery of Lewis's death: Vardis Fisher, David Leon Chandler, Richard Dillon, and Stephen Ambrose. Also of invaluable assistance was the staff of the Lewis & Clark Trail Heritage Foundation, Inc., which furnished back issues of their publication, *We Proceeded On*, a gold mine of scholarly information on Lewis and Clark. Jonathan Daniels and William C. Davis have both written excellent books on the Natchez Trace. Ms. Pat Choate, director of the J. H. Warf Public Library of Hohenwald, Tennessee, was most helpful. Linda Gavin gave us a fascinating tour of the Blackburn farmstead in Lewis County. My wife, Margaret, accompanied me up the Natchez Trace, camped with me on the grounds of the Meriwether Lewis National Monument, and served as a sounding board throughout. Dennis Jones, Carl Kuttruff, and Guy Weaver all aided me regarding the current location of Fort Pickering. Becky Hill provided information about DNA testing. Paul Lemke gave me advice on Louisiana law. And last, but hardly least, were my editors, Coates Bateman and Jennifer Sawyer Fisher, who encouraged this project from start to finish, and my agent, Peter Rubie.

In this work, the author, for simplicity, has adopted Grinder's as the name of Lewis's last stopping place because that version of the name has prevailed in popular history. It should be noted, however, that the proper spelling of the name is Griner, and Griner is the version still favored in that part of Tennessee.

▦ PROLOGUE

It was midnight and the November wind raked the eaves of the great house. Inside one of the bedrooms, the tall man stared out through the window from his seat at the long writing table. Overhead, his pet mockingbird flew from one end of the room to the other, finally settling on the man's shoulder.

He was sure he'd heard a sound outside, a jingling of harness. Ordinarily, a visitor would not arrive this late, but the man was expecting someone, and he dreaded what the visitor was going to say.

Perhaps it had been his imagination. He drew his woolen robe close and settled back to consider the papers spread before him. Nine months had passed since the burden of office had been lifted from his shoulders, but there was no such thing as retirement. He was immersed in the building of a great university, whose buildings he was designing himself, and his social life was as busy as ever, for scientists, inventors, and diplomats all sought him out. It was only late at night, when his guests had retired, that he could be truly alone.

But tonight his mind was not on his studies. Too much troubled him: A trusted friend was dead, and it was the details that the tall man had to learn. The details were all-important. What had his friend found out? What had he told others? What evidence had his friend possessed? There were sinister forces at work, and now, with the country again on the verge of war with a foreign power, the nation's survival could depend largely on what a dead man had known.

1

The tall man rose and went to the cabinet in one corner of the room, where he took out the decanter of water and poured himself a drink.

Damn it, he should never have put a friend in that position. The pressure had been too great and there were signs his friend had cracked under the weight. But what else could he have done? The man he'd appointed first had been the author of the present trouble, and the tall man had needed someone to assess the extent of the damage.

As he stared out through the window at darkness, a soft knocking reverberated from the door.

The man sighed. His hearing had not lied: The visitor he expected had arrived and there was no delaying the inevitable. He went to the mirror, gathered his graying red hair into a knot at the back, and tied it. Then he took a deep breath and turned back to the door.

"Yes?"

The door opened slowly, revealing the face of one of his servants.

"A visitor, Master Jefferson. He said you were waiting for him."

Thomas Jefferson, lately president of the United States, but now a gentleman farmer who dabbled in politics, nodded gravely.

"I have indeed. Please show him in."

Almost two hundred years later, that was how I imagined it happening. Two hundred years too late . . .

☰ONE

The headstone leaned at an awkward angle, a gray slab with a single name chiseled on its face:

LOUIS

Below the name was a legend:

Died July 3, 1863

The crypt was like the others in the cemetery: old bricks, once faced with cement, but most of the cement had long since flaked off, with gaping cavities in the sides of the vault where tree roots had tunneled.

I gazed around at the other stones, crooked teeth biting at the September wind.

"At first I thought it was a slave's grave," the young woman said. "The single name and all. A faithful servant, buried in the family plot."

I nodded. It was what I would have thought, too, looking at the crypts of those who had owned Désirée Plantation over the last two hundred years.

Eleanor Hollings Hardin Fabré
born August 21, 1834
died September 12, 1906
Our Mother

And a few yards away:

> *Sarah Elizabeth Hardin*
> *born May 22, 1829*
> *died November 19, 1835*
> *Our Love, Now with God*

And near the center, the tomb of the patriarch:

> *Dr. Charles Franklin Hardin*
> *born March 4, 1770*
> *died December 12, 1825*
> *A Loving Father and Dear Husband*

It was a small cemetery, confined by a wrought-iron fence to the top of an ancient Indian mound. A live oak threw half the little plot into afternoon shade and its dead leaves danced across our feet.

"This is the one who wrote the journal, Alan." She pointed out a grave to the left of the patriarch's and I looked down:

> *John Clay Hardin*
> *born June 30, 1803*
> *died March 11, 1865*

"The journal mentions Louis," she explained, brushing her blond hair away from designer glasses.

There were three of us there: myself, Alan Graham, contract archaeologist; the middle-aged black man who ran the place; and the woman, whose name was Pepper. Thirty years old and as determined as she was attractive, she'd agreed to serve as historical archaeologist under our contract with the Corps of Engineers to survey a stretch of Mississippi River levee just upstream from Baton Rouge. We'd worked together before, more or less. Which is to say, we'd survived our mutual differences. We'd almost gotten to the point where we liked each other.

"You know Miss Ouida, the owner?" I asked the caretaker.

"I know her," he said and that was it. His name was Brady Flowers and I got the feeling he wished we'd go the hell away. But it wasn't because he was busy working on the plantation house: Désirée was slowly falling to pieces and there were no indications that anybody cared.

"She ever say anything to you about this Louis?" I asked, nodding at the grave.

"She didn't say nothing," Flowers said. "All we heard he was a pirate or something. That's what the old people say. Don't matter to me. Don't know why it matter to *anybody*. Now I gotta go take care of my bees."

I looked past the oak to a collection of white bee boxes at the foot of the levee. Beyond the earthen embankment stretched the gray expanse of the river. A slight haze hung over the far bank, from the refineries on the east side.

Too bad the river couldn't talk.

I got out my camera and took a roll of pictures while the others watched, photographing each headstone and recording the direction and subject of the shot in my notebook.

"Well, thanks for showing us," I said, zipping up my camera bag. "We may come back and take some rubbings."

Flowers grunted. It was clear he didn't think much of archaeologists.

I let the other two go ahead while I unloaded the film from my camera. Then I picked my way down the mound into the shady field behind the big house, where Pepper waited. I tried to picture the place as it had been in 1850, when John Clay Hardin had been its master and a man with only the single name, "Louis," had lived in one of the wooden outbuildings that was now long gone. A scene from Gone With the Wind hovered in front of my mind, but I knew better: Plantation life wasn't a succession of balls given by Old Massa while happy slaves sang in the fields. It was tough work for everybody, the plantation owners included. We skirted the pond with the cement figure of a black boy fishing and came to the little wooden chapel where the owners had worshiped. We halted, but Flowers had already gone the other way, to his bees.

"Pierre Fabré built the chapel when he bought the plantation right after the war," Pepper said. "The original owners weren't Catholic, but Pierre wanted his own church on the grounds. I guess he didn't want to have to cross the river to go to mass."

Good enough reason, I thought, and followed her across

the lawn toward the big house. The grass came to our ankles and the house itself hadn't been painted in a quarter century. Not, I thought, since Pepper was a child. Suddenly I felt old.

We came around to the front of the house, where an avenue of live oaks stretched along a gravel drive to the two-lane blacktop a quarter mile away.

"They're just letting it fall apart," Pepper said with disapproval, indicating the sagging balcony and leaning pillars. "Word is that they want to sell it for a plant site."

"They?" I asked.

"The administrator of the estate. Nick DeLage. He's the nephew of the owner, Ouida Fabré. He sells insurance. Got her declared incompetent and stuck her in a rest home. But he didn't know she took some of the old papers with her."

I stopped at the red Blazer in the driveway and reached for my car keys.

"Well, let's go see Miss Ouida," I said.

We headed back across the river to Baton Rouge, a city that has long spread beyond its initial Spanish nucleus to encompass a university on the south and a cauldron of chemical refineries on the north. The nursing home was in the southern part of the city, in a commercial area that had been pasture when I was growing up here over thirty years ago. Now it was a clogged asphalt two-lane with restaurants, doctors' offices, and a couple of branch banks. The nursing home itself was set back from the street at the end of a circular drive. The sign said GREENOAKS RETIREMENT SHELTER, like it was advertising a mutual fund. I parked in the lot and checked my watch. Four-ten.

"We'll make it right between nap time and dinner," Pepper said.

"We call it supper down here," I said, smiling, and she heaved an exaggerated sigh.

"Rub it in," she said, coming to the big glass entrance door. I held it open and she hesitated, then laughed and walked through.

"Alan, you'll never change," she said. "What worries me is I'm not sure I want you to."

There was a time when we'd been at daggers' points, after she'd come down from Boston a year ago and announced her intention to run me out of business as a contract archaeologist. But we'd ended up working on a couple of projects since then, almost getting ourselves killed the first time out, and that made for a strange bond, whatever the differences of age and upbringing. Besides, I told myself, watching her slim figure precede me, with curves in all the right places, she was a damned nice-looking young woman.

It was the *young* part that bothered me. She was young enough to be my, well, *protégé*.

"We'd like to see Miss Ouida Mae Fabré," she told a thin woman behind a big glass panel. "Is she feeling like having visitors?"

The receptionist's narrow face cracked into a smile.

"I'm sure she is. She doesn't get many. Weren't you here just the other day?"

"Yesterday," Pepper said.

The skinny receptionist nodded. "I'll buzz and see if she's up."

I turned away from the window, shivering. It was cold in the hallway, but it wasn't just from the air conditioning. Pepper's hand touched my arm and I looked up.

"I really appreciate it, Alan."

"How's that?" I knew what she was going to say, but I wanted to hear it all.

"Catering to me. I mean, this is just a sort of tangent. All you hired me to do was research the historical background of the plantation and conduct some artifact analysis. I guess I let myself get carried away by the unanswered questions."

I felt an archaeological lecture coming on but caught myself.

"Tangents can be productive," I said.

"And they can be costly, too. A couple of years ago I'd have said none of this fit into the model."

"I'll leave that to Bombast," I said. Bertha Bomberg, a.k.a. La Bombast, was our contact at New Orleans District, Corps of Engineers. She doled out the projects under our current contract and then did her best to hinder us as we worked on them. At least, that was from a contractor's point of view. I'm sure we were all simply money-grubbing vermin to her.

"I just got caught up in it," Pepper went on, as if an apology for enjoying one's work was necessary. "When I thought of this poor man, Louis, and how no one really knew who he was, not even his last name, even though he lived there all those years on the plantation . . . And his last words, calling for the president . . . There has to be an explanation. And that's why I thought maybe you could sweet-talk her into lending us the diary long enough to get it copied.''

"I'll try," I said.

A young, perky woman in white appeared in the hallway. "Miss Ouida's in the dayroom," she said. "If you'll come this way . . ."

We followed her down a well-lit corridor that smelled vaguely of fried food. We turned a corner and emerged into a large room with a couple of television sets turned low and a handful of card tables. At a couple of the tables there seemed to be games going on, but most of the players stared straight ahead, like mannequins.

"Here we go," our guide said brightly. "Miss Ouida, you have company."

The old woman in the wheelchair looked up, frowning slightly. She had cottony white hair and translucent veins under a palimpsest-thin skin. She wore a housecoat and there was a blanket on her lap.

"I know you," she said to Pepper. "You came here yesterday to talk about the plantation."

The attendant flashed an especially bright smile, as if her charge had done something clever, and patted the old woman on the shoulder.

"I'll leave you all to visit," she said and melted away.

Pepper took Miss Ouida's hand.

"That's right. You showed me your books, the ones you got from your father."

"Yes." Miss Ouida considered me with pale blue eyes. "Is this your young man?"

Pepper blushed and I grinned.

"We work together," I said.

"Oh." The answer seemed to satisfy her.

"I brought you something," Pepper said, reaching into her bag and handing the old lady a box of chocolates. "I hope you can have them."

"Elmer's," Miss Ouida exclaimed, taking the box with both hands as if it were a fragile artifact. "I love them." She sighed. "Not many people come to visit, you know. Just my nephew, and I haven't seen him since . . ." She frowned, letting the sentence trail off.

"That's Nick," Pepper said to me.

"Nicholas," Miss Ouida corrected. "Do you know him?"

"No, ma'am," I said.

Pepper leaned over so she wouldn't have to speak loudly.

"This is Dr. Alan Graham. He was interested in what you told me about the plantation and the people who used to own it. I told him about the man called Louis. He thought it was an interesting story, too."

Miss Ouida nodded slowly.

"Very interesting." Her fingers started to work on the candy box, but the cellophane wrapping defeated her, so I picked it up and tore the end off, and then took the top off the box.

"Thank you." She looked down, hesitated a second over which candy to select, and then opted for a chocolate cherry.

"I haven't had one of these in ages," she said, chewing slowly, her eyes closed. "You're so kind."

"Our pleasure," Pepper said. "You said there were stories even in your time about this man?"

Miss Ouida chewed, oblivious, and for a moment I thought she'd forgotten the question. Then she spoke again:

"There was a story he was the Man Without a Country. Somebody said that, anyway, but I don't know. I always thought that story was made up."

"It was," I said. "There was a Philip Nolan, but he wasn't court-martialed at Fort Adams, Mississippi, and, from what I remember, he actually died a good many years before the story was supposed to take place."

"Then I don't know," Miss Ouida said. "I just know the grave was always there and the colored people were scared of it, called him Boogie Louie, something about he was murdered, but, of course, that's not true. They just made all that up."

She found another chocolate and we watched her chew it and swallow.

"I'll tell you one thing, though, I got the scare of my life up there when I was little. I had an uncle who loved to frighten us, make us believe there were spooks, and he dared us to go up there one Halloween. Said Boogie Louie was going to get us. Well, I had to take the dare and, of course, he was waiting, with a sheet over his head.'' She laughed under her breath. ''I can still feel how my heart just stopped.''

Pepper bent lower, her mouth near the old woman's ear.

''Miss Ouida, do you think Dr. Graham could have a look at your books?''

Miss Ouida dropped her eyes. ''Did Nicholas send you?''

''I don't know him,'' I said. ''We're just interested in history. We're trying to write the history of the people who lived at Désirée: your family. We don't want it to be lost.''

''There's a lot of history there,'' she agreed vaguely.

I took a deep breath. ''If I could have your diary for just tonight, I could copy it and get it back to you tomorrow.''

''Copy it? Oh, you mean on one of those machines.''

''Yes, ma'am.''

''I really don't know.''

''I understand,'' I said, knowing it would do no good to push.

''He was your great-great-grandfather, wasn't he?'' Pepper said. ''John Clay Hardin, who wrote the diary?''

''Yes, I think that was it. Papa explained it once.'' Her voice faded and I straightened up to go.

''The plantation was something back then,'' the old lady said. ''Sugar and cotton. And all those Negroes to work the fields. They say it was really something. Not like now.''

''No,'' I agreed.

''Have you been out there?'' she asked suddenly, her watery eyes fixing on my own. ''Have you seen it?''

I nodded. ''Yes, ma'am.''

''Nicholas said he was going to take care of it. He promised when he brought me here.''

Pepper and I exchanged glances.

''I miss it, you know. The people are nice here, but it isn't the same. Nicholas said I couldn't keep up the old place, that I'd fall, hurt myself, but I told him I always had help, that they could look after me.''

I didn't say anything.

''He didn't mean it, though. Nicholas never cared about Désirée. All he sees is money. He'd sell it to the first buyer.'' She looked past us into a world that didn't exist any longer.

"You have to understand: The diary is all I have."

"Sure." I gave her hand a pat. "Take care, Miss Ouida. Thanks."

I glanced over at Pepper and she nodded. It was time to go. Then, unexpectedly, she bent down and gave the old lady's cheek a quick kiss. She looked away when she saw my eyes on her.

"Let's go," she said under her breath.

We turned and started out, but we only made it a few steps before Miss Ouida's voice caught us.

"Wait."

We turned around.

"Yes, ma'am?" I asked.

"Call the girl and tell her I need to go to my room for something. You can have the books."

Two

I took Pepper to her apartment on Delgado, in University Acres. She sat in my vehicle with the door open for a long time.

"I knew Nicholas was a sleaze," she said. "That old lady isn't any more incompetent than I am."

"No," I said.

"So why are you staring at me?"

"Oh, nothing," I said, smiling.

"What, I'm not supposed to have feelings just because I'm a Yankee?"

"I never said that."

"No." She nodded at the brown paper parcel on the seat between us. "Well, at least we got the diary."

"Yep."

"Call me tomorrow," she said. "Tell me what you think after you've read it."

I watched her walk down the driveway to the garage apartment that once had been a source of embarrassment to her. The defensiveness of last year had all but disappeared. If only I were ten years younger . . . Nah, it would never work.

I drove back through the Louisiana State University campus, quiet now on a Thursday evening. I'd gone to school here a long time ago, studied, dated, taken long walks under the moss-dripped oaks. The students looked younger these days and there were more buildings crowded into what had once been tree-shaded space. Sometimes I felt very old, but on days like this one, in the early fall, with the first hint of crispness in the air, my spirit roused itself. I loved this time of year.

And besides, I had something to look forward to: the diary.

I went through the north gates into the war zone called Tiger Town. In the daytime students frequent the restaurants, stores, and bars, but at night the hoodlums come out. Freaks, muggers, psychos—this part of town has them all. Contract archaeologists, too. This is where our office is located.

I pulled into the parking lot behind the big frame two-story that we rented in a cul-de-sac off State Street, in the heart of the ghetto. It was after five and the place was deserted. Not even any winos sleeping on the back porch. I went up the steps with the paper bag in one hand, avoided the weak floorboard, and unlocked the door. Once inside, I punched my private number into the keypad and saw the indicator light go green.

The big central room that served as a lab seemed cavernous. Two long tables in the middle held neatly sorted piles of potsherds, lithic flakes, and bits of glass from one of our excavations, and the filing cabinets along one wall contained site records and contract data. The place smelled of dirt— hardly strange considering that most of the material on the tables had lain in the earth for hundreds of years.

I went into my office, an erstwhile bedroom that had been divided by drywall and paneled with oak veneer. Two walls were covered by bookcases salvaged from yard sales and the window behind me framed a shell parking lot that had once been a backyard. I flipped on the light and regarded the stack of papers on my desk.

A couple of draft reports to be read over prior to submission, a note from my associate, David Goldman, telling me he and his crew would be leaving early to go to the Atchafalaya Basin to start a Corps project, and a message from Rosemary Amadie, the president of the local archaeological society.

I groaned as I read it. A teacher who lived with her old father, Rose Amadie was the kind of amateur who could take all my time through sheer enthusiasm, if I let her. Still, she meant well and I'd just have to see what she wanted.

Then I spotted the folder with Marilyn's printouts of our latest balance sheet. I stuck the folder in my desk drawer to get it out of sight, because just knowing it was there was depressing. There was a note pinned to it reminding me to hassle a dermatologist who'd gotten fifteen grand's worth of work out of us for a subdivision he was developing and who, four months later, was still stalling on payment, because the Corps was slow in issuing his wetlands permit.

The part of my job I hated.

Well, it would wait. I hadn't gotten into archaeology to read balance sheets. I'd gotten into it to have fun and because a certain part of me felt more comfortable with the dilemmas of history than with the trials of real life.

I unwrapped the parcel Miss Ouida had given me and looked down at what was inside.

There were three of them, leather-bound daybooks of the kind popular in the last century. Each consisted of a set of pages bound between two covers and used for journals and ledgers.

I sat down behind my desk and opened the first one. On the top of the first page I saw the name *John Clay Hardin* in a flowing, black script, and below it the date *December 12, 1825.* The ink was faded and the pages yellowing, but the cursive was easy enough to make out, even with the misspellings.

I read the first entry:

December 12, 1825. *This day my father, Dr. Charles Franklin Hardin, was taken from us at the age of 55 years. Now I become the master of Désirée, may God help me. I will miss you, Father, but the pain is made less by knowing you are with my dear Mother.*

December 14, 1825. *Father was buryed today, on top of the mound. I comanded Tom and Dickens to dig the grave but a strange thing hapened. Louis, who seems particularly afected, insisted on digging the grave himself so I let him, though it is not white man's work and I would not want the negroes to think the wrong thing. Later, after the service, I talked to Louis & he told me no man had been kinder to him than Father, who took him up out of the river after the tremors fourteen years ago. I was much afected myself by this. I wish I knew* *more about Louis, who he was and his people, but he says he does not remember anything before coming here. He may have fallen from a flat boat, but Father always said he had the air of a gentleman. Poor Louis. Poor all of us.*

I sat back, trying to remember. I'd heard about the 1811 New Madrid quake. It had been the most destructive in U.S. history. It wouldn't have been good to be on the river when it hit.

I leafed through the pages, curious now to learn more about the strange man called Louis whose grave I'd visited a few hours before.

But the better part of the ledger entries were mundane.

March 4, 1826. *Day cold, fog heavy untill 10:00. Planting corn.*

March 5, 1826. *Still cold. Edward's little Amelia ill. Dont know if she will survive. Ploughing for cotton. Saw a bear in the back field & shot but missed.*

March 10, 1826. *Miss Mason and Miss Fournet in evening. Dr Sparks came by to treat old Abe, who was thrown by mule.*

And then, on July 14:

Ainsworth elected to legislature. We will see how he turns out. The man has always acted above himself & mistreets his negroes something terible. News reached us yesterday of the death of Pres Jefferson on July 4th. Information had a strange effect on old Louis, who imediately asked how he had died and for all information, etc, etc. He left his work (He is reparing a gin at Cotters place) and I saw him walking by the river. Seemed more melancholy than usual. Asked him if he had a special affection for Mr Jeffsn & he said only that the man had often been in his dreams. Lost a good dog to snake bite today.

I reread the entry and silently cursed John Clay Hardin for his brevity. Why would an amnesic drifter be particularly affected by the death of an ex-president? But then, why should the man be amnesic to begin with? Might that not in itself point to some mental problem? And didn't people with severe mental problems experience distorted thinking? Who knew what connection Louis might have imagined he shared with Thomas Jefferson? I skipped through several more entries. Louis appeared only one more time before the end of the year.

December 4, 1826. *Tomorrow to be happiest day of my Life, when I wed Miss Judalon Fournet. Wish Mother & Father could be here. Louis insists on giving her horse he has worked with since a colt. I have noticed a strange look in his eyes lately, as maybe he is thinking what his life might have been. Have talked to him many times over years, but his life before coming here is unknown to him. Most of time seems happy in his little cabin near overseers place, with little garden and fixing things. Excelent gun smith and knows more about natural history than any man I ever met & is versed in remedies for cholic, fever, etc. But other times seems excessively melancholy. Sometimes when his door is locked I think he is taking spirits but he has never appeared outside in a disorderly state. Wonders if he has a family somewhere, etc. Last year, when he had ague I went with Dr Sparks to his cabin. Poor Louis was lying on the floor, on his bed of animal skins—He never has acustomed himself to a reglar bed. He was deranged & talking about making sure boat didnt sink, was iron, too heavy. Have never heerd of iron boats & Dr S said it is most likely his indisposition talking. When he came to himself he said he couldnt remember anything. From scar on his head I wonder if he was shot once.*

The ledger ended with the year 1830. As time passed, John Clay Hardin had become less conscientious about his diary: After 1829 he seemed to have lost the energy to make daily entries, saving his pen for what he considered important events: the birth of a child, the death of a family member or slave, an economic, political, or social occasion of note. I wondered if it had something to do with the death of his firstborn, Adam, whom he buried in 1829, at age eleven months.

I went to the next book, which covered the years 1831 to 1855. As with the last year of the first book, the entries in this ledger were sparse. I read complaints about Jacksonian politics, including a lengthy diatribe against the state constitution of 1845, which he felt slighted the planters, and apparent satisfaction with the pro-Whig constitution of 1852, which replaced it. He mentioned the births and deaths of two more children, the sales of crops, and the status of his slaves. The writing was less disciplined now, more of a scrawl, and the entries briefer, as if a weariness had leached the joy from his soul. There were only occasional references to Louis.

I closed the book, moved it to the side, and stared down at the scuffed leather cover of the final volume.

We were wasting our time, I told myself: Bombast only wanted a report, with the usual boilerplate and a dry recitation of the pertinent facts. That was, after all, what contract archaeology was all about. You were paid to assist your client, whether private or public, to obtain an environmental clearance, and the two things that counted most were price and speed. Only academics were given the luxury of following the twists and turns of a line of data simply out of interest.

Well, the hell with Bombast, I thought, and slowly opened the cover of the last volume.

There were few entries for 1856 through 1860. But thereafter, as the secession crisis deepened, there were more comments of a political nature.

January 1, 1861. *Day cool, clear. Negroes working on back field. Mr Chambers came to visit. News is secession likely & welcome. Mr C feels they will let us go in peace, Lincoln weak reed, etc. I am less hopefull, depends on England, cotton market, etc. Mr C said "God willing." I said I wish I could be sure the Almighty was involved.*

And three weeks later:

*Spoke with old Louis. Very feebel now, must be almost
ninety years, maybe more. Still plants his little garden
behind house, wont let the negroes fool with it. Com-
plaining his eyes bad, cant see to gather herbs. Getting
silly I think. Talked about dreams of prairies and rivers,
going there, almost like the negroes talking about
heaven. I went to his cabin yesterday, saw him looking
at his little steel box. Asked him what he kept in it &
he said only a few old papers, but seemed not willing
for me to see them, so left him alone. I remember Father
said he had papers in an oilskin when he was found by
the river & how he looked at them & made no sense,
so left them & afterwards the papers disapered. He fig-
ered Louis had buried them, because he was so protecting about it when they found him, etc. Maybe this
is whatever he keeps in the box. Asked him what he
thought about secession & he said hoped it wouldnt
hapen, etc. Not sure he understands much these days,
though.*

A few months later:

April 15, 1861. *It is War though what kind of war no
one knows. Talked to old Louis about it but dont think
he understood. Was busy in his garden, though dont
know what he expects to grow there. Old fellow hasnt
much longer I fear. Bay mare gave birth to colt this
evening & all well.*

The last entry concerning Louis appeared on July 10, 1861:

*The end came for old Louis this morning just after 6
oclock. Last night he sank into a sleep from which he
awoke just before dawn, when my wife called me saying
he wished me there. When I arrived he was awake, eyes
clear, etc, & he took my hand with a force I didnt expect
& told me I was to bring his box to the president if
anything hapened to him & I was to promise to do that
on my honor as I had saved him, etc, etc & I was to
give it to the Presdt personaly, etc. He said the Presdt*

would know about the artichokes, which must refer to his garden, tho I never knew artichokes were planted there. Clear he thought I was Father & seeing he was close to the end I gave my word and he sank back with a look of peace good to see and half an hr later stoped breathing intirely & went to his Maker. Have his will, poor old fellow, which he wrote some time ago, gave to me for safe keeping, but not much to bequeeth, but will file it as requested, etc. Thus ended a strange life We will probably never know the all of & have given orders he is to be buryed in the family plot near Father as he was truely a friend & member of the family even though we do not know even his last name, which only the Maker of all of us knows. Cannot explain the weight I feel on me as if everything is ending.

Searched for the lock box later & could not find it. May have been taken by a negro. Will search in quarters for it though cannot believe any of mine have done such a thing.

Thus the strange Louis vanished from the journal of John Clay Hardin. The journal itself lasted only two more years. I read news of the war, falling cotton prices, the Union occupation of Baton Rouge, and the unsuccessful Rebel effort to retake the city in August 1862, all leavened with an increasing cynicism. And then, at the end of November 1864, the journal stopped. I checked my notebook. John Clay Hardin had died in March 1865, at the age of sixty-one. I didn't know the cause of his demise, but I knew that during the Civil War many plantation owners had succumbed to the combinations of stress and the usual diseases of the day.

I rubbed my eyes and reread the section detailing Louis's last hours: *He said the Presdt would know about the artichokes* . . . How was I supposed to interpret that? Was there some logic to it, or was it the raving of a dying man? John Clay Hardin had described the old man as awake, with clear eyes. But Hardin was no physician: Clearly Louis had been seeing something that happened long before, and if that was the case, who was to say his memory wasn't the invention of a tortured mind?

Now I knew why Pepper had insisted I read the journals.

The story of Louis was an intriguing problem. It might never be solved, but it was still worth looking into, if for no other reason than our own intellectual satisfaction.

I rewrapped the journals and locked them in my desk drawer. Then I went to the bookshelf in the lab room and looked for a reference on West Baton Rouge Parish. There was the *Louisiana Almanac,* which gave general information, and a slim, privately published history of famous plantations along the river, by one Adrian Prescott. I thumbed through it, found a reference to Désirée, and put the book in my pocket for background reading at home. Then I drove back to the old house on Park Boulevard. I had grown up there and inherited it when my parents had died. Now it was still filled with what, for want of a better term, could be called memorabilia. I put the journals in my study, fed my mixed shepherd, Digger, who tried to climb into my lap (all seventy-five pounds of him), and checked my answering machine. Nothing.

I changed into running shorts. I couldn't do anything about my age (mid-forties) or slightly receding brown hair, but I could duke it out with the extra ten pounds that kept creeping up on me. After a couple of miles around the lakes, I came back, showered, changed, and, feeling virtuous, went down to the Country Corner on Perkins and got a few links of boudin. So much for resolve. When I'd eaten, I drove out to the university library and looked up some sources on antebellum plantation life. I read until ten and drove back home, watched a tape of *The Caine Mutiny,* and went to bed. In my dreams I kept seeing the strange old man called Louis, waiting on the banks of the river like a lost soul; waiting for the boat that would take him home.

The image was still hovering in my mind the next morning when I wandered into the office, turned on my computer, and found out somebody didn't want me to learn more.

 # THREE

It was the only E-mail message waiting for me and it was to the point:

DO NOT GO BACK TO DESIREE. IF YOU DO, WHAT HAPPENS
WILL BE ON YOUR HEAD.

I stared at it and then at the gobbledygook of letters at the top that stood for an address. I walked into the lab. A couple of workers were sorting potsherds at one of the long tables and a thin young man with thick glasses sat at a desk in the corner, inputting data into a computer. L. Franklin Hill was the lab supervisor as well as our resident computer guru. I caught his eye and he got up and followed me into my office. I motioned him around the desk and pointed to the computer screen.

"Thing crashed again?" he asked, frowning. "I thought I fixed that."

"Read the message," I said.

He bent over and then looked up at me.

"Is this a joke?"

"I don't know. Not that many people know we're working at Désirée."

"Ummm." He drummed his fingers on the table. "Maybe Freddie?"

Freddie St. Ambrose was one of our local competitors, an unscrupulous operator with dubious credentials who would close his eyes to tearing down the Great Pyramid for a parking lot if the price was right.

"He's not above it," I said. "But there would have to be something in it for him. Can you trace this back to the place it was sent from?"

Frank Hill shrugged. "Theoretically. But nobody who'd send this kind of thing would do it from their own computer. Let's see . . ."

His fingers began to dance over the keyboard while I paced back and forth. Minutes later Hill grunted.

"About what I thought. This comes from the computer lab at the university."

"Meaning?"

"Well, you can find out who this address belongs to, but I don't think it'll help you."

"Why?"

"Chances are somebody forgot to sign off and your mystery messenger cruising the lab found it. Happens all the time. Kind of like one of these Xerox machines with an access code. Somebody forgets to cancel their code when they've finished and the next person, if they're not honest, just charges it all to that account."

"Great." I looked over his shoulder at the words on the screen and then sighed. "But how did they get my E-mail address?"

He gave me a pitying look. "Isn't it on your business cards?"

"You're right. Thanks, Frank."

I let him get out of the little office and then printed out the message and stuck the paper in my top drawer. Then I exited the Internet.

It made no sense. My business cards were all over town. But the last person I remembered handing one to was Brady Flowers, the caretaker of Désirée, when we'd stopped by a week ago to ask permission to look around the place. But Flowers hadn't seemed very interested and had told us he didn't care what we did as long as we didn't tear things up.

I went into Marilyn's office. Tiny, efficient, and feisty, Marilyn served as office manager, bookkeeper and receptionist. Only twenty-five, she swore at least twice a month that she was looking for another job and at least twice a month I coaxed and flattered her into staying.

"I'm going to see Sam," I told her. Sam MacGregor was my ex-professor and mentor, the man who'd started the company and invited me to work with him when I'd returned from New Mexico some years back, after a failed marriage and no prospects. Today he lived in retirement in a plantation on the River Road and was always free with a glass of whiskey and advice.

Marilyn jerked her head away from her computer screen to consider the source of the distraction.

"You can't call him?" she asked. "We really have to go over these balance sheets."

"It's Friday," I said. "Can't it wait until Monday?"

"Monday you'll want to put it off till Tuesday."

"Got me," I said.

"And Rosemary Amadie called again. She wants you to talk to her class."

"Can't somebody else handle it?"

"She wanted *you*."

"It's wonderful to be famous," I said. "Tell her I'll get with her in a day or two."

"Like Monday?"

"Marilyn, you get smarter every day."

"And there was a woman named Goforth who's with one of the television stations. She said she heard we were working at Désirée and she wants to do an interview."

"How did she find out?" I asked.

Marilyn shrugged. "Is it a secret? I'm sure everybody in Port Allen knows. It's only the other side of the river."

"Probably," I agreed. "Well, I need Corps clearance to give interviews."

"I told her."

"Is that it?"

"Alan, you really need to call Dr. Ardoin and get him to pay up."

"I'll do it as soon as I get back from Sam's," I said and felt her disapproving eyes follow me out of the office.

It took me half an hour to reach Sam's house, partly because I stopped to pick up a bottle of Dant's, mainly because I followed the winding River Road instead of taking Nicholson, which cut off most of the curves of the river. But it gave me a chance to get my questions in order. When I got there, though, the place was closed and I remembered vaguely something Sam had said about taking a trip in the fall.

I could have called first, of course, but the drive had given me a chance to go over things in my mind, and to try to tell myself that the man buried in the mound across the river was just one of the hundreds of anonymous travelers who'd struck out for the old Southwest, as this part of antebellum America was called, and never been heard from again.

And I could have believed it if I hadn't seen the same dark car behind me on the River Road as I made my way back that I'd noticed behind me on the way down. By the time I reached Gardere Lane, on the outskirts of the city, it was gone, taking, I supposed, the short route back to town.

≡ FOUR

When I got back to the office, more urgent business pushed the car out of my mind. La Bombast wanted an update on our survey at Désirée and, as usual, took it as a personal affront that I wasn't in the office when she'd phoned. The television reporter had called again and wanted to appear at one o'clock with a camera crew. A man in Lake Charles needed an immediate quote on a pipeline through the wildlife refuge. And Rosemary Amadie, substitute schoolteacher and amateur archaeologist, was seated in a chair with her hands in her lap, looking nervous.

"I'm sorry, Alan," Marilyn whispered, following me into my office. "She just showed up."

I sighed and put down the pink message slips.

"It's okay. I'll return the calls when she leaves."

I went out to the lab room and put on a smile.

Once, I figured, Rosemary Amadie had probably been a beauty. But ever since I'd known her, which had been four or five years, she'd had the worn look of someone who'd been beaten down by the system. Now in her late forties, she had auburn hair that was stringy and gray-streaked, and worry lines etched her thin face. It came, I figured, from teaching a horde of young hellions and then going home to care for an aged parent. Truth was, I felt too sorry for her to be rude.

"Dr. Graham," she cried, jumping up. "I hope I'm not interrupting . . ."

"It's okay," I said. "What can I do for you, Mrs. Amadie?"

She told me her class was studying Indians: "Dr. Graham,

25

I hate to ask you, but would it be possible for you to come speak to the students about archaeology?''

I told her I would and she shook my hand gratefully and promised to call and set a time for me to come. I saw her out, happy to get away with such a short visit, and then turned to the message slips.

The estimate for the pipeline was priority, so I called the prospective client and told him to fax me the survey plats. Then I took a deep breath and called Bombast's number. She was in a training session so I left a message. Then I called the reporter, who was also out, and left a message that I couldn't do an interview without running it through the Corps first. These tasks accomplished, I called Frank Hill into my office and, unlocking my desk, took out the Hardin journals.

"I want you to go over to Printing Tech. Use one of the self-service machines and make a good copy of every page of these three books," I said.

"Something wrong with the machine out there?'' he asked, gesturing at the lab room where our own copier sat.

"This will take a while,'' I said. "I don't want to have to interrupt any of our other work.''

Frank left, Marilyn handed me the faxed maps from the pipeline man, and I worked on the estimate until noon. I inserted the estimate into our standard agreement, faxed it back, and was just trying to decide where I wanted to eat lunch when the phone buzzed and Marilyn told me a Mr. DeLage was on the line.

I pressed the button. "Hello?''

"Dr. Graham?''

"What can I do for you, Mr. DeLage?''

An imitation of a chuckle echoed from the other end.

"How about lunch?'' Nicholas DeLage said. "I'd like to hear what you're finding at the plantation.''

I thought for an instant and then made up my mind.

"Tell me where, Mr. DeLage.''

"How about the Camelot Club? I like to look out at the river. Say half an hour?''

"I'll be there.''

After I replaced the receiver, I sat back, trying to decide what it meant. Either he was fishing or he wanted to make a proposition. Or maybe a threat disguised as a proposition.

I reminded myself to try to find out what color car he drove. Then I called the history department and asked for our historian.

"Alan? How nice to hear your voice."

That was Esmerelda LaFleur, a true member of the gentility. Left with a modest insurance policy from her husband, at age fifty-five she'd taken a doctorate in history at the University of New Orleans and now worked part-time for us while teaching a couple of classes at LSU. A native of Natchitoches, on the Red River, she was an expert on antebellum Louisiana history and I'd learned never to underestimate the nooks and crannies of her mind, which seemed filled with esoteric bits of knowledge.

"Has Pepper talked to you about the Louis grave?" I asked.

"Indeed she has. It's as intriguing as hell, if you'll pardon my use of the vernacular. I've just finished the chain-of-title research in the Port Allen Courthouse, but I didn't find any will on file. Of course, not having a full name to work with leaves something to be desired, and I really didn't find anything that remotely fit the description. But I'm going to check the Hill Memorial collection after lunch."

"Why?" I asked. "What's there?"

"Charles Fabré's collection, according to the archivist I called. Fabré donated his papers before he died."

"Go to it," I said, deciding that telling her about the threat wouldn't accomplish anything.

"And Pepper?" she asked.

"What about her?"

"Nothing. But you know you can talk to your aunt Esme anytime."

I groaned. She never gave up trying to put us together.

"All right, be hardheaded. I'll tell you what I find out at the library."

And she hung up before I could protest.

The Camelot Club is at the top of one of the tallest buildings in downtown Baton Rouge, the tallest being the state capitol. It's a members-only restaurant for lawyers and bankers and I'd eaten there only twice before, both times by invitation.

On the previous occasions I'd worn a coat and tie; this time all I had was my usual guayabera and if they didn't like it I figured I could let Nick DeLage straighten out the misunderstanding.

But they were expecting me because the maître d' met me as I emerged from the elevator, and when I told him my name he escorted me to a corner table where a man was already seated.

The man, who had an empty martini glass in front of him, jumped up when he saw me and extended a hand. Maybe forty-five, he had longish blond hair and a tan that probably came from Cancún. His hand tightened on mine for an instant and then just as quickly let go, as if he'd done what was required and didn't want to be seen holding hands with another man.

"Dr. Graham?" he said, trying to smile. "Glad you could come. How about something to drink?"

"I'll take tea," I said.

The waiter at his elbow scurried off and another one brought a menu. I gave mine a quick look and then let my eyes creep over the top edge to study DeLage's face.

The best I could say about it was that the smile didn't go with the eyes. The smile was broad, but his eyes were close-set and hard. I wondered how many of his properties had turned into crawfish farms.

"I like the chicken cordon bleu, but everything's good," he said.

I ordered sensation salad and the soup du jour.

"The usual," my host said, handing his menu back to the attendant. "And hit me with another martini."

He turned to me, one hand playing with an edge of the tablecloth.

"I don't know any archaeologists," he said. "I thought you'd have a bullwhip and a pistol."

"Only when I'm on a movie set," I said.

DeLage forced a smile and nodded at the window, which framed a view of the river.

"Nice, isn't it? You can almost see Désirée from here. Can I call you Al?"

"Alan's better."

"Fine. In my business we use first names a lot." He leaned forward and I held my breath, waiting for the hard sell: "Call me Nick."

"All right, Nick."

His smile was lopsided.

"Alan, I called you because I'm curious about what was going on at Désirée. I hear somebody talked to my aunt Ouida."

I nodded. "She's the owner of record and your caretaker said she was in a nursing home. We try to interview people we think might have historical information."

"Right." He nodded, fingers drumming the table. "Old Flowers said some people had asked for permission to walk around the place."

"That's right." I picked up a piece of melba toast and took it out of its cellophane wrapper. "Is there a problem, Nick?"

"None at all," DeLage said. "But I was curious when I heard you were asking questions about the plantation. I thought it was just the levee the Corps was interested in."

"Technically," I said as my iced tea arrived. "But they like us to try to get as much historical information on nearby properties as possible. The river's taken a lot of the land in the last few hundred years, so where you put a levee now might be square on top of some historic feature or even an Indian site. What was Désirée Landing before the Civil War is in the river now and the place they want to put the levee is where an old store is shown on the maps. So the idea is to get as much information as possible about a given holding and see if the improvement will impact anything that might be buried there."

"Fascinating," DeLage said, trying to sound sincere. "And that's why you went to see my aunt?"

"We thought she might know some of the folklore of Désirée. Talking to people is one of the best ways to get an idea of what went on at a place."

DeLage lifted his glass. "Cheers."

I half lifted my own and watched him guzzle.

"But, you know, Alan, Aunt Ouida is pretty confused these days. That's why I had to have her put in the nursing home. I don't think you'll get much from her." He attempted a laugh.

"Really," I said. "She seemed pretty lucid to me."

"She has her moments," my host said. "But the thing with Aunt Ouida is you never can tell. She can be clear as glass one minute and in outer space a few seconds later. That's why we had to put her under supervision."

The waiter brought our plates and DeLage ordered another martini, then started sawing at his cordon bleu.

"How's the salad?"

"Very good," I said.

"I'm glad. Bring a lot of clients up here. Never had any complaints."

He chewed almost angrily and then jabbed his fork at the river.

"Ever go down to the gambling boats?"

"No," I said.

"Smart," he answered. "You can't beat the house. I learned that a long time ago. Just like you can't fight City Hall. You can buy 'em, but you can't fight 'em."

He speared a piece of broccoli. It headed for his mouth, then halted with the fork midway up.

"I hear Aunt Ouida loaned you some papers."

"That's right."

"What kind of papers?"

"Diaries of John Clay Hardin," I said. "They cover about forty years."

The broccoli continued to hover in midair.

"Never heard of 'em," he said. "Sounds like Aunt Ouida's been holding out on me."

"I assumed the diaries were hers."

"All the family papers were part of my grandfather's estate." This time his smile let me know he was sure I understood.

"Well, we aren't going to keep them," I said. "We just needed to look through them as part of our background research."

He nodded. "Was there anything interesting in them?"

"It was all interesting," I told him, "if you're trying to get a feel for what a planter's life was like in the years before the Civil War." I played with a piece of lettuce and decided I might as well say the rest: "And there were some references to somebody named Louis, who's buried in the family cemetery.''

DeLage snorted. ''I know the grave you're talking about. The blacks used to be scared to death of it. I must've heard a dozen stories about old Louis, every one of 'em different.''

''Really? What did you hear?''

''Oh, Christ . . .'' He set his fork down and sat back in his chair. ''Let's see, have you heard the one about the Man Without a Country?''

I nodded.

''And then there's the one about how he was a rich man's son in the East, a doctor, who took to drink and fell off a boat and washed up at Désirée. And then there was one that said he was a traveler on the Natchez Trace, who was being followed by robbers all the way from Nashville. They were supposed to have followed him to Natchez and tried to finish him off after he got on a boat for New Orleans.''

''The Natchez Trace,'' I said thoughtfully.

''Sure.'' He coughed. ''It went from Natchez to Nashville in the old days.''

''Of course.''

He asked a few more questions about archaeology, but I could tell that the subject didn't really interest him. Finally he wiped his mouth with his napkin.

''Coffee, Alan?''

''Thanks, I've got to be getting back.''

''Sure.'' He got up. ''By the way, Alan, if you dig up something, who does it belong to?''

''The owner,'' I said.

''I thought so.''

''Were you planning to sell the property?'' I asked.

Nicholas DeLage shrugged. ''I've had a few feelers. Nothing definite.''

It isn't polite to call your host a liar, so I just stuck out my hand and told him goodbye.

''One more thing, Nick.''

''Yes?''

''How did you get my phone number?''

DeLage looked faintly surprised. ''It was on your business

card. Old Flowers gave it to me when he called to tell me some archaeologists had come by.''

We left the restaurant together. Nick's car, I noticed, was a red Camaro. Clearly not the car that had followed me from Sam's.

▰ FIVE

Nick's car was the wrong color and make, but maybe that other car hadn't been following me after all. Because Nick was too good a suspect to pass up. He was a slimeball who'd put his old aunt in a home so he could control her assets. And now he wanted to know if there was something there that made the property worth more than he'd thought. Worse, the last person I'd given my business card to was his man Flowers, and Flowers had passed it to Nick.

A threat via E-mail, from a man who sold insurance and thus had time of his own to cruise the university computer lab and find an open machine.

So what was it about a man who'd been dead for almost a century and a half that made him worth all this trouble? I went over the stories DeLage had recounted: Our Louis wasn't the Man Without a Country, because that story had been fiction. He may have been a wastrel younger son, fleeing from the East after some misdeeds, as the other account had it. And he might easily have traveled the Natchez Trace to reach the Mississippi River and taken a flatboat south.

But was there truth in either of these two stories? I knew how unreliable family lore could be. A kernel of truth could be misinterpreted, twisted, embellished. A story set in one place or time could be inadvertently borrowed and made to fit another place and time. And yet often there was that single grain of truth.

Was that the case here?

I got back to the office just after one. The copies of the

Hardin journal were neatly stacked by my computer, beside the original bound chapbooks.

I lifted the receiver and punched in the number for my lawyer, Stanley Kirby, a.k.a. Dogbite. He'd earned his nickname when he'd taken the case of a three-hundred-pound center on the Southern football team who, after being savaged by a Pekingese, professed a phobia for small, furry animals. Most days, Dogbite spent his hours practicing putts on the rug of his office on France Street, waiting for a really good toxic spill or oil well fire, but true disasters were hard to come by. Like the Maytag Repairman, he sometimes seemed like the loneliest man in town, so I wasn't surprised when he answered on the first ring.

"Law Offices," he said quickly.

"Sorry, Stanley," I said. "It's just me, Alan."

"What's up?"

"Got a question for you," I said. "Ever hear of a guy named Nicholas DeLage?"

"DeLage? I saw him in court once. They had him up for coke possession, but he got out of it. I hope you didn't do a deal with him. He owns slum property all over town, but his rent income goes up his nose. If he's trying to get you to do some kind of historical assessment you're gonna lose your ass."

I explained about the journals and my lunch at the Camelot Club.

"Can he claim these journals for his own?" I asked.

"I don't know."

"He says they're part of his grandfather's estate."

"Maybe they are and maybe they aren't. Does the will mention them? Is there even a will at all? Louisiana probably still had forced heirship when the owner died; the law was only changed a few years ago. The administrator of the estate could have disposed of things like the journals. I'd have to see what the judgment of possession said. There's a chance her father gave the journals to his daughter before he died, in which case they're hers and not part of the estate."

"But if she's been declared incompetent . . ."

"Has he been appointed her curator?"

"That's what I hear."

"Then he can take them into his possession if he thinks

she'll destroy them and they have some monetary value. Do they?''

"It's possible. Can he do anything he wants with her possessions?''

"No. He's required to take care of them and not to commingle her assets with his own. The court should have appointed an attorney to look after her interests.''

"Can you find out who that is?''

"No problem. Maybe he'll sue you and I'll make some money.''

"Thanks, Stanley.''

"Just joking, Alan.''

I hung up and called Bertha Bomberg. She was in this time and I had to listen to a litany about how we never kept her up to date. I apologized and promised to mend my ways. Then I called Pepper at her Perkins Road office.

"I read the journals,'' I told her. Then I recounted the E-mail threat and my lunch with Nick DeLage.

"You haven't noticed anybody following you, have you?'' When she said no, I told her about the dark-colored car on the way back from Sam's place. "It might have been my imagination, but it seemed to keep far enough back so I couldn't see the driver or the make and whenever I slowed down it did, too.''

"You think DeLage is behind this?'' she asked.

"I keep coming back to my business card and wondering who else.''

"I have a bad feeling about this, Alan. He's up to no good and poor Ouida's in his clutches. He has to have somebody at the nursing home reporting back to him to know about the journals.''

"I agree. But all we can do now is bring the journals back to her. We can't keep 'em.''

"No.'' Pepper hesitated. "Did you make copies?''

"On my desk. Why don't I swing by? We can take back her originals.''

"I'll be here.''

Ten minutes later I pulled in at the little complex of offices off Perkins, in the southeast part of the city. Pepper had rented offices here when she came down from the East a year ago,

though she seemed to spend more time at our shop these days
than at her own. Still, I knew having her own suite gave her
the sense of independence she needed, a place where she
could have her own space and her privacy. Sometimes I didn't
see her for days and I knew at such times she was holed up,
immersed in her studies and the occasional jobs that came her
way.

I was just opening my door when she came out, smiling,
and I felt a brief surge of something I tried to keep hidden
except when I was in active pursuit.

Understand, I love women. But this was professional and
P. E. Courtney, Ph.D., as she'd originally presented herself,
wasn't the most approachable woman I'd ever met. Over the
past year I'd learned she wasn't exactly the iceberg she'd
pretended to be, either, but if we were going to work together
there was no sense muddying the water with extracurricular
feelings that would never go anywhere.

"I ran down to the drugstore while I was waiting for you
and got some chocolates," she said, getting in. "I don't think
Miss Ouida gets many presents."

We drove to the nursing home in silence. It was midafternoon, and for all I knew the patients were sleeping, but I
didn't feel like hanging around the office. There was too
much on my mind.

I parked and we went to the reception window and asked
for Ouida Mae Fabré. The thin receptionist lifted the phone,
said Ouida Mae's name, and listened. Then she replaced the
receiver and turned back to me with an apologetic look:

"I'm sorry. She's having a bad day."

"Is she? That's too bad, because we have something of
hers we promised to bring back."

"Well, you can leave it right here," the woman said, smiling. "I'll see that she gets it."

"Fine. You'll need to sign a receipt and I'll need it to be
witnessed," I said, placing the receipt on the counter for her
to see.

She held it up and frowned.

"What's all this *In the matter of possible evidence . . .* ?"

"Legal gobbledygook," I said. "Chain of custody, they
call it. When there's a lawsuit, they call everybody who handled the evidence, who might have tampered with it . . ."

The smile was replaced by alarm.

"Lawsuit? Just a minute." She left her desk and disappeared through a side door. I heard her heels in the corridor. I checked my watch and exchanged grins with Pepper. The receptionist was back in eight minutes.

"The supervisor says you can give whatever it is to Miss Ouida," she said. "Mrs. Krogh will take you to her room."

Unlike the sylphlike attendant who'd assisted us yesterday, Mrs. Krogh was six feet tall and weighed more than some football linemen. She did not seem eager to assist us.

We followed her around a corner and down a corridor with a series of doors on both sides. She opened one at the end without knocking and stood aside as we entered.

Miss Ouida sat in a chair, staring out the window, a shawl draped over her thin shoulders. At first I didn't think she realized anyone was there. But then her head turned so that she was staring at us.

"Miss Ouida," I said. "We brought your books back."

"Oh," she said. "Did you talk to Nicholas?"

"Yes, ma'am."

"He was upset," she said. "I don't know why. I told him you'd bring them back. They're not his anyway."

"No."

"Sometimes Nicholas can be so mean. My sister spoiled him, you know."

"That's too bad," I said.

Pepper handed her the chocolates and I laid the journals down on the bed.

"We brought some more candy," Pepper said and I heard Mrs. Krogh suck in her breath behind us.

Miss Ouida reached out a frail hand and looked past us at the woman in the corner. "I'm not supposed to have candy, they tell me. Against the rules." She started to open the box, but I took it, tore off the cellophane, and handed it back to her.

She extracted a chocolate cherry. "Pooh. What do they know?"

"I know it's gonna mess up your blood sugar," Mrs. Krogh pronounced.

"Pooh," Miss Ouida said again, fishing out a second cherry. I had a feeling the two pieces were all she was going to get, but there was nothing I could do about that.

"Thank you for letting me borrow your journals," I said, taking her hand in my own. "You've been very kind."

"I wish I had a nephew like you," Miss Ouida said. "Sometimes I think Nicholas doesn't care at all."

"Now, that ain't true, Miss Ouida," Krogh said, moving between us. The nurse turned to face me. "You're going to have to leave now."

"Thank you, Miss Ouida," I managed before the yeti-like attendant pushed us out.

On our way to the car I checked my watch.

"It's just three now. I think I'd like to talk to Brady Flowers."

We crossed the Mississippi on the new bridge, just beating the Friday afternoon exodus from the city, and took the four-lane bypass north around the little riverbank community of Port Allen. There were stalks of cane littering the road where they'd dropped from the trucks, and twice we whipped past tractors pulling heavy burdens of cut sugarcane. I thought about the man called Louis and wondered what he would have made of the new mechanized harvesting process. According to the journals he'd been good at mechanical things, so I supposed he would have approved. Then I thought of John Clay Hardin, whose wealth depended on what slaves could harvest. What would he have made of labor-saving inventions? Would they have been welcomed or would they have been seen as a threat?

At the end of the bypass we bumped across a railroad track and onto a narrow blacktop, with cane fields on either side.

The blacktop dead-ended a quarter mile ahead at a cluster of tenant houses and rising up on our right was a pair of brick pillars, marking the entrance to Désirée. I turned into the shell drive. Someone had lowered the chain that usually blocked the entrance and we drove up to the front of the house and parked.

The great mansion loomed in front of us, its shadows deepened by the failing light. I looked up at the boarded windows and the sagging shutters. Everything seemed the same as the last time we'd been here.

"Should we go to the back and try to find Flowers?" Pepper asked.

I nodded. "You want to wait here?"

"Not on your life."

We walked around the side of the house and looked out over the pond, but Flowers was nowhere in view.

Without speaking, Pepper started back toward the mound and I followed. We took the little path between the pond on our left and the old wooden chapel on our right, and when we reached the foot of the mound Pepper hesitated a second, as if uncertain. She looked over at me.

"Want to say hello to our friend?"

"Why not?"

We trudged up the side of the hill and emerged in front of the little cluster of brick vaults that marked the family graves.

"Hi, Louis," she said. "Just thought we'd pay our respects."

I stared down at the grave and knew what she was thinking, because I was thinking it, too. But we were both wrong. Nothing had changed, no one had been up here to dig him up, everything was the same as when we'd last been here.

I looked past the graves to the bee boxes at the foot of the levee. No sign of the caretaker. The place seemed deserted.

We made our way down the side of the mound and started toward the river. As we neared the bee boxes a menacing buzz greeted us and I saw tiny black bodies darting about in the air. I hurried past them and stumped my way up the levee to stand looking out over the river.

"You must not like bees," she said.

"I've stepped on too many hornet nests during surveys to feel very close to the little buggers."

She laughed. "You have a way with words."

"Yeah."

In front of us was a willow-fringed borrow pit from which the earth had been taken to make the levee. The pit was almost dry now and a small dirt bridge connected it with the riverbank. We went down the slope and across the dug-out area to the water's edge.

"You really want to find out who he was, don't you?" she asked.

"I always said I was an unreconstructed romantic." I gave her a half smile. "And it looks like you're becoming one, too."

She smiled, picked up a piece of wood, and spun it out over the speeding water. It made a splash, bobbed to the surface, and then headed downstream.

"It must've been a lonely life, living all those years as somebody's guest and not knowing who he was." She swept her hair away from her sunglasses as she stared out over the waters. "I wonder if he ever fell in love, wanted to get married."

"I don't know. Maybe he'd have made a lousy husband." She turned to look at me.

"Is that why you never remarried?" she asked. "Were you afraid you wouldn't make a good husband?"

I exhaled. I didn't like to remember Felicia and our divorce.

"You never mention her," she said. "Does it still hurt that much?"

I shrugged. "It did for a while. I'd kind of gotten used to feeling that way until . . ."

"Until what?"

"I dunno." I felt myself grinning. "I guess life just got more interesting."

"Really." She smiled again and I wished I could see her eyes behind the dark lenses.

"You know, Alan, the first time I saw the name Moundmasters and realized it was an archaeological company I thought it was silly," she said. "Then I realized it wasn't silly at all. It just took me a while to figure out what it meant."

"Which is?"

"I think you were reminding everybody—and yourself—not to take the world so seriously. That archaeology could still be fun."

"You read me like a book," I said.

"When I came here I'd just about forgotten," she said, turning back to the water. "They leach so much humanity out of you in graduate school."

"It's called professionalism," I said dryly.

"And I was so determined to find my brother."

Her older brother, the only link to her family past, had taken off while she was in high school, and the last she'd heard he was driving a truck somewhere in the South. She'd gotten a card from him, postmarked Monroe, Louisiana, and had come south hoping to locate him. But I knew she hadn't had any luck.

"Someday," I said, trying to offer hope.

"Yes." We stood side by side watching the driftwood bob past on the current. "Do you think he really could have been some traveler on the Natchez Trace?" she asked.

My turn to kick at the ground. "I don't know. All we can do is follow where the trail leads."

"And if it doesn't go anywhere?"

"Then we turn it loose."

"Alan . . ." I felt her hand on my arm and goose bumps prickled my flesh.

"Yes?"

"I'm glad things have gotten better—about Felicia, I mean."

I drew in my breath. "Do you?"

"Yes."

"Not as glad as I am."

She took a step toward me and I gently lifted off her sunglasses. A cloud of butterflies suddenly fluttered through my belly. My God, was it really happening? Was she really inviting me to reach out, touch her?

"Pepper . . ." My mouth went dry. Her hands came toward me and then quickly drew back as I heard steps behind us. I wheeled

Brady Flowers, armed with a heavy stick, was standing a few feet behind us and he didn't look happy.

▰ Six

The old man glared at us from deep-set eyes.

"What you doing here?"

"We were just checking some things," I said.

"Before you come on this land, you talk to me."

"You weren't around," Pepper said.

"People come here, they dig holes, steal things, take gravestones. I won't have none of that."

"I talked to Mr. DeLage at lunch," I said. "He doesn't seem to have a problem with us being here. Neither does Miss Ouida."

"They ain't taking care of the place. I am."

I couldn't argue with that.

"Why don't you call Mr. DeLage?" Pepper said.

Flowers grunted. "I don't have to call nobody."

"We were leaving anyway," I said and took Pepper's arm. I started toward the land bridge and then stopped and took out my wallet. "By the way, thanks for giving Mr. DeLage my card. Here's another one."

I handed him my business card and when his eyes dropped to look at it I guided Pepper past him and back toward the levee.

"Mr. Nick DeLage don't do nothing for this place," Flowers shouted after us. "I been here fifty years and he ain't never done nothing for it. It belong to Miss Ouida, you hear?"

We climbed back over the levee and down again, leaving the old man to his anger, and started back alongside the pond.

Suddenly Pepper stopped and pointed.

"Look."

I followed her finger to the fresh dirt that lay scattered at random on the surface, twenty feet off the path, between the dilapidated little chapel and the levee.

"Somebody's been digging," I said, as we walked over to inspect the fresh excavations. "I guess we walked right past this earlier."

She nodded. "Somebody made sure to cover their shovel holes pretty well." She bent and lifted a handful of dirt. "But they're fresh. Not many leaves have blown on top of them. I'm willing to bet these were dug today."

"So that's what Flowers meant by people digging holes," I said and then, from the corner of my eye, caught movement on the levee. "Let's get on before he comes over and raises some more hell."

We went back to the footpath. To our right a bass plopped in the pond, sending ripples across the surface.

"I wonder what they did with the dirt when they dug this thing," I said.

"Used it for the levee?" she asked.

"Maybe, but most of the levee came from the borrow pit."

"Then they would have probably spread the pond dirt in low spots," she offered. "Look, the door of the chapel's open. Wasn't it closed last time we were here?" She frowned. "Do you think somebody broke it open?"

"I doubt Flowers was in there praying," I said.

I glanced behind us and saw the caretaker standing beside the bee boxes, stick in hand, his eyes taking in our every move.

"Come on," I said. "I don't want to cheat the bees out of a chance to sting the old bastard."

An hour later we were seated at the Library Restaurant on Chimes Street, just across from the university. They made good hamburgers, as well as the best muffaletta sandwiches in town, and it was a Friday tradition for the archaeological community to congregate there at the end of the day. The wooden building itself was probably fifty years old and the music could deafen a rock band. But up until eight or nine it was a pleasant place to be. Later than that, the freaks came out and Chimes Street wasn't a good neighborhood if you carried much cash.

Most of the faculty crowd hadn't arrived yet and the only other customers were a trio of students playing pool. A television over the bar droned CNN news, but it wasn't so loud that we couldn't hear ourselves talk at our little table against the wall.

"You remember the business about artichokes when old Louis was dying?" Pepper said, blowing on the foam in her beer cup. "I'm thinking he buried the box in his garden. And the pond is where his garden used to be."

I shrugged and popped a peanut into my mouth. "It's a good possibility."

"Then what were the fresh holes for?"

"Somebody obviously doesn't see it that way," I said.

"So what could be so important about what's in the box?" she asked. "It's been a hundred and fifty years."

"I don't know." I swept the peanut hulls into a little pile and shook some fresh shells out onto the table. "It may be more a question of what somebody *thinks* is in the box."

"But if somebody knows enough to have found out about the box in the first place, they're more than just your ordinary pothunter. They must have read John Clay Hardin's journal and come to the part about old Louis asking Hardin to bring his box to the president."

"I agree." I sipped from my bottle. "And that's kind of interesting in itself."

She nodded and picked a peanut out of the pile.

"I'll say. It sounds like somebody thinks the old man's ramblings ought to be taken seriously. And that means . . ."

"Somebody with a good handle on the history of the times," I finished and saw her nod.

"But, Alan, that brings us back to who the man was and what he was doing on the Mississippi to begin with in 1811."

I pondered and took a another swallow.

"Madison," I said finally.

"What?"

"The president in 1811 was James Madison."

"That's right. He was the president during the War of 1812, when the White House was burned by the British."

"What else do we know about him?" I asked.

Pepper made a wry face. "You mean besides the fact that he was Dolley's husband and that he wrote the Constitution? I can't think of much. He was followed by Monroe, of the Monroe Doctrine." She screwed up her face. "Alan, do you think the papers in the box had something to do with the war? Maybe something about the British? Do you think our man Louis was a spy?"

"Could be," I allowed. "Maybe *artichokes* was a password."

"Like for a secret group?" she asked. "A cabal of some sort. Aaron Burr and his people. Wasn't the time about right for the Burr conspiracy?"

I tugged an ear, trying to remember. "As I recall, Burr's trial was five or six years before. He was accused of trying to take part of the Louisiana Territory and create his own country. He was tried before the chief justice of the United States, John Marshall, and acquitted. And if I have it right, he died at the start of the 1812 war. But he never stopped plotting."

"So it could have been a Burr group," she declared.

"Or any other group that wanted to carve out a slice of the pie. Kentucky was a pretty wild area then, and a lot of Kaintucks came down the river to New Orleans as adventurers. And St. Louis, where the Missouri and Mississippi Rivers meet, was the gateway to the whole Louisiana Territory. There were all kinds of people there—French, Spanish, British, Americans, Indians. There's no telling what schemes were being hatched."

Suddenly I realized the young woman across the table from me was smiling again.

"Do you always peel the label off your beer bottle when you lecture?" she asked.

I looked down at the shreds of gummed paper in front of me.

"Only when I get wound up," I said, feeling my face flush.

"That's okay." She reached out, put a hand on mine. "I like your lectures."

"Really."

"Mostly." She slipped out of her chair as the bartender called my name, and before I could say anything she was retrieving our order from the counter.

"God," she muttered, setting the cheese fries on the table. "We're both going to have to run a hundred miles to work this off."

"Fifty, anyway," I said, popping a fry into my mouth. "Wait till you see the size of the muffaletta."

"I'm afraid to," she said. "By the way, I hear you're a pretty good cook."

"I do okay with your usual dishes," I said. "Jambalaya, gumbo, things I can feed people when we have a poker game."

As soon as I said it I knew I'd screwed up.

"That's something I've been meaning to ask you about," she said and I groaned inwardly.

"Isn't that your cheeseburger they're putting on the counter?" I asked.

"No, that's somebody else's." She leaned toward me over the table. "Look, Alan, about the poker games . . ."

I was saved by the door opening, spilling daylight into the dark room. To my surprise, I saw Esmerelda LaFleur standing in the entrance, red hair ablaze from the sun.

"Ahhh, there you are!" she cried.

"Esme, what are you doing here?" I asked, beckoning her to the table.

"I'm looking for you two," she said. "I called the office and Marilyn said you'd gone off together, which is fine and none of my business, because you're both adults and single and healthy, but I thought you might be interested in what I found. So I asked Marilyn where you might be and she said to try this place and here I am."

"Sit down," I said. "What can I order for you?"

Esme slid into a chair and looked down her nose at the bar.

"It's a little early, but I'd take a sloe gin fizz."

I went to the bar, placed her order, and watched the barkeep shake his head.

"I'm serious," I told him.

Two minutes later he handed me the glass and I returned to our table.

"So what's up, Esme?"

She gave a catlike grin.

"I've been in the archives at Hill Memorial," she said.

Hill Memorial was the oldest of LSU's libraries and held rare materials and manuscripts.

"You've found out something about Louis," Pepper declared, her voice excited.

Esme sipped from her cup and then pursed her lips, as if unsure whether the drink met her approval.

"Yes and no," she said.

"Want to explain?" I asked.

"Go get your food," she ordered, as the barkeep called my name. I brought Pepper's burger and my muffaletta.

"You're not going to eat all of that, are you?" Esme asked, incredulous.

"I may take some of it home," I said. "Now what's the news?"

"Can I try a little piece?"

"Here." I handed her half the kaiser roll. "Now, about the archives . . ."

"Oh. I'd forgotten."

"Don't lie," I said.

"You're so rude," Esme complained, lifting the bun to her mouth and biting off a small piece.

"Esme . . ." I said.

"I can't speak with my mouth full."

She chewed another few times, swallowed, and wiped her lips with a paper napkin.

"About the research . . ."

"We're waiting," I prodded.

"You remember, I told you I looked in the courthouse for the will and couldn't find that any record of it had ever been filed."

Pepper and I nodded together.

"Well, I found it in the Fabré Collection in Hill Memorial."

I set down my beer bottle.

"Are you serious?"

"Perfectly."

"Signed and witnessed?"

"Absolutely."

Pepper and I looked at each other and she spoke for both of us: "Hallelujah."

Esme held up a hand.

"Don't get too excited. It doesn't answer everything. Still, there's at least one interesting thing about it."

"Did you copy what it said?" Pepper asked.

"No," Esme said primly. "I abased myself sufficiently that the archivist let me make a photocopy."

She delved into the canvas shoulder bag that served both as purse and document case.

"It doesn't provide an answer," she warned.

I took the paper and held it to the light, as Pepper bent her head to read the long, slanted pen strokes.

Last Will and Testament

Under the heading were only a few lines:

Being of sound mind and sensible of the frailty of life, I hereby make this, my last Will and Testament.

I leave to my friend John Clay Hardin my watch & my collection of natural history specimens.

I leave to Judalon Hardin, wife of the above John Clay Hardin, my drawings & paintings, pore as they are.

I leave my rifle to Louis Rayfield Hardin, my godson.

I leave to Eleanor Hardin Fabré, wife of Pierre Fabré, the furniture I made with my hands.

My money, & tools I leave to John Clay Hardin to dispose of as he sees fit.

Signed at Désirée Plantation in the Parish of West Baton Rouge, in the State of Louisiana, on this Tenth Day of October, in the Year of Our Lord One Thousand Eight Hundred & Fifty-Seven.

But it was the signature that got my attention, because there, above the scrawl of John Clay Hardin, who had signed his name as witness, was a single name, and the spelling was unmistakable:

Lewis

≡ SEVEN

"L-E-W-I-S?" Pepper spelled.

"Interesting, isn't it?" Esme said. "It's the only thing we have in his handwriting and he spells his name the Anglo rather than the French way."

I nodded. "So all the references to L-O-U-I-S in the journal and the spelling on the gravestone are based on how the Hardin family thought it *ought* to be spelled."

Esme smiled. "And since this is south Louisiana, they naturally spelled it the French way."

"Wait a minute," Pepper said. "If John Clay Hardin witnessed the will, then he saw how the man spelled his name. Why would he spell it differently on the grave?"

Esme shrugged. "Old habits die hard. And remember, orthography—spelling—as we know it was a lot less rigorous in those days. People weren't nearly as concerned about how a word—or a name—ought to be written."

"True," Pepper agreed. "But there's something else about the will: It doesn't mention the metal box."

"You noticed that, did you?" Esme said. "Good girl. Most wills have what's called a residuary legatee, who gets everything that isn't specifically mentioned. But there's no clause like that in this one. He leaves certain specific things, but he's very careful not to make Hardin the owner of the things he didn't mention."

"So what do you make of it, Esme?" I asked.

She picked off another fragment of my sandwich.

"I'm not sure. But I know somebody who may be able to help."

"Oh?"

"Shelby Deeds," she said. "He retired from the University of New Orleans a couple of years ago. He's a specialist in the early statehood period for Louisiana and Mississippi. He's also an authority on the Natchez Trace."

Pepper nodded. "I think I read a book of his about the history of the Mississippi Territory," she said.

"That's Shelby," Esme said. "He's living in Abita Springs now. It was so sad: He had to take early retirement because of his drinking. His marriage broke up years ago and he just sort of went to pieces after that." She sighed. "But once he left New Orleans he got control of himself. He joined AA and I don't think he's had a drink for four or five years. I called him and he said he'd talk to us tomorrow. I told him we could be there right after noon." She looked from one of us to the other. "We can, can't we?"

Pepper looked over at me. "Alan?"

"Sure."

It was just past nine when I parked in my driveway. I disarmed the alarm, went inside, and dropped my attaché case beside the door. The house seemed unusually lonely, despite the dog pawing at the back door. I got out a big can of dog food, opened it, and let Digger in to eat.

"I know," I said. "It's way past suppertime. I'm sorry."

But he was devoting his full attention to his bowl.

I went into my study and for the first time in over a year took the little gold-framed photo of Felicia and me on our wedding day out of the drawer where I kept it and stared at the two happy people smiling up at me.

Was it really over with? All the times before when I'd taken out the picture, it had hurt to see it. Sometimes I'd taken it out just so that it *would* hurt, as if hurting somehow reminded me that I was alive.

I'd dropped Pepper off just minutes before, found myself standing at the foot of the wooden steps that led up to her tiny garage apartment.

"Alan . . ."

I knew she was going to invite me up, but I needed time to sort out my emotions.

"Tomorrow," I said and gave her a quick, brotherly hug.

Now I was telling myself I was a fool, that all I'd had to do was hold the hug a second longer. I could be with her now, instead of by myself in a house that was more like a museum than a home.

Sure, and then what? I'd had flings since breaking up with Felicia. There was Peggy Lipscomb, the spacey biologist who wore a crystal to bed and whom I'd found, one morning at six, after a night of torrid lovemaking, seated in a yoga position on my back porch, stark naked. There was Yvette, who was driven by her biological clock and wanted nothing so much as to snare a man before it was too late. And there was Lucy Moran, who, after I'd gotten to know and like her, had confessed to some bizarre notions about religion and race.

I'd broken up with all of them and hadn't really regretted it. But now I was beginning to wonder if I hadn't chosen them for their eccentricities in the first place. Maybe I hadn't been ready for something permanent, and now perhaps I was.

I took Digger for a late-night walk to City Park and back, feeling safe in the umbrella of the camphor trees that lined the silent boulevard. When we got back, I showered, had a light scotch and water, and went to bed.

In my dreams, Bertha Bomberg pushed a line of chessmen who resembled Roman legionnaires inexorably along a levee, the pawns in the front of the column falling helplessly into the waters below.

She was down to her rooks and a bishop when the sound of Digger barking shook me out of my sleep and made me sit up in bed.

There was a noise downstairs.

I fumbled for my clothes and tried to clear the sleep out of my mind. How could they have gotten past the alarm?

Then I heard a car start on the street and I realized they must have been on the front porch. I grabbed the heavy walking stick, left over from an old field injury to my leg, and raced downstairs, taking the steps two at a time.

I jerked open the front door and looked out. The porch light spilled into the front yard and there was no one there.

I walked out of the house and down the sidewalk.

So far, so good.

Then I saw my Blazer.

Both tires on the driver's side were flat and its red surface had been sprayed with white paint. As I approached I saw that a piece of paper had been stuck under the windshield wipers.

I plucked it off and held it up, my hand shaking with anger.

The writing was in block letters an inch high, done with a black felt pen.

I WARNED YOU ONCE.
THERE WON'T BE ANY MORE CHANCES.

# EIGHT

I spent the morning getting my car towed to a Texaco station just north of the university. Putting on four new tires would be no problem. But I'd need a paint job, which they didn't do. They'd be happy to send it to a body shop, but I wouldn't have it back until Tuesday.

I shrugged and told them to do it, then walked the half mile to our office. I called my insurance agent. He took the information, told me to make a police report, and half an hour later I was standing on my office porch making a report to a bored-looking patrolman with a paunch. He took the information, but I knew the case would get priority just above a stolen bike, and there was a better chance of catching the bike thief.

At ten-thirty I called Esme and asked if we could use her car. She agreed immediately and I asked her to swing by the office.

As a precaution, I checked the copies of the Hardin journal, but they were still locked securely in my desk. If somebody wanted them, they'd have to get past our alarm.

I sat back and closed my eyes. I kept seeing old Brady Flowers and his angry face.

But this didn't seem like the kind of thing he'd do. People like Flowers were direct. If they were angry, they told you to your face. They didn't wait until you were asleep and vandalize your car. And they sure didn't slip into the campus computer lab and send you a threat by E-mail.

It was the style of somebody like Nick DeLage.

I was roused from my meditations by the sound of Esmerelda coming through the front door.

We were halfway to Pepper's when she started her routine.

"So are you and Pepper done playing games with each other?"

"What?"

"Oh, Alan, stop pretending. Do either one of you think you can fool an old fool? I may be a Natchitoches blue-hair, but I've played all the games and I've told all the lies—to my lovers and to myself. Mr. LaFleur was the only man who could see through it all. Aren't you a little old to still be pretending?"

"I don't know what you're talking about."

"No? Well, listen to your aunt Esme: A woman doesn't care about age in a man. That's your own stupid obsession. Pepper is crazy about you, but you've got her scared to death."

"Esme . . ." I squirmed in the seat, wondering if we was going too fast for me to jump out.

"She's scared you aren't for real. She's scared you don't want her."

"Look—"

"But most of all, she's scared you'll leave. She's a lot more insecure than you think. She's still working through some problems from her family life. You know how she grew up, her father going off to Vietnam and never coming back, then her brother disappearing—"

"Okay, okay."

We were turning onto Delgado, the boulevard that led into Pepper's subdivision, and the driveway to her apartment was just ahead.

"What she really wants is for you to swoop down and carry her off."

She turned into Pepper's driveway and I jumped out of the Gran Prix before she could protest. I loved Esme, but this was getting ridiculous.

I raced up the stairs and was relieved when Pepper opened the door.

Not that I'd expected anything-bad to have happened to her, but you never knew.

A few minutes later we were on the interstate, leaving behind the traffic that kept us a mere ten miles above the posted limit. Esme was a terror on the road. She collected speeding tickets like some women collect jewelry. But she also had good reflexes and the kind of Old South charm that got her a second chance from many highway patrolmen.

I waited until we were out of the city and then told them about my experience last night.

Pepper gasped and Esme's mouth set in a grim line.

"Alan, this is really rather serious."

"I had the same feeling, Esme." I shut my eyes as she fit herself between two speeding eighteen-wheelers.

"Someone could kill you," she pronounced.

I looked at the INFLAMMABLE LIQUID sign on the back of the tanker truck ten feet in front of us and nodded.

"That's for damned straight."

"I remember being threatened when I was in high school. A boy was insanely jealous if I looked at another male. He began to pester me and to make the most outrageous threats. I finally faced him down and told him I simply wouldn't have it. He was broken after that. He joined the Army and I heard later he did quite well. In the enlisted ranks, of course."

"Of course," I said and heard Pepper giggle.

I tried to imagine Esme as a young Natchitoches belle, growing up in the late fifties, absorbing all the gentility of life in the oldest community in Louisiana and yet, at the same time, acquiring the steeliness that saw her through the death of a husband, subsequent graduate work, highly successful investments, travel, and, from what I could judge, a number of love affairs. But no man she'd met had ever measured up to the legendary Mr. LaFleur, the love of her life, who'd carried her off on a cloud of poetry and then dropped dead ten years later.

"But one great passion," she'd once confided, "is as much as anyone can expect in a lifetime."

Right now I was concerned mainly with not abbreviating my own time on earth. Maybe, I thought, my anonymous assailant had merely been warning me about Esme's driving.

It took just over an hour to reach the turnoff to Abita Springs, a tiny community in the pine woods. Before the Second World War people used to go there for the medicinal value of the waters. Today they go there to escape the cauldron of vice and violence called New Orleans, on the south side of the lake. A microbrewery produces a decent beer and the atmosphere is unpolluted by exhaust fumes. A good place for a man like Shelby Deeds to retire.

We found a burger joint on Main Street and after we'd eaten, Esme pulled out the sheet of paper on which she'd written Deeds's directions.

"Poor Shelby," Esme lamented. "I think he could have done well at Harvard or Stanford. Instead, thanks to his problem, he was stuck for his whole career at a state university."

"Esme, you sound like an elitist," I said.

"I never claimed to be anything else."

She slowed at a shell driveway and then turned in. Ahead was a low frame house with lots of windows, and a dark blue Buick Regal under the carport. In the yard was an ancient live oak, with a bird feeder hanging from one limb.

A rubber welcome mat greeted us at the front door and Esme raised her hand to knock, then paused and turned to Pepper and me.

"I adore Shelby, but he's so *tragic*. You almost have the feeling he ought to be in a Eugene O'Neill play."

She knocked, and when the door swung slowly open I understood what she meant.

The man in front of us was slight, not over five-foot-five, and he leaned on a cane. His khaki trousers and white suspenders gave the impression of old gentry, as did the maroon bow tie. But it was his face that demanded attention. With a drooping gray mustache and pools of sorrow for eyes, I immediately thought of William Faulkner.

"Esme, it's so good of you to come," he said, giving the tall woman a kiss on the cheek. He took Pepper's hand and said, "I'm charmed."

Then he offered me a hand and we shook. I noticed that his skin was soft and his fingers long and delicate, like those of a pianist.

"Shelby, what have you done to yourself?" Esme asked, nodding at the cane.

He gave her a sad smile.

"When was the last time you were up here, Esme? One year? Two? None of us is getting any younger." He turned around and hobbled forward, motioning for us to follow him into the house.

"You'll have to forgive the study. It's a little untidy, I'm afraid."

"Don't be ridiculous," Esme said.

He led us down a hallway and into a large room that reeked of cigarette smoke. The room protruded from the rest of the house so that there were windows on three sides. Under the windows were bookshelves and two-drawer filing cabinets. The shelves were crammed with books of every description, some standing upright and others lying on their sides atop one another. Several accordion files were stacked on the floor. Against the center wall, just under a window, was a desk, and on it I saw an ancient manual typewriter.

"Please sit down. Can I get you some iced tea?"

"That would be wonderful," Esme said, slumping into a cane chair and kicking off her sandals.

Shelby Deeds nodded gravely. "I have it already brewed." He turned to Pepper and me: "Would either of you care for some homemade tea?"

"That would be fine," I said, answering for both of us.

Our host hobbled off and Esme shook her head.

"Do you see what I mean about tragedy? He just exudes it. All old gentry are like that, but Shelby has it in spades."

Deeds came back with a tray, napkins, four glasses, and a glass pitcher. He poured gravely, saving himself for last, and then raised his glass.

"Cheers," Esme said. Pepper and I lifted our own glasses and Deeds raised his halfway.

Esme sipped, eyes closed, and sighed.

"What you've told me is very interesting," the old scholar said finally, taking out a pack of cigarettes. "I can't think of another situation quite like it." He shook his head slowly from side to side: "A man from nowhere, who can't remember who he is, and at the end of his life demands that certain papers be shown to the president of the United States. I'd say it was unique."

Esme smiled. "I knew it would appeal to you, Shelby."

"And it certainly does. Did you bring a copy of the will?"

Esme delved into her shoulder bag and produced the piece of paper.

"Of course you have other copies," Deeds said, taking it and shifting his unlit cigarette to his other hand.

"Of course."

"Good." He studied the document for a long time, held it to the light, and then laid it down flat on his desk.

"Amazing," he muttered.

Pepper and I looked at each other.

"It means something to you, then?" Esme asked.

Deeds shrugged. "I need to do more study. Would it be possible for you to leave it with me?"

"Of course. That's why I brought it."

"Excellent." He lifted the paper again, as if this time he might see something he'd missed before.

"Yes, it's very suggestive."

"Of what?" I asked.

He ignored the question. "Might I borrow the journals?"

I told him about Miss Ouida and how I'd had to make a copy.

"We can copy the copies," I said.

"That would be of some value. But hardly ideal." He sighed, got out a silver lighter, and lit his cigarette. "An historian always prefers to work with the original documents. But a good copy might be sufficient at this stage."

Esme leaned forward. "I know that light in your eyes, Shelby. You're on to something. So how about telling us what you have in mind?"

Deeds drew on his cigarette, closed his eyes, and exhaled. "Then you also know how much I hate making a fool of myself."

"I understand," I said. "But let me ask you this, Professor Deeds: Does it seem likely that our man came from the East, or from St. Louis, or from the Natchez Trace?"

Deeds turned his head slowly and fixed me with his doleful eyes.

"If I'm right, I'd say all three."

Pepper made a little sound of surprise.

"Care to elaborate?" I asked.

The old man sat back, the sad eyes alive now with excitement.

"What do you know about the Natchez Trace, Alan?"

I frowned. "It was an old Indian trail that the government

expanded into a wagon road back in the early 1800s. It went from Natchez to Nashville. I think the National Park Service has restored parts of it.''

Our host forced himself up, hobbled over to his bookshelf, and extracted a volume.

''As Esme may have told you, I threw some of the historical materials together a few years ago and wrote this book. It's called *The Old Natchez Trace*. Got a few decent reviews.'' He shrugged and Esme tisked.

''It won a National Book Award,'' she said.

''There wasn't much competition that year,'' Deeds said disparagingly. ''In any event, the Natchez Trace wasn't much more than a footpath until Thomas Jefferson decided the country needed a land route to unite the eastern states to the Mississippi River. He made treaties with the Choctaw and Chickasaw Indians and had the army start to widen the trail into a road in 1802. It wasn't finished until 1809, and it served as a route for mail riders and travelers until the development of steamboats in the 1830s.''

I nodded, waiting.

''Alan, try to imagine how it must have been: miles and miles of nothing but a dirt track, twenty feet across, with trees leaning up from the sides, and no other white people in sight for days. Maybe an occasional party of Indian hunters appearing around a bend or at your campfire. When you came to a stream you had to ride across, unless it was one of the few with a ferry. Two weeks is what it took to get from one end to the other, but sometimes it took a lot longer.''

''All I can say,'' Esme pronounced, ''is that it makes the fifty-five-mile-per-hour speed limit sound good.''

''And then there were the robbers,'' the old man explained. ''Gangs like Murrell and the Harpes, and Sam Mason, although, to be truthful, traveling the Trace was probably safer than walking through the New Orleans French Quarter after dark.''

''Of course,'' Esme quipped. ''The robbers on the Trace didn't have Uzis.''

''Eventually,'' Deeds went on, ''people put up inns along the Trace, every couple of days' ride or so. But these weren't hotels like we think of them: They were generally a log cabin for the innkeeper and his family and another cabin for travelers. The innkeeper usually sold cheap whiskey and his wife cooked a meal of corn mush. Basically, all it amounted to was a roof over your head, a place to shelter your horse, and other human company."

"And Louis?" I prodded. "You think he was headed down the Trace from Nashville, then?"

A tiny smile curled the old man's lips. "No."

I shook my head. "Then I'm confused."

"Well, I don't want to add to the confusion. Because it's likely that my conjectures are wrong." He gave another little head shake. "In fact, they almost *have* to be. I need more information. I need time. Then, I promise, I'll tell you exactly what I think."

"You think there really was some kind of plot?" Pepper asked.

Deeds sucked on his cigarette again, as if trying to decide how much to say. Finally he exhaled and looked from one of us to the other.

"What do you know about Jamie Wilkinson?"

Esme cocked her head slightly. "Do you mean General James Wilkinson?"

Deeds nodded. "The same."

Esme shrugged. "As I remember, he was from Maryland, a bit of a prodigy. He was a doctor before the age of twenty, and in the Revolution he fought at Saratoga under Horatio Gates. After the Revolution he eventually ended up in New Orleans, as a general."

Shelby Deeds stubbed his cigarette out in the ashtray. "There's a little more to it. After the Revolution he settled in Kentucky, reenlisted in the Army, and entered into the Aaron Burr intrigue. He ended up betraying Burr to Jefferson, which covered him just in time, because there were some other rumors making the rounds about him."

"Such as?" Pepper asked.

"That he was also on Spain's payroll."

"Nice guy," I said.

Deeds chuckled. "Wilkinson was a slippery character. He managed to worm out of just about everything he was ever accused of, usually by blackmail and informing on his friends. The incredible thing was that in time he came to be the ranking general in the United States Army. He was the general

Jefferson ordered to build the Natchez Trace, using soldiers.''

"Of course," Esme said. "Now it's coming back."

"He was court-martialed several times," Deeds went on, "but he was never convicted. Most historians think it was because it would have been too embarrassing to the administrations he served to have an important general shown to be a traitor and a thief. When Wilkinson turned on Burr, for example, Jefferson couldn't afford to expose his chief witness, so he made him governor of Upper Louisiana and sent him to St. Louis, which was the territorial capital."

"Sent him as far away as possible?" I suggested.

"Yes. But it was an important post. And after he ended his term as governor, he was stationed in New Orleans, with a large contingent of troops, many of whom died or deserted because he pitched camp in a fetid marsh south of the city."

"Incompetence or intention?" I asked.

"A little of both. He was cheating his troops of their rations, feeding them substandard food, and pocketing the difference. In 1809 he was ordered to Washington to explain himself at a court-martial."

"But he was exonerated, wasn't he?" Esme asked.

"I wouldn't use the word *exonerated*," Deeds said. "But, yes, he was acquitted."

"What finally happened to him?" I asked.

Deeds smiled. "He botched a campaign in the War of 1812 and left the Army in disgrace. He went to Mexico, got a Texas land grant, and died before he could do anything with it. But he does have a county in Mississippi named after him."

"Serves him right," I said.

"Well," Deeds said, "that's not the end of his story. Just after the Spanish-American war, an American historian went through the Spanish archives in Havana. What he found was secret correspondence from the Spanish government, dating to the first part of the last century. It proved what had been rumored in Wilkinson's lifetime: that Wilkinson was on Spain's payroll all the time he was an officer in the United States Army. Even while he was the senior general in the Army. In fact, he made a tidy sum from his reports to his Spanish contact."

"An American general," Pepper declared. "It's hard to believe."

"Oh, it's well proven," Deeds told her. "And part of the proof is the trouble he went to in order to hide his treason. He insisted that, in his dealings with the Spanish representative, a code name be used. He called himself Number Thirteen. But the Spaniards, among themselves, referred to him by name, so we have the best proof possible."

"And you think old Louis found out about Wilkinson's treason?" I asked.

"Found out and may have had the documents to prove it."

☰ NINE

I thought of the old man's dying words.

"Yes," Deeds said. "Whoever the man at Désirée Plantation was, he might have been able to prove something that
would have ended Wilkinson's career and sent him to prison."

"Then this Louis must have been a spy," I said. "An
Army officer sent to check up on Wilkinson."

"Right," Pepper cried, "and the locked box Louis had
before he died might tell us."

"But why," Esme asked, "is someone trying to keep all
this secret so many years later?"

Shelby Deeds shook his head.

"There are always people who don't want things to come
out. You know old families: Some descendant may be afraid
something may come to light and embarrass the lineage. It's
happened before."

"That may be," Esme said. "But every family has its
black sheep. And some families are proud of them."

"Then look at it from the point of view of our contemporary
cutthroat academic world. Who stands to profit?"

"You mean from publishing any papers from the box?"
Esme asked. "If they're genuine, they could make a wonderful little monograph."

"You mean tenure," Pepper said.

"Tenure, promotion, academic kudos. You know the
game," Deeds said.

"There's only one problem," I said. "Nobody seems to
have gotten interested in this before a couple of days ago and

they've had years to look for the box and publish the papers in it if there's anything to be found."

Deeds nodded. "I admit that's a problem." He tapped the photocopy of the will with one finger. "About all I can do is follow up some ideas. It's really quite fascinating and I appreciate your bringing it to me."

"Shelby, you're a dear," Esme said.

I stood up. "You've been very helpful, Dr. Deeds. Since we're using your time, I hope you'll bill us as a consultant."

He shook his head. "I haven't done you any good yet," he said mournfully. "But any excuse to see Esme is worth it."

"You're such a flatterer, Shelby," Esme cried as we moved toward the door.

"Wait a minute." Deeds hobbled off into the back of the house and Esme and I looked at each other. She gave a little shrug and then broke into a smile when he reemerged with a bottle of wine.

"Here. It's an excellent vintage. Cabernet sauvignon. I've had it for years, ever since I stopped drinking. I hate to pour out something someone else can enjoy. Take it. You'll have to share it, of course."

"Shelby, we couldn't . . ." But she was already reaching for it. "You're such a darling."

Esme pecked him on the cheek and we moved out of the house and into the yard.

Deeds looked up at the trees, where squirrels were chattering. "Going to be an early winter, I think. The squirrels have been unusually busy lately."

An hour later Esme dropped me at my office. I made copies of the journals while she waited and asked her to take them to Deeds for further study. And the way things were going, I'd feel better with an extra copy in someone else's hands.

As the door closed after her, I looked around the empty office. Sorting table, trays of artifacts, bookshelves, everything was frozen as it had been left when the day had ended. The only movement was the little red light blinking on the answering machine by Marilyn's telephone.

A message. But nothing that couldn't wait until Monday or they would have called at home. Still . . .

I went over and, against my better judgment, pressed the playback button.

A mechanical voice gave me the time and date: To my surprise, the message had been logged just half an hour ago.

Probably a wrong number, I thought.

I was wrong.

"Mr. Graham," a voice rasped, "this is Brady Flowers. You told me to call. So if you hear this, come out here at six o'clock. I won't wait."

I stared at the answering machine for a long time and then called Pepper.

"I don't know what it's about, but he wouldn't have called if it wasn't important."

"I'll pick you up at five."

"Actually, I was thinking you might lend me your car."

"And go there by yourself?" she asked. "Not a chance."

"Look, Flowers is a queer old cuss. There's no telling what he's got up his sleeve."

"And that's why you can't go by yourself."

"Pepper . . ."

"It's settled."

And that was how, just before six, with darkness still an hour away, we found ourselves on the blacktop road between the cane fields, with the brick pillars of Désirée just ahead. Down the street I glimpsed the tenant houses, awash in the evening sun. A car sat motionless at the edge of the cane field like a dark insect, and a boy on a bicycle circled lazily in the street and then pedaled slowly away.

The driveway chain was still on the ground and we drove up to the front of the house and parked.

The great mansion loomed in front of us, its shadows deepened by the failing light.

"Should we try to find Flowers?" Pepper asked.

I nodded. "I'll go ahead."

"Not without me."

We walked around the side of the house and looked out over the pond, but Flowers was nowhere in view.

I was about to suggest we walk back to the bee boxes when I felt Pepper touch my arm. I turned and saw what she was pointing at: The back door of the house was open.

"Maybe he's inside," she said.

We started toward the house together.

"Do you smell something?" she asked, halting on the porch steps.

I sniffed. She was right. Mixed with the scent of dust from the house and the reek of river mud that permeated the air was another odor, something pungent. I walked across the porch to the open door and poked my head inside.

"It's gasoline," I said.

Before Pepper could answer, a rush of hot air slapped me backward as the fumes ignited.

The flash lasted only a split second, but in that instant an image of the back room etched itself in my mind—cabinets, shelves, counters, an overturned trash can, and the body of a man.

"Alan, get away!"

"It's Flowers," I yelled. "He's inside. I have to get him."

"You'll be killed."

But I wasn't listening. The flames were coming from the hallway, not the kitchen, and Flowers was half in and half out of the two rooms. With any luck I ought to be able to reach him . . .

I plunged inside, choking on the suffocating mixture of smoke and fumes. In the gloom I saw his outline just ahead and, out of the corner of my eye, on one wall, just over one of the counters, an extinguisher. But Pepper was already reaching for it.

"Get out of here," I barked, but she ignored me, jerking the metal canister from its moorings.

The flames were licking up now from a rat's nest of tinder in the hallway, and once they reached the walls the house would become a bonfire.

I stooped and grabbed the fallen man under the shoulders. I started to pull and he slid across the floor. Then, without warning, a gust of air slammed me in the face and fire scorched my arms. I heard a door slam on the other side of the house and I rocked back, dropping the inert man.

Pepper shoved past me and seconds later the hallway was filled with a white fog. I grabbed Flowers again and dragged him back, into the kitchen, half aware of her form limned in

the hallway entrance, extinguisher in hand. I tried to warn her
to step back, but the words died as a croak. My lungs craved
air and my head was starting to swim. I tugged Flowers to
the open doorway, gulped in the saving air, and tried to clear
my head.

Pepper was still inside!

I wheeled and plunged back into the house. I felt my way
toward the hallway and almost tripped over her, seated on the
floor, back against the wall. I reached down and the fire extinguisher rolled away on the floorboards.

I pulled her upward and she managed to stagger to her feet.
She looped her arm over my shoulder and I helped her
through the kitchen and out the back door. We both collapsed
coughing on the grass.

"Fire . . ." she finally managed, pointing. "I think I got it.
The man . . ."

I shook my head and sucked in more air. Twenty seconds
later I got the words out: "It's Flowers. I think he's dead."

I fell back onto the ground, sucking in the air, and it was
what seemed an eternity later that I heard her voice.

"Look," Pepper said, raising herself on one arm. "He's
got something in his hand."

I removed a crumpled fragment of paper, brittle with age,
and stared down at the black, flowing letters, just visible along
the undamaged right margin:

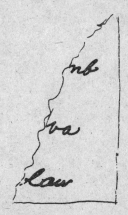

We both stared at the letters for a long time and then I carefully replaced the paper in the dead man's fingers.

What had the last message said?

I WARNED YOU ONCE.
THERE WON'T BE ANY MORE CHANCES.

I felt as if I was going to be very sick.

TEN

The ambulance took us to the emergency room and they stuck us in two curtained cubicles, side by side. After checking our vitals (excellent) and examining us for burns (minor), they gave us oxygen to inhale and then let the West Baton Rouge deputies interview us. Pepper drew a middle-aged Cajun named Sonnier. I got a wiry man with white hair whose name tag said Spano. I told him we'd gone to Désirée to see Flowers about our archaeological investigation and that he needed to call Nick DeLage.

"You friends of his?" the deputy asked.

"Not especially."

Spano grunted. "Man's got a bad reputation in our parish. They say he's into drugs."

He squinted at me with sky blue eyes, but I tried not to react.

"You know Miss Ouida?" he asked.

"We've met."

"Nice old lady. She didn't deserve what that bastard did."

He seemed to be daring me to disagree, but I didn't.

"You know anything about people digging up the grounds?" he asked then. "DeLage called us the other day to complain."

"No."

"But you dig, don't you? That's what archaeologists do."

"I saw the holes. They were round."

He frowned. "So?"

"Archaeologists make square holes."

"So you don't know nothing about this."

"Somebody sent me an anonymous letter by E-mail," I told him. "And somebody trashed my car. You can check the Baton Rouge police report. I don't know if it had anything to do with what happened tonight, though."

"You got any idea why anybody would kill old Flowers?"

I thought about the lock box. But bringing it up would only lead to a horde of deputies digging up the grounds.

"It must've been burglary," I said. "Somebody opened the front door right after the fire started."

"But why would they try to burn the place down?"

"Destroy the evidence?" I asked. "Maybe Flowers caught him in the act and the burglar killed him and then decided to try to burn everything up to cover his tracks."

He stared at me with the ice-cold eyes.

"He had a piece of paper in his hand," Spano said. "Looks like the killer tried to get it away from him and he ended up holding an edge." He scratched his chin. "From the looks of it, the paper's pretty old."

I tried not to show any reaction, but the blue eyes bored into me.

"What does the paper say?" I asked.

"I thought maybe you'd know."

"It's hard to read something while you're trying to get your breath," I equivocated.

Spano brought out a pocket notebook and showed me what he'd copied. "It says something about the law. Some kind of threat, maybe?"

"Your guess is as good as mine. But you might want to have it looked at by an expert."

"I thought you were an expert."

"In archaeology, not documents. You need a forensics document examiner." I thought for a moment. "There was a dark-colored car up the street. It may have belonged to the killer. And there was a kid on a bike. He may have seen something."

Spano shook his head. "Nobody saw nothing. The other deputy knocked on some doors and called me while you were waiting for the doctor." His eyes narrowed slightly. "Any other ideas?"

"Yeah," I told him. "Look for somebody with burns.

Whoever splashed that solvent and set fire to it probably got singed.''

He nodded, put away the notebook, and left me to the nurses.

When they let us go it was almost midnight. It was too late to call somebody to pick us up, so we took a cab. Pepper was groggy and I wasn't much better. When the cab stopped at her apartment I had to help her out.

I told the cabby to wait and gave her my arm as she went up the steps one at a time. When we got to the top she fumbled for her key and I had to take it out of her hand and open the door.

She stared into the dark room for a moment and then turned around.

"Alan, don't go."

"I'll pay off the cab," I said.

When I got back to the room she was slumped on the couch. Her flowered Mexican blouse was smeared with soot and her hair was an ashen tangle. A black smear striped her forehead like Indian war paint. She looked very small and very vulnerable.

"There's some wine in the cabinet under the sink," she said. "Would you get me a glass?"

I came back with two glasses of burgundy. Jealously, I wondered who she drank with when I wasn't there.

She took the glass and sipped. I collapsed into the armchair, an involuntary groan escaping me.

"Are you hurting?" she asked. "I hardly asked about your burns."

"They aren't anything," I said. "Only my hands got a little singed."

"You saved me, you know."

"I don't know," I said. "You're the one who put out the fire."

"Seemed like a good idea," she said sleepily.

"You know, I was thinking about that piece of paper Flowers had in his hand," I said. "I wonder if it could have come from the box."

But she was already asleep.

I went to the couch, moved the wineglass, and started to

cover her with the afghan, but her eyes opened halfway as I touched her.

"I want to go to bed," she mumbled. "I want to sleep in my room."

She let me help her up and made her way through the doorway into the dark bedroom, with me just behind in case she stumbled. She fell onto the bed and I lifted her feet the rest of the way.

"Good night."

"Where are you going?" she asked in a small voice.

"To the couch," I said.

"I don't want you to." Her hand reached up out of the darkness, touched my own. "Please."

"All right." I kicked off my shoes, took off my mangled guayabera and settled down onto the bed next to her.

"Ummm," she mumbled and turned toward me, already falling back into sleep.

I lay beside her, listening to the branches scraping the window in the midnight breeze. My life with Felicia seemed like a distant dream now, something that had happened in my imagination. What was real was tonight, and the woman beside me. I turned my head to look at her.

Just think of her as your daughter.

Right.

I fell asleep.

When I woke up, sun was streaming through the window and I heard water running nearby.

I turned my head to Pepper's side.

She was gone.

I raised myself, moaning from the stiffness of my joints, hauled myself to the side of the bed, and fumbled on the bedside table for my glasses.

The running water sound was coming from the bathroom. She was taking a shower. I glanced down at the floor by the closed bathroom door and saw her clothing from last night in an untidy little heap. Then I looked at my arms.

They looked like I'd been playing in a charcoal bin and my jeans weren't much better. My body reeked of gasoline and wood smoke. When I ran my hand through my hair I felt soot particles.

I had a sudden urge to sneak away before she could see me like this.

Then the running water stopped.

I got up quickly and slipped into the front room. After all, she might come out of the bathroom half dressed, forgetting I was there.

I busied myself looking over the books on her shelf (the standard archaeological works plus an assortment of biographies and, amazingly, romance novels) and the CDs beside the stereo. I was looking through the names of unfamiliar rock bands when I heard the door open behind me and turned.

She was wearing a pair of cutoffs and a T-shirt, sans bra.

"Hi," she said. "I was scared for a minute you'd taken off."

"I heard you in the shower," I said, sliding the book back onto the shelf. "I didn't know . . ."

She smiled and then walked over and, quite unexpectedly, reached up for my head, brought it down to her level, and gave me a kiss on the lips.

"You're so old-fashioned," she said.

"Sorry, but—"

She touched my lips with her fingers. "Please, Alan. Don't change."

I waited, unsure what to say.

"So how do you feel?" I asked finally.

"Fine," she said. "But you're a mess."

I nodded.

"You can shower, if you want to," she offered. "But I don't have any clothes for you to wear."

"I better get home." I sighed. "And Digger'll want to be fed."

"Little problem," she said. "My car's still across the river."

It took an hour for the cab to come and another half hour to get to Désirée. Pepper's white Integra was still parked where we'd left it, but now there was a sheriff's cruiser beside it on the grass, a bored deputy reading the Sunday newspaper with his door open. After some argument and a call to his superiors, he released the Integra and we drove back across the bridge.

We passed down Park Boulevard, quiet and shaded in the

morning light, and she made a U-turn around the median and pulled in before my house.

Sudden inspiration hit me.

"Want to come in for some breakfast?" I asked. "I'm a pretty good cook."

"*Huevos rancheros?*" she asked, opening her door.

"A snap," I answered.

I let us in and turned off the alarm. Digger was pawing at the back door and I let him in. He rushed in to nuzzle my hands and then went to inspect Pepper. She let him sniff her hands and legs and smiled when he tried to jump up to lick her face.

"You passed the test," I said. "He likes you."

I went to the cabinet, took out a couple of cans of dog food, and started to open them.

"I'll feed him," she offered. "If you want to get your shower."

She was offering to feed my dog. A good sign. I nodded and made my way upstairs to my room, the room where I'd grown up, still adorned with some of my airplanes and ships and a baseball autographed by the 1960 Pirates.

I hummed a little tune as I lathered myself, taking comfort in the warm water as well as in the thought that she was still here, hadn't left, was even doing one of my chores.

And I'd always found Digger to be a good judge of character.

When I came down twenty minutes later she was frying the eggs.

"Thought I'd get a head start," she said.

I put some frozen tortillas in the skillet with oil, and started to slice a tomato. Five minutes later we were seated on the screened back porch, our plates in front of us.

"You know, this is the first time I've been in your house," she said. "I mean, besides just inside the front door."

"An oversight," I said, lifting my glass of orange juice. "As you can see, the garden could use some work."

She eyed the tall grass in the backyard.

"It has a lot of potential. I like the banana plants. You could put in a deck . . ."

"And a swimming pool," I suggested.

"In the corner," she said. "But not so big that it would

take away some of the area from the rock garden.''

''Rock garden?''

''I love rock gardens. And, of course, the pool would have a hot tub.''

''I wouldn't build one without it.''

She pushed aside her empty plate and wiped her mouth with a paper napkin.

''Mind if I inspect the grounds?'' she asked and went down the steps into the yard. Digger gamboled over and I watched, thinking how she looked almost as if she belonged here. Then the dog whined and ran to the water oak in one corner of the yard.

''What's wrong with him?'' Pepper asked.

''He's been after a possum for the last week or so. It comes down into the yard at night and steals the food out of his dish. I think it's got young ones.''

''It's pretty brave,'' she said. ''Digger's a big dog.''

''Ever see a mad possum?'' I asked, walking down the porch steps and into the sunlight.

''I thought possums just played dead,'' she said.

''When nothing else works. But generally they put up a pretty good fight.'' I reached down to scratch Digger's ear. ''The old fellow's got a scar on his nose to prove it.''

She patted the dog's head.

''Poor Digger: He ought to know not to oppose a female.''

I followed her to the board fence that divided the back of my yard from the service alley between my house and the neighbors.

''I like this fence. Did you build it?''

I nodded. ''I like privacy. When I was little the old lady who lived across the alley could see everything I did. I got in trouble a lot because of her.''

''Is she still there?''

I laughed gently. ''God, no. She's been dead twenty years.''

Pepper half turned and looked up at me with a twinkle in her blue eyes.

''Then there's nobody who can see us back here now.''

''No,'' I said, my throat suddenly dry.

That was when Digger started barking. Someone was at the front door, ringing the doorbell.

"Hell," I muttered. "I'll be right back."

I went into the house, prepared to kill whoever was outside and couldn't wait.

I jerked open the front door and saw Nick DeLage.

▰ Eleven

"Sorry to bother you on a Sunday," he said. "I tried calling, but . . ." He shrugged.

I remembered then that I hadn't checked my answering machine.

"May I come in?" he asked, leaning forward like a vulture.

I stepped aside. "Sure."

"They told me you hadn't been hurt," he said, sinking into my sofa. "They said there was a woman with you. Is she all right?"

"I'm fine," Pepper said from the hallway and DeLage's head twisted in that direction.

He grinned lewdly. "I can see that."

Pepper advanced into the room and took a seat out of arm's reach, as if she half expected DeLage to pounce. I settled into my stuffed chair and waited.

"What can we do for you, Mr. DeLage?"

"You can give me some idea why somebody wants to burn down my plantation and kill my caretaker," he said, one hand playing with his trousers cuff. "I was at the sheriff's office a little while ago, trying to get something out of those idiots, when the deputy radioed in and said you were there to get your car. I drove over but you'd already gone."

"Too bad," I said. "But the short answer is we don't know much more than you do. Flowers called me and told me to come see him. When we got there he was already dead."

"But why? It doesn't make sense. Why would Flowers call you? That isn't like him." DeLage corrected himself: "*Wasn't* like him."

"I assume he found something. But why he wanted to see me about it I'm not sure. He didn't seem like a very helpful sort of fellow."

DeLage rubbed his chin. "He must've been on to something. And it must've been worth killing for."

I searched his face, trying to detect some evidence of his lying, but it was useless. A man like DeLage was a master of the art.

"You know, those deputies didn't want to give me the time of day. But they asked me a lot of questions, and one they asked was about a piece of paper in the old man's hand."

I nodded.

"Didn't make much sense," DeLage went on. "Something about the law. But it wasn't in Flowers's handwriting. Got any ideas?"

"Not really."

DeLage blew out his breath and looked from one of us to the other.

"Where do you folks stand in your study for the Corps?"

"We have a little more fieldwork to do," I said. "And we have to write up the results."

DeLage nodded and summoned up a smile. "I don't guess the Corps wants to get tangled up in murder, does it? And I guess they pretty much restrict you to the area at hand. I mean, except for the historic research, they probably wouldn't pay for digging at Désirée.

"Right on both counts."

"I figured that. And it's got to be a bitch working for a federal bureaucracy. All the red tape and regulations."

"There's that," I agreed.

"So I was thinking," DeLage said, leaning toward us, "maybe you'd want to follow up your work for the Corps with some work for me. You do work for private individuals, don't you?"

"Yes."

"Good." He put on his sincere face. "Alan, I love Désirée. It's where my family lived for generations. If there's something there that's historical, I want to find out as much as anybody. And you seem to be the person who knows the most about it."

"You're suggesting a privately financed survey of Dési-rée," I said.

He nodded again. "Exactly. Without any of the crap you have to put up with from the government. On your schedule, not theirs. And when it's over, you get the credit, not some bureaucrat in New Orleans."

"You make it sound irresistible," I said. "But these things aren't cheap."

"Of course not. And I'd expect you to be paid what you're worth. I can raise the money. Don't worry about that." He gave his little-boy grin: "Besides, I've always been interested in archaeology. Hell, I might want to come dig holes with you."

My turn to nod. "Give us a day or two to look at our schedule and talk it over," I said.

"Fair enough." Nick DeLage stood up and stuck out a hand. "But don't wait too long. I want *us* to find whatever's there, not some trespasser."

"Of course," I said.

"And one other thing."

"Yes?"

"I don't want to upset Aunt Ouida. I think it would be better if we didn't say anything about Flowers to her, don't you?"

I walked him out to his car.

He paused, out of earshot of Pepper.

"Nice-looking girl," he quipped and gave my shoulder a nudge. "I knew I should've been an archaeologist."

I watched him drive away and turned back to the house, fists clenched.

"Well?" Pepper asked from the doorway.

"Where's my roach spray?" I asked.

"Yeah, he's pretty slimy. All he wants is somebody to do his work for him."

"You got it."

"So are you really going to consider it?"

"I want access to the property," I said. "But I don't want his money. In fact, I don't know if we'd ever *get* any of his money. He's not the kind whose check I'd base our payroll on."

"All he wants to do is hunt for treasure."

"That's right. It's what most people's idea of archaeology is. But this time there seems to be something to it."

"Do you think he knows about the box?"

"I'm not sure what he knows. That's why I don't want to make an enemy out of him—just yet. If we do, we may not ever find out who Louis was and whether his box has historic papers in it."

Pepper nodded and put a hand on my arm. I got goose bumps again.

"But he said something else outside, didn't he? Something that upset you. I could tell from your expression."

"Nothing," I said.

She frowned. "Did it have something to do with me being here when he came?"

"The man's a slug," I said.

"Alan, the hell with him. Who cares what he thinks?"

"I guess I do," I said. "I won't have him dragging your name through the mud."

She touched my face with a hand. "Did I ever tell you that you were old-fashioned?"

"A few hundred times," I said.

The phone rang then and it was Esme.

"Alan, thank God you're all right. I picked up my paper this morning and there was your name and Pepper's, and a story about this gruesome business in Port Allen."

I groaned. My newspaper was still on the lawn, wrapped in its protective cellophane.

"We're okay," I said. "Just a little tired."

"Then I'm coming over. I'm going to bring a pot roast. You both need to rest and somebody needs to look after you."

I thanked her, knowing it would do no good to argue. When Esme decided to be the Earth Mother there was nothing anybody could do.

Pepper squeezed my hand. "At least we'll get a free meal," she said.

"Have you ever eaten Esme's cooking?"

"That bad?"

"Worse."

Pepper smiled wickedly. "Well, she won't be here right away."

I heard a car door slam and turned, crestfallen.

"No. David beat her to it."

David Goldman came hurrying up the walk, his wife Elizabeth at his elbow. Seconds later they were seated on the sofa listening to our story and David was promising to stay all night, in case the killer came back.

"You didn't tell me about this threat business," he accused.

"You were out of town," I said. "And I didn't take it seriously."

By the time Esme arrived with her pot roast, Gator Kelly and Frank Hill appeared with a twelve-pack of beer. Gator grinned toothlessly.

"Thought we'd make sure you were okay," he said, popping a tab. "We came for the poker game last night, but you weren't here."

"I was busy getting burned," I said.

"We figured it was something like that," Gator said. "But I brought a deck in case you want company. Never can tell who might be lurking around."

"I'm overwhelmed," I said, as Esme emerged from the kitchen and announced that the pie was ready.

"Sounds great," Gator said. "Hey, where's Frank?"

"In the study," David said. "Probably on Alan's computer."

I sighed. "Make yourselves at home," I said.

Pepper rose.

"I think I'll go see a friend of mine in a nursing home," she said. "It's a little less crowded there."

I started up, but she shook her head.

"Call me later if you want."

I watched her go and stared around me at my bounty of friends.

David had already gotten the folding table out of my study and Gator was shuffling the cards.

≡ TWELVE

Monday morning I awoke with Digger licking my face. When I staggered downstairs I saw a disaster of beer cans and playing cards scattered on the rug, overturned chairs and table, and, in the middle of it all, a body.

When I looked closer I saw that the body belonged to L. Franklin Hill. He was alive, if mere breathing counted, and there was a note pinned to his shirt:

WE HAD TO LEAVE FOR THE FIELD.
FRANK STAYED TO GUARD YOU.
WE FED DIGGER THE REST OF THE POT ROAST.

It was signed, THE GUYS.

I surveyed the wreckage and then made my way to the kitchen, where I got a can of dog food out of the pantry for Digger.

"Sorry about the pot roast," I told him. "Maybe this will make up for it."

I dressed, ate a bowl of cereal, and then shook the dead man awake.

"I fold," he mumbled.

"Give me your car keys," I told him.

"Didn't bring it," he muttered and went back to sleep.

I threw up my hands, went back to the garage, got out my bicycle, and inflated the tires with a hand pump. What the hell? It was only two miles to the office. Nice day for a ride.

I needed something to wake me up anyway. Last night, just after eleven I'd excused myself from the commotion and gone upstairs to bed. Elizabeth Goldman had long since dragged David away and Gator and Frank were playing some game that had black cards wild, while they watched *Beavis and Butthead* reruns on the television. I called Pepper from my bedroom and got her on the second ring.

"Don't say anything," she said softly. "It wasn't your fault." A giggle: "I had no idea how much you were loved."

"So how was Miss Ouida?" I asked.

"Fine. We had a very nice visit, despite Nurse Krogh. Miss Ouida kept asking for her newspaper and Krogh kept saying they'd run out of copies. But I don't think Miss Ouida was fooled."

I looked over at my clock: eleven-thirty.

"If I had my car . . ." I said.

"Go to sleep," she said sensibly. "There's no hurry. And maybe it's a good idea for us to have some time to think."

And now, as I coasted down the hill past city park, I reflected on her words.

Some time to think.

It was what I'd been most afraid of. What had happened had been a spur-of-the-moment thing, caused by our being thrown together in the face of death. Now that she'd had a chance to reconsider, she was backing off.

Right when I was having to face the fact that I just might be in love with the girl.

Marilyn met me on the porch.

"What do you mean not calling me?" she demanded. "I called five or six times yesterday morning and all I got was a recording."

"I forgot to check the machine," I said sheepishly.

"And when I called last night all I got was a drunk who asked if I thought he ought to draw to three of a kind, whatever that is."

"Gator," I said. "He was keeping me company."

"I figured that out." She turned on her heel and preceded me into the sorting room. "And where's Frank? There's work for him to do on the Cosway report."

"He's sick," I told her. "I'm sure he'll be in by noon."

"Well, somebody better get out and get a new answering tape for the office machine, because the police came and took the old one away. Alan, what in the world is going on?"

I explained about Flowers's call and watched Marilyn's round little face go from red to white.

"Jesus Christ," she cried. "What does *she* want?"

I followed her shocked gaze: A woman had barged in through the doorway, followed by a man with a videocam. The woman was about thirty, chunky, with curly black hair and a smudge of lipstick for a mouth.

I'd seen her on the local news several times over the last year doing exposés, and she reminded me of a pug dog.

"Dr. Graham," she said, thrusting out a hand like a challenge. "I'm Sarah Goforth, with Channel 7 news. I'd like to talk to you about your work at Désirée Plantation."

"I don't have anything to say," I told her.

The videocam was aimed at my face and I knew it was running.

"But you *were* hired by the Corps of Engineers to do archaeological work there, weren't you?"

"Well, yes . . ."

"Is it usual for the government to do work on private land?"

Oh, shit.

"It's for a levee setback. We're working along the river. Look, you really ought to talk to the Corps."

"But you've been working on the plantation itself, haven't you?"

"We've been doing background research. You really need to talk to the Corps—"

"Is it true that Lafitte's treasure may be buried at Désirée?"

"Lafitte's treasure is buried all over the state," I said sarcastically. "Also Jesse James's money and Spanish gold."

"But you do think there may be some other kind of treasure on the plantation?"

"Anything is possible," I said.

"You were there when the caretaker, Brady Flowers, was killed, weren't you?"

"Yes."

"Can you tell us how you feel about that?"

I said a rude word.

She frowned.

"Cut that part," she ordered. Then back to me: "Do you

have any idea who'd do something like that, or who'd want to burn down the plantation?''

''The usual suspects, I guess.''

She chewed her lip, frustrated. ''Just one more question, then, Dr. Graham.'' And to the cameraman: ''I want a tight shot.''

She was getting ready to slip me one . . .

''Dr. Graham, do you think the police suspect you of any of this?''

''Goodbye, Miss Goforth.''

The sour note continued when two detectives from West Baton Rouge Parish appeared and went over my statement again in detail.

''What do you think the killer was after?'' one of them, a scrawny little man named Duplessis, kept asking.

I said some old family papers mentioned a man who'd lived there before the Civil War and maybe somebody thought he'd buried something. I told them his will was in the LSU library, and I even had a copy, which I showed them. As they could see, the old man had nothing of value to bury. They shuffled out, unmollified, and I called Dogbite.

''How much do I have to tell them?'' I asked.

''Depends on what they ask. You don't have to talk to 'em at all, if you think they have you in mind for the crime. Do they?''

''I don't really think so, but you can't ever tell.''

''You can say that again. If you're the closest target you could just be the one they decide to grab.''

''You always make me feel so good.''

''Feel-good is for shrinks. I'm a lawyer.''

''Yeah, I forgot.'' I shifted the phone to my other ear and eyed my office door, to make sure there weren't eavesdroppers.

''Listen, I'm worried about what'll happen if they get the idea there's something out at Désirée that ought to be dug up.''

A snort came over the line.

''Yeah, when I was an assistant D.A. I saw what happened when cops try to do forensics anthropology. Well, if they ask you anything else, refer 'em to me. But if you say anything at all, make sure it's the truth.''

''Cross my heart,'' I said.

After I hung up I sat quietly for a minute, thinking.

It was true I didn't really think they considered me a suspect. But I didn't want to give them the details of our research because I didn't want our work spread all over the newspapers. It was bad enough I'd been ambushed by Sarah Goforth. If any of it aired, there was no telling what the killer would do next.

I punched in Pepper's office number, but all I got was her answering machine. I left a brief message asking her to call and then tried her apartment. Another recorded message. I hung up and tried her cellular. No answer.

Anxiety started to gnaw me. What if the killer had decided to pay her a visit? What if he'd waylaid her on the road?

Then I told myself to calm down: There were a million good reasons why she might not be in telephone contact.

Suddenly I was resentful that she didn't have a pager. But she usually put her cell phone in her handbag, so her failure to answer meant either that she was separated from her bag or the phone wasn't on.

Or that she was somewhere that microwaves couldn't penetrate, or the battery had run down . . .

Or that she'd been grabbed and the phone had been tossed out the car window . . .

I stared at the mountain of work on my desk and then went out into the lab. To my chagrin the only worker present was the Mahatma, a late-blooming flower child in his mid-thirties who'd left Alabama for the West Coast fifteen years ago and never gotten past Baton Rouge. These days, he took occasional courses in anthropology and environmental science and lived in a rat trap on Chimes Street, when not communing at one of the local coffeehouses.

"Is your car running?" I asked.

The Mahatma smiled. "Absolutely."

I thought of the rainbow-colored VW van that was always jacked up in his driveway and wondered what that meant.

"Then drop what you're doing and go to the following addresses." I wrote down Pepper's office and apartment addresses on a sheet of paper. "Knock and see if anybody comes. Try the door. If you see anybody around, ask if they've seen Pepper Courtney. If you see anything suspicious at all, call back here. Or if it won't wait, call the police."

The Mahatma, whose real name was Dean Callahan, nodded.

"You think there's something wrong?"

"I doubt it. But I can't get Dr. Courtney on the phone. If you read the paper this morning, you know I'm kind of nervous right now."

"I don't read newspapers. Too many trees have to die to make them. But I think everything's okay." He touched the crystal hanging from his neck by a leather thong. "I have a sense when something's wrong."

"Go," I said.

The phone rang in the outer office and a few seconds later a reserved Marilyn appeared in my doorway.

"That was Mrs. Amadie reminding you about the talk this afternoon."

"What?"

"Remember? You promised to give a talk to her class at one-thirty."

"Oh, Jesus." I'd forgotten entirely. "What did you tell her?"

"I said you'd be there. You can use my car."

"Bless you."

"Alan, where did Dean go off to?"

"There was something I needed him to check," I said vaguely.

"I hope it was important. We're short of workers and sending one of them off without telling me leaves a big hole in our schedule. According to the Gantt chart I showed you, meeting our deadline on this project requires everyone to stick exactly to the schedule I developed. And one person I expected already hasn't shown up this morning."

"I apologize," I said, wondering if Frank Hill would make it in today at all. "I'll try to find more people."

"That would be nice. But I don't know what you expect to pay them with," she snapped and went back to her desk.

I got my lecture materials from the file where I kept them. For talks such as this one I usually brought some artifacts, showed some slides, and handed out some pages with the Louisiana prehistoric culture sequence on them.

For an instant I considered calling Rosemary and asking to reschedule, but I might as well get it over with. And talking to students often got my mind off whatever was preying on it at the time.

By noon, when the Mahatma hadn't come back, I was frantic.

What if . . . ?

I called home and as the answering machine finished its message a sleepy voice came on the line.

"Are you just waking up?" I demanded.

"I guess so," L. Franklin Hill admitted. "Where's everybody?"

I had him check for messages, but aside from Pepper's calls there weren't any.

Half an hour later I left the office in Marilyn's green Tercel, grabbed a couple of tacos at a cholesterol factory near the campus, and, against my better judgment, swung by Pepper's apartment. No sign of Pepper, no sign of the Mahatma. Then I cut over to Perkins and stopped in the parking lot in front of her office. An ancient black hearse was taking up two spaces in front of her door. Not, I thought, a good omen.

I was trying her locked door when a familiar voice startled me.

"Hey, boss, what're you doing here?"

I wheeled and saw the Mahatma beaming at me.

"Where's the van?"

"At home. I'm keeping the hearse for a guy who's walking around the world for brotherhood. He didn't need it."

"He might be surprised," I said, turning toward Pepper's door. "No luck, huh?"

"The real estate guy with the office next door said he saw her this morning. She was in a hurry. Said something about having to meet somebody. A doctor friend."

"A doctor friend?" I gulped.

"That's what he said."

I swallowed my alarm.

"Okay, Dean, thanks. Might as well get yourself some lunch and go back to the office."

I knew there was an explanation. People had doctor's appointments all the time. Maybe, heh-heh, she just needed to get a birth control prescription.

Or maybe she had an incurable disease.

But why had she said a doctor friend? That didn't sound

like an appointment. It sounded more, well, social.

Damn. I was acting like a teenager. I should be glad at least that she hadn't been snatched by the killer.

So why hadn't she kept her cell phone on?

The school was a Catholic institution in the eastern part of the city. The cars in the parking lot looked relatively new and there was no cyclone fence. The one-story brick building was less than ten years old and actually had windows.

Rosemary Amadie met me at the office. We shook hands, and she told me she'd read in the newspaper about my horrible experience.

"I just can't imagine what you go through," she gushed. "I'm allergic to bee stings and our last class field trip almost sent me to the hospital with poison ivy." She pointed to a pink swatch on her arm, as if to emphasize her vulnerability. "I'm the world's biggest buyer of calomine lotion. But here you are dealing with *murderers*."

"It isn't by choice," I assured her as we entered the hallway with its faintly wax smell. We passed a door that led into a neatly ordered library and one that showed a set of desks with computers. A well-furnished school, I thought, not like the public ones, with their sagging ceilings and flaking walls.

The class was sixth-graders, all in neat uniforms with the school name stenciled on the boys' shirts and the girls' blouses. I set up the slide projector, handed out my information sheets, talked a little about prehistory and the tribes of the area, and passed around some artifacts for the kids to examine. When I was finished answering questions and the bell had rung, Miss Amadie walked me back to the car.

"You don't know how much it means to me to be able to get them involved," she cooed. "There's such a problem with young people today. No respect. They aren't taught values at home." She shook her head. "I was always taught *my* father was a great man and so many of them don't even know who their fathers are!"

"But this is a private school."

"Yes, it's better here. But even here it's hard to get them interested. They're so used to TV. That's why having you come here is important. It breaks the monotony. I'm a firm believer in the hands-on approach.''

And, as if to emphasize the fact, she put a hand on my arm.

''It works sometimes,'' I said and opened the car door on the passenger's side.

''I hope you don't get involved in any more murders,'' she said, and I noticed my personal space had decreased significantly.

''Me, too,'' I said, placing the slide tray and the bag of artifacts on the car seat and shutting the door.

''I hope you'll come to the next meeting of the archaeological society,'' she added, her face only inches from mine. ''I'd love to have you as a speaker. Come to think of it, you haven't given us a talk since I've been president . . .''

''Give me a call,'' I said and then, excusing myself, opened the car door and drove away. In my mirror I saw her staring after me.

Poor woman. She was probably as frustrated as I was.

I pedaled my bike home at five, resentful of the cars whipping past. There were no messages on my machine and Frank Hill had managed to find his way out. The place was still a wreck, and reeked of beer. I reflected on my good fortune in having friends to protect me.

Worse, the refrigerator had been cleaned out and I vaguely remembered my visitors taking out frozen meals and opening cans.

I considered Digger's food, decided against it, and gave him a can.

''You don't know how lucky you are,'' I told him and got a woof in return.

I could always put on some red beans and rice, but it would take time and I was tired. Instead, I made myself a peanut butter sandwich, poured myself a glass of low-fat milk, and flopped in front of the TV, trying to block out the disaster zone around me.

The pug face of Sarah Goforth greeted me, talking breathlessly into the camera, and I noticed with shock my office building in the background.

''To many, the word *archaeologist* conjures up the image

of a man wearing a pith helmet and cracking a bullwhip. And while archaeologists as a whole deny the accuracy of this view, it may not be that far off. Today we spoke with archaeologist Dr. Alan Graham about a murder that took place at a West Baton Rouge plantation, and about what he thinks may be buried there.''

The picture flashed to a front view of Désirée in all its dishabille.

"Saturday night, the caretaker of Désirée plantation, Brady Flowers, was found dead under mysterious circumstances. According to West Baton Rouge deputies, Flowers had been stabbed in the hallway of the plantation home and an attempt was made to burn the house itself.''

There was then a close-up of yellow crime scene tape strung across the lawn and a clot of officials milling in the background.

"A burglary? A crime of passion? The indications today are that there may be more to the story.''

Back to my building.

"This house, near the LSU campus, is the headquarters of a private archaeology firm known as Moundmasters.''

Pan to our sign, at a slight angle where one of the wood screws had pulled loose.

"Moundmasters is run by Dr. Alan Graham, a specialist in the field of environmental consulting. We asked Dr. Graham what might have been behind the murder of the elderly caretaker.''

The face of a middle-aged man with glasses, looking slightly put-upon. *My* face.

"... You do think there may be some kind of treasure on the plantation?''

My expression was definitely surly.

"Anything is possible.''

"You were there when the caretaker, Brady Flowers, was killed, weren't you?''

"Yes.''

Cut back to the pug dog.

"Dr. Graham, do you think the police suspect you of any of this?''

My face went red and I told her goodbye.

"As you can see, Dr. Graham definitely did not want to

talk to us. We'll just have to wait and see what develops in this mysterious case of the old plantation and the murdered caretaker."

I punched the off button with a vengeance, just as my phone started ringing.

"By God," Dogbite Kirby intoned, "I never saw a guiltier look."

"You're funny as a child molester in a Santa Claus suit," I said.

"Well, don't admit to anything, Hoss."

"With you for a mouthpiece I wouldn't dare."

I had to get out of the house before anybody else called. I changed into jogging shorts and got Digger's leash. Fifteen minutes later I was standing next to the lake that stretches from the foot of the golf course to the university. The interstate, reaching from one side of the lake to the other, was reflected in the brown water and a flotilla of ducks paddled by a hundred feet from shore.

Suddenly I found myself thinking about Louis again. When he'd been alive the lakes had been swamp, cut by a small bayou. Where I was standing now had been the back acreage of a plantation, and the only sounds would have been the cries of ducks and herons.

Maybe, I thought, Louis had come here, paddling along the bayou in a pirogue, flintlock rifle in the bow. I tried to imagine him and conjured up the image of a lean, leather-skinned man in a cotton shirt, straw hat shading his face.

He'd adapted, in spite of the blankness that was the first half of his life. But when he was alone in the pirogue, he must have had glimpses of another world.

Or was it all a pretense? Maybe he really was running away and his amnesia was only feigned. Maybe he knew there were people who would kill him for what he knew. Maybe they'd already tried, and his only hope of escape was to pretend ignorance. Maybe, after years, the knowledge of having failed in his mission had driven him insane.

Maybe . . .

I jogged back, put Digger in the backyard, and checked my answering machine. Nothing but a credit card company. I erased it and went upstairs to shower.

Midway through, as the warm water cascaded down over

my head, I thought I heard movement in the bedroom. I turned down the water and listened.

Imagination, I told myself. *The old house settling.*

I finished the shower and stepped out onto the bath mat.

A floorboard creaked.

This time I knew it wasn't my imagination.

I fastened a towel around my middle and looked frantically for a weapon. But the only thing I could think of was my father's old .32 Colt revolver, stuck away on a closet shelf with ancient shells that might not even fire.

In desperation, I looked around for something heavy and grabbed a jar of multivitamins. At least I could throw it at the intruder and maybe that would give me a chance to get in a punch.

Or run naked down the stairs.

I tiptoed to the door and listened.

Clothes rustling.

Someone was standing between the bed and the closet, probably going through my things.

But surely he'd heard the shower stop. Why hadn't that alerted him? Maybe he was really just outside the door, waiting for me to step out.

Maybe, for that matter, there were two of them.

I took a deep breath. It didn't matter: I couldn't stay in here forever. I raised the vitamins in my right hand and reached slowly for the doorknob with my left.

Count to three and then do it.

With a wrenching movement, I jerked the door inward and then, with my left arm lifted to block a blow, jumped into the bedroom with the vitamins ready to fly.

"I've never been threatened with One-A-Day," Pepper said, arms crossed.

She was standing beside the bed, a whimsical expression on her face, and her smile broadened as I felt my face turn red.

THIRTEEN

"Are you just going to drip water on the floor?" she asked.

"How did you get in?"

"You left your door unlocked. I heard the water going and I guess I let my curiosity get the better of me."

"What would your doctor friend say about you being in my bedroom?"

She smiled. "You mean Fitz."

"Fitz?"

"Do you remember that consulting job I did last year at Pirate's Landing?"

"The one you stole from under us?" I asked.

"Don't be jealous," she said. "I underbid you."

"How could I forget?"

"The subdivision was owned by Fitzhugh Griffin."

"And?"

Her smile widened. "I did it for a hundred dollars."

"A hundred dol—" I went mute, mouth half open. "Four acres? With a known prehistoric site?"

"I took a loss to get a track record for this area."

"Obviously."

"Don't be miffed. I can charge anything I want. And he wasn't one of your scum-sucking developers; he was building a retirement community for old people. I did a good job."

"I'm sure," I said.

"Anyway," she said, "that's how I met Fitz."

"*Fitz*," I said.

"He's a very nice man."

"I'll bet." A surge of jealousy twisted my stomach.

"He liked the report I did for him and we got to be friends."

I waited. "And?"

"He even took me to the symphony last year, when they played Schubert."

"I didn't know you liked classical music."

"This is different. Fitz is so intelligent, so knowledgeable. They played Schubert's Unfinished Symphony and Fitz told me how it was only in two movements instead of four, sort of like Schubert's life, because he died when he was only thirty-one, and when I heard the music I wanted to cry and . . ."

I could imagine Fitz handing her a silk handkerchief.

". . . he told me if I ever needed anything to come to him."

"What did you need?" I asked.

"Fitz is professor emeritus of medicine at the LSU medical school. His specialization is geriatric psychiatry."

"Emeritus?" I asked. "You mean he's retired?"

"Of course. He's seventy-three years old. But his mind is as sharp as a needle."

I started to relax. Although old age wasn't an absolute guarantee against licentiousness.

"So what do you need a geriatrician for?" I asked. "That's for the diseases of old people." But even as I said it I began to have a glimmer of the answer.

"I wanted him to talk to Ouida," she said.

"You wanted . . . ?"

"I wanted him to go with me to see her, as a friend, and form his own opinion. I want an independent judgment of whether she's competent."

"You probably just broke fifteen different laws."

"If that nice old lady is being kept in a nursing home by that crooked nephew of hers, the law needs to be broken," she said.

"And it didn't bother your friend Fitz that he might be getting into trouble?"

"Fitz said he'd given up his license to practice medicine when he retired and there wasn't much they could do to a man his age. Anyway, it wasn't an official examination: I just wanted his impression."

I was beaten and she knew it.

"So what did he say?" I asked.

"He said he didn't see anything wrong with her. He asked her questions about her past and then about recent things and he asked her what kind of activities she liked, and when he was finished he told me he thought he could get her attorney to agree to a formal hearing on her competence."

"Formal hearing."

"Sure." She nodded at my towel. "But maybe we want to talk about it downstairs."

Damn.

Much later, when she was gone and I was tired of cursing myself for letting her go, I fell into bed. I dreamed of a pirogue, gliding across the lake. Pepper was with me, seated in the bow, except that it wasn't Pepper, because she had long black hair that flowed down her back. There was a splash in the water behind me and I turned around. When I looked back at the bow of the dugout Pepper was gone, and I wasn't sure she'd ever really been there.

I was calling her name, yelling soundlessly into the wilderness of swamp, when the jangling of the telephone shook me out of my dream.

I groped for the receiver, almost dropping it.

"Hello?"

"Alan?" It was Esme's voice. "I'm sorry to bother you this late."

I glanced at the bedside clock. Eleven-thirty. "What's up?"

"It's Shelby. He's here with me."

I tried to imagine Shelby and Esmerelda.

"That's your business."

"Alan, don't be dense. Shelby came here to do research. That's why I'm calling."

"About his research?"

"Yes, for heaven's sake." There was a muffled sound, as if she'd put her hand over the phone. "Look, you really ought to come over."

"Now?"

"Yes."

"Why?"

"Because, Alan, as I've been trying to tell you for the last two minutes, Shelby has finished his research, or, at least, enough of it, and we thought you and Pepper would want to know. She is *there,* isn't she?"

"Not exactly."

"Then you're a fool. Call her and then both of you get over to my place, now."

"Because Shelby finished his research," I repeated.

"Because he finished his research *and* he has the answer."

"What answer?" I asked.

"Alan, don't act dull. Shelby thinks he knows the identity of our friend Louis."

▰ FOURTEEN

It was almost one in the morning and a cold fog hugged the ground. Pepper had driven over, still half asleep, after getting my call, and now she slid her car into the driveway of Esme's condo on the lake. Across the dark water a few dim lights winked, but otherwise the night was black. The pale square of her picture window was the only sign of human life in the two-story complex.

"This better be worth it," Pepper mumbled as we hurried across the lawn. "I was having such a nice dream."

We mounted the concrete stairs to the second floor and I'd just raised my fist to knock when the door opened.

Esme stepped aside, gave us a smirk, and then closed the door behind us. The room was hung with the paintings of artists she expected would one day be worth money, and there was a stone fireplace against the far wall. One side of the room was a bookshelf and on the other side was a bar.

Shelby Deeds rose from the sofa as we entered and set his coffee cup down on the glass-topped coffee table. A welter of books and documents littered the sofa, coffee table, and rug. The wrinkles in his face seemed deeper in the bright light of the floor lamp and his sad eyes had retreated even farther into his skull. The usual flowery aroma of Esme's apartment had been destroyed by the smell of tobacco, and a crystal ashtray on the coffee table was filled with butts.

"I'm sorry to call you out at such a late hour," he said. "But Esme said you'd never forgive either one of us if we didn't tell you as soon as we were sure."

I shrugged. "I don't guess there's some coffee handy?"

"There's a fresh pot in the kitchen," Esme said and vanished into the back.

"The handwriting's the same," Deeds said, but I didn't know if he was talking to me, because there was an odd glaze in his eyes. "I'd be willing to stake my reputation on it."

"Handwriting?" I asked.

Esme came back with a pot, two coffee cups, cream, and sugar on, of course, a silver salver.

"Sit," she commanded, pointing to a pair of woven cane chairs.

Pepper and I sat down and fixed our coffees. "Now can you tell us what's going on?" I asked.

"It was murder," Esme said gravely. "Except that he wasn't really killed."

"Flowers?" Pepper asked, her sleepiness vanishing.

"No," Esme declared. "The man buried on top of the Indian mound with the Hardin family. The man without a past."

"Somebody tried to murder him," I repeated. "Is that what you're saying?"

Shelby Deeds nodded. "Exactly."

"You've found a record, then," Pepper said.

Deeds nodded again. "Oh, yes. We even have his picture."

Now I was awake.

"What?"

Deeds reached into the papers and handed me the photocopy of a portrait.

Pepper and I huddled together, staring at it.

The man in the painting was in his mid-thirties, dressed in a black coat, with a white cravat. Dark hair spilled carelessly down over a high forehead, and intelligent, deep-set eyes stared into the distance. His nose was straight and aquiline, his chin strong, with just the hint of a dimple. But what got my attention were his lips, slightly pursed as if he had just tasted something and was unsure whether it met his approval.

"Where did you find this?" I asked, incredulous.

Deeds gestured toward the books. "In these. It's all documented. You only have to look in an encyclopedia for the basics."

Now I was sitting on the edge of my chair.

"Then this isn't just some unknown traveler."

Deeds shook his head.

"No."

Pepper looked up from the picture to Deeds and then over at me, and the truth began to hit us both at the same time.

"My God," I heard myself say.

Shelby Deeds smiled grimly. "It happened on October tenth, 1809, at a place called Grinder's Stand, about seventy miles west of Nashville. The accounts say he died early the next morning, either by suicide or murder. He's buried there. Or *somebody* is buried there. It's a national monument today."

"Louis," Pepper and I said together. "The spelling in the will . . ."

Esme smiled like a cat. "Yes. The second governor of the Upper Louisiana Territory. Thomas Jefferson's protégé. The man who made the greatest exploration in American history, who traveled all the way to the Pacific Ocean and back with William Clark. Meriwether Lewis."

I got up slowly. "Wait a minute . . ."

Esme held up a hand. "You probably think we've lost our minds." Her hand was shaking and I didn't know if it was from excitement or the caffeine. "But you know we wouldn't invent something like this and we wouldn't have called you here if we weren't sure."

Deeds reached for his coffee cup and drank slowly, then set the cup down on the table and took out his cigarette pack.

"When you came to me on Saturday, what you said rang a bell. But I couldn't put my finger on it. After all, Meriwether Lewis was supposed to have died two years before this man turned up at Désirée. But there were some odd coincidences—the need to send a message to the president, for example—and the name was interesting. It was L-O-U-I-S on what was written about him, but in the one document in his own handwriting, he spelled it differently. I only knew of one Lewis who figured in the history of that era. Not to say there may not have been others. There probably were. But there was only one who could be checked historically. There was only one person who had samples of his handwriting readily available, that I could compare with the copy of the will that Esme brought me."

"You have copies of Meriwether Lewis's handwriting?" I asked.

The old man smiled and held up a book.

"It's not that hard. Some years ago, the writer Vardis Fisher published a study of Lewis's death, with all the evidence he could find for and against the theory that Lewis killed himself. To illustrate his case, he reproduced a number of letters Lewis wrote toward the end of his life, to show the extent to which his handwriting had changed as the result of the pressures he was under just before he died." He opened the book to its midsection and passed it to me. I saw a plate that was the photograph of a handwritten document. "I drove to Baton Rouge today to see the will in the library collection at firsthand. An historian always prefers original documents. Then all I had to do was compare the will and the examples in this book."

"They were the same?" I asked.

Deeds shrugged and lit his cigarette. "Let's just say close enough to make a believer out of me. But make up your own minds."

Pepper and I compared the various sheets of slanting cursive, the well-formed letters.

"Notice the backward hooks on *d*'s and some of the *e*'s," Deeds said. "And the way some of the terminal *s*'s sort of die off in midstroke."

Pepper nodded. "It looks the same to me. But I'm not an expert on handwriting."

"Nor am I," Deeds admitted. "There are differences, but we're also looking at fifty years of time. The handwriting of the will seems more, well, deteriorated, you might say. Nevertheless, it's the sort of thing that requires the eye of a forensics handwriting expert. I know a man who used to work for the FBI as a specialist in questioned documents. He and I worked together as expert witnesses on an old land-claim case a few years back. I hope you don't mind if I contact him."

"Not at all," I said. "If it will settle the matter."

Deeds sighed and blew out a pungent cloud of smoke. "I wish it were that easy. In the sixties a writer named Clifford Irving made a fortune with a diary he said was written by Howard Hughes. Several top handwriting experts vouched for it. A major magazine paid a million or so for the scoop. Trouble was, Irving forged it himself.''

''I remember something about that,'' I said. ''There were a lot of red faces.''

''Indeed there were.''

''And even if your expert says it's real,'' I pointed out, ''that doesn't explain how Lewis managed to convince people he was killed and then showed up at Désirée two years later without anybody knowing who he was or recognizing him during the trip.''

''That raises another issue,'' Pepper said. ''Just how *was* he supposed to have been killed?''

''And what was he doing on the Natchez Trace?'' I asked.

Deeds got up slowly, limped over to the window, and gazed out over the dark lake.

''Lewis and Clark returned from their exploration, in 1806, famous. They went east, so that Lewis could make a report to President Jefferson. The expedition was something Jefferson had planned for a long time. Even before he acquired the area as part of the Louisiana Purchase he'd planned to send explorers to the northwest to see if there was a water route to the Pacific and to try to keep Britain and Spain from edging out American trading interests.''

He turned around from the window and faced us.

''He chose Meriwether Lewis because Lewis was a soldier, a fellow Virginian, and because Lewis had been Jefferson's private secretary. So Jefferson had a chance to prepare the young man and observe him closely, and it seems that he made the right choice.''

We waited while Deeds drew on his cigarette. Somewhere in the distance I heard a siren, the sound keening over the waters and then dying away.

''The expedition was a great success. In twenty-eight months, Lewis and Clark took forty-five men across an unexplored continent. They saw new animal species and described Indian tribes that other Americans had never heard of. It was a fantastic accomplishment.'' The sad eyes looked away. ''But as soon as Lewis got back things started to go wrong for him.''

''Too much success?'' Pepper asked.

''It's hard to say,'' Deeds said. ''Meriwether Lewis was an

unusual man. He could act decisively in a life-or-death situation, command a body of men in a wilderness, but he had trouble making lasting relationships with women. He never married and yet never gave up hope that he'd somehow find his soul mate. He was a meticulous observer who could write copious notes about animal behavior and describe zoological and botanical specimens, and yet he could never settle down and publish the journal that he'd promised Jefferson, and that Jefferson had promised others, would be one of the great accomplishments of the expedition.''

"But he kept a journal," Pepper said. "I remember seeing it in bookstores."

"Certainly. But he was sporadic in writing it. There are gaps in his journal, some of them lasting for months. We don't know if he never wrote those sections or whether he did and the originals are lost."

"Odd," I said. "So a lost journal could pop up at some point."

"It's quite possible," Deeds said. "But in nearly two hundred years nothing has surfaced. Whatever the case, Jefferson needed to have the journals of the expedition published to justify the tremendous amount of public money he'd spent on the trip. Lewis kept promising to deliver the draft to the printer and never came through. It had to be done by others, using Lewis's original materials, after Lewis was dead."

"Sounds like a lot of graduate students who never get their theses written," Esme said.

"I'm sure there were reasons for delay in the first months after getting back to the East after almost three years away from civilization," Deeds said. "But after some weeks, after Lewis had seen his mother and visited Jefferson, the president appointed him governor of the Upper Louisiana Territory, which had its capital in St. Louis. I suppose Jefferson thought this wasn't only a fitting reward, but also a chance for Lewis to get his journals into shape. But Lewis seemed to be in no hurry to get back there. And when he finally did go, he immediately fell afoul of the man who'd been in charge during his absence, Frederick Bates. Bates was the territorial secretary, sort of a lieutenant governor, and he and Lewis became bitter enemies."

"What about Clark?" Pepper asked.

"Jefferson made him territorial Indian agent. He and Lewis were too close by now to go their separate ways. But Clark seems to have avoided the acrimony between Lewis and Bates. In fact, he even tried to act as intermediary, though it didn't work: Bates was too petty, too jealous. He was from Virginia, too, and he'd applied for the position as Jefferson's secretary several years before. The fact that Lewis had gotten the job and then went on to glory obviously grated on him. So he set out to undo Lewis in every way he could."

"Old story," I said.

"I'm afraid so. What made matters worse was that by the time Lewis arrived as governor, in 1807, Jefferson's term as president had expired and he'd been succeeded by James Madison. The Madison administration decided on a program of austerity and when Lewis began submitting expense vouchers to the War Department, his vouchers started getting rejected. Most of the expenses were quite legitimate. The reasons given for rejecting them were usually that Lewis hadn't gotten permission for the expenditure from Washington first. Not very practical when you consider that, as governor, he had to make decisions on the spot and Washington was weeks away by mail."

"Sure he wasn't working for the Corps of Engineers?" I asked.

"Just the usual clerks in the War Department," Deeds said. "But they were carrying out the orders of the Secretary of War, William Eustis. And when they'd finished, poor Lewis was ruined financially. Oh, not that he didn't make some risky investments while he was governor, and he may have had a bit of a drinking problem, but what he had to deal with would have driven anybody to drink. Finally, in desperation, he packed up copies of his vouchers and set out with his servant, a man named John Pernier, to go to Washington and confront the people in the War Department in person."

"Hear, hear," I said.

"But he was killed on the way," Pepper said. "Is that right?"

"Well, *something* happened," Shelby Deeds said. "But historians have never known just what. He started downriver, with the plan of reaching New Orleans and then taking the coastal route by sea until he got to Washington. But when he got to Fort Pickering, at what's now Memphis, he changed his mind and decided to take the overland route instead.''

By now I was caught up in the saga.

''Does anybody know why he changed his mind?'' I asked.

Deeds walked over to the fireplace and stared at the grating as if the answer might be there. Then he turned back to face us and shook his head.

''Ostensibly it was to avoid being captured by English raiders. He had all his notebooks from the expedition with him. But there's a lot of confusion about that, because the officer in charge of Fort Pickering, a Captain Gilbert Russell, later said Lewis was so distraught when he reached Pickering that Russell had to guard him to keep him from killing himself. Supposedly, Lewis had tried to kill himself on the trip downriver by boat before they got to Pickering. But after a few days at Pickering he recovered, allowing him to start out on the Trace, with his servant and an Indian agent named Major James Neelly, who just happened to pop up at Fort Pickering while Lewis was there and who offered to look after Lewis on the Trace.''

''Are you saying this Neelly . . . ?''

Deeds shrugged. ''Nobody knows. The point is that if Lewis had continued downriver to New Orleans by boat, he might have run smack into somebody else who was coming upriver. Somebody who was already in trouble because of his dishonesty and incompetence, who was on his way to answer charges in a military court.''

''General Wilkinson,'' I said.

''Number Thirteen,'' Esmerelda said. ''He was here when Lewis changed his mind and decided to head overland, via the Trace.''

''Here?'' I asked.

Esme nodded and gave her cat's smile.

''In Baton Rouge.''

▰▰FIFTEEN

It was my turn to walk over to the window and stare out, trying to see through the darkness and into the past.

"So Lewis took the Trace instead," I said.

Shelby Deeds nodded and reached for another cigarette. "And that brings us to Grinder's Stand, seventy miles south of Nashville, on the afternoon of October tenth, 1809. It wasn't much more than a couple of cabins linked together with a makeshift breezeway and a barn some distance to the rear. It was just off the Trace, which ran alongside the clearing where the Grinder house was located. The people who lived there were Robert Grinder; his wife, Priscilla; several young Grinder children; and two slaves, a boy named Peter, thirteen, and a girl named Malinda, twelve years old. That evening, Robert Grinder was twenty miles away at their other farm, on Duck River."

I tried to visualize it: a lonely homestead, not even on the main track, a woman with crying children, her husband gone, and only a pair of young servants to help her with chores . . .

"A mail rider would have passed every few days," Deeds went on. "Other than that, the only visitors would have been unannounced travelers on horseback. Also, since they were on the edge of Indian territory, there were roaming bands of Chickasaw Indians, which couldn't have made Mrs. Grinder feel that comfortable, especially since the Indians probably were hoping to find liquor to trade for."

"Not exactly the bright lights," I allowed.

"Just before sunset on that day, Mrs. Grinder looked up and saw a horseman coming up the path. He wore a white, blue-striped gown, or duster. Usual riding garb for those days," Deeds said. "It was Lewis, riding alone. Later, it came out that Neelly had stayed at their last camping place to round up some packhorses that had strayed. And Lewis had outpaced the two servants, his own and Neelly's, who were behind him a half hour or so."

I nodded. So far, so good.

"According to what Mrs. Grinder later said, Lewis acted deranged and walked around talking to himself. Since her husband wasn't at home, she was scared, so she put Lewis up in her cabin and slept in the other one, which served as a kitchen. The two servants slept in the barn, two hundred yards behind the cabins."

I watched Esme make a steeple of her thin fingers.

"Around three in the morning," Deeds went on, "Mrs. Grinder heard two shots from Lewis's cabin. The servants woke up and they all went in and found Lewis wounded. He'd been shot once in the head and once in the chest. He begged for water and she gave him some. He died a little while later. When Major Neelly came up, some time after dawn, Lewis was already dead."

"Any last words?" I asked.

Deeds laid aside his cigarette. He picked up a book and opened it to a marked passage.

"When they went into the cabin and found him he's supposed to have said, and I quote, 'I've done the business, my good servant. Give me some water.' "

"Convenient, huh?" Pepper said. "But how many suicides do you know of who needed two bullets to kill themselves?"

"A point," I said, "though with the guns of that day misfires were pretty frequent."

"True enough," Deeds admitted. "Anyway, Major Neelly says he saw to the burial, gave Lewis's servant, Pernier, fifteen dollars for travel, and then continued on to Nashville with Lewis's effects. When he got to Nashville he reported to the local Army official, a Captain Brahan, who wrote letters to Jefferson and to his own superior, the Secretary of War, based on what Neelly told him. Then Neelly himself wrote a personal letter to Thomas Jefferson, who was in retirement at Monticello."

"What did Jefferson have to say about it?" Pepper asked. "It seems to me that's a key point."

Deeds shrugged. "He took Neely's word that it was suicide. And so did Lewis's best friend, William Clark, who'd accompanied Lewis on the famous expedition."

"That's interesting," I said. "They knew Lewis better than anybody and if they thought it was suicide . . ."

"Maybe," Esme said then. "But remember, they were going on what they were told. And they also knew Lewis was under tremendous pressure. The man *was* upset and depressed, or he wouldn't have taken off for Washington to plead his case. The bureaucracy really *had* ruined him financially."

Deeds nodded. "And don't forget that Jefferson was a politician. It might not have been in his interests to stir up a scandal. The country was on the eve of war with Britain, and Spain was lurking on the borders, ready to snatch anything it could get. The Spanish had even sent out an expedition from Santa Fe to try to intercept Lewis and Clark during the exploration, on Wilkinson's recommendation, no less! Jefferson was the kind who might have wanted to let sleeping dogs lie, even at the risk of leaving his friend unavenged, especially if Wilkinson was involved. How would it reflect on his administration if everything about Wilkinson came out?"

"You think Lewis had evidence of Wilkinson's treason?" I asked.

Deeds pursed his lips. "I don't know."

Outside, the fog had thickened into a soup and smothered the surface of the lake. I tried to visualize the dying Meriwether Lewis lying on the cabin floor in the chill morning of that long-ago October day.

I turned around to face them. "So what are we saying? That the official account's wrong and Lewis somehow managed to find his way down here two years later, with amnesia?"

Pepper rubbed her hands against her thighs. "I think we're saying somebody else was buried at Grinder's Stand and that most of the so-called witnesses were wrong about who it was."

Shelby Deeds and Esme both nodded agreement.

"Was the body ever disinterred?" I asked.

"Supposedly," Deeds said. "In the middle of the last century, the Tennessee legislature appointed a commission to erect a monument at the grave site. But you'd hardly call it a study in forensic pathology."

"So now," I said, "we're proposing to reopen the case on the grounds that whoever is buried there is the wrong man."

"Exactly," Deeds said, putting the remains of his cigarette in the tray.

I raised my palms, frustrated. A headache was starting to throb somewhere behind my eyes.

"But all we really have is the handwriting," I said.

Esme looked over at Shelby Deeds and the old man nodded for her to respond.

"There's a little more than that," she said. "There are the resemblances between Meriwether Lewis and the man who lived at Désirée, as recounted in John Clay Hardin's journal."

"Oh?"

Esme picked up a sheet of paper with handwriting and I saw it contained a numbered list.

"First," she said, "the man at Désirée was about the same age as Meriwether Lewis. Second, the man at Désirée was noted for his knowledge of natural science and Meriwether Lewis was an excellent self-taught naturalist. Third, he had a knowledge of herbs; the real Lewis's mother was known as an herbalist and a healer. Fourth, Meriwether Lewis was mechanically astute and we have references to Désirée's Louis repairing cotton gins and guns. Do you remember the reference to the iron boat? I think Hardin mentions it as something Louis talked about when he was delirious with fever. Well, Thomas Jefferson and Meriwether Lewis designed a boat with an iron frame, that was to be collapsible and that could be used on the expedition. It never worked, but it makes sense of what the old man was raving about. Fifth, old Louis slept on animal skins, on the floor of his cabin. That was something Meriwether Lewis was known to do—a habit from his trip with Clark. Sixth, there was Hardin's report of how Louis reacted when he found out about Thomas Jefferson's death: The real Lewis had been Jefferson's secretary, a member of his household, one of Jefferson's most trusted confidants. It would have been in character for the real Meriwether Lewis to have reacted to news of his benefactor's death, even if most of the memories stayed buried. Seventh, Meriwether Lewis tended toward the depressive—what they call a bipolar type these days. Energy alternating with feelings of hopelessness. He may have had an alcohol problem. In fact, his behavior was erratic enough during his trip from St. Louis to Grinder's Stand that his death was considered suicide at first. Hardin mentions Louis being melancholy and once suspects he may have been holed up in his cabin, drunk.'' She looked at her fingers, which she had used to tic off the points.

"Don't forget the scar," Deeds said.

"That's right," Esme said. "Hardin writes that his Louis had a scar on his head. Meriwether Lewis was reported to have been shot in the head at Grinder's Stand.''

"Well," I said, "it's all interesting, but it isn't proof.''

"No," Esme said. "But look at the handwriting." She brought out the Vardis Fisher book. "This is one of the last letters Meriwether Lewis is known to have written. It's a letter to President James Madison, dated September sixteenth, 1809, less than a month before Lewis died. The handwriting's almost the same.''

"Similar," I said. "But handwriting tended to be more uniform back then, because of the way people were taught cursive.''

Esme started to protest, but Shelby Deeds held up a hand.

"He's right to be skeptical. But it would be hard to imagine all these coincidences not meaning *something*.''

"You know there's only one way to prove it," I said.

"Yes." Pepper nodded. "We exhume them. Both of them.''

≡ Sixteen

I felt their eyes on me. They were right. There was only one way to prove the case.

"Of course," Pepper said, "we'd have to get some descendants to give blood samples so we could make DNA comparisons."

"And we'd have to have the right kinds of remains," I said.

"What do you mean?" Esme asked. "I thought you could do it on bones."

"You have to have the right parts of bones," I explained. "You need material from the medullary cavity—marrow, in other words. Long bones—the legs, the arms—are best, but teeth are good, too, if there's pulp left."

"Is there likely to be any so long afterward?" Deeds asked.

I shrugged. "It's hard to tell. In this area the soils are pretty acidic. There might not be anything left. On the other hand, if he was buried in a cypress coffin or in an iron casket, the bones might be in pretty good shape."

"And the grave in Tennessee?" Esme asked.

"Another problem," I told her. "It's part of a national monument. That means we'd have to get permission from the National Park Service."

"That may be a real stumbling block," Deeds said.

"I agree." I picked up the photocopy of the will. "I think the sooner we can establish that the will is genuine, the better. And we need to have your expert look at the Hardin journals, too."

"Absolutely," Deeds said. "And then there's the little

matter of pinning down our man's whereabouts between October of 1809 and 1811.''

"But how?" Esme asked. "Where in the world would you look?"

Deeds blew his breath out slowly and his mustache rippled.

"I think I'd start in Tennessee. Maury County, to be precise."

"You mean where he was killed?" Pepper asked.

"Yes. It's a favorite research topic there. I've already taken the liberty of calling someone I know in Columbia, the county seat."

"A historian?" I asked.

"A retired librarian, Dorcas Drew. She knows the literature on Lewis's death better than anyone alive."

"But what could she have that hasn't already been published?" Pepper asked.

"I don't know," Deeds said, "but when I talked to her today she seemed surprised. She said I was the second person who'd called her about it."

The room went silent and a thin whistle of wind came from the fireplace.

"Who was the first person?" I asked.

"She couldn't remember the name. She said it was five or six years ago. This man was supposed to come up and see her, but he never showed and she forgot about it until now."

"Well, it could have been anybody," Pepper said.

Deeds smiled. "I don't think so. Because I explained what we were interested in—the possibility that Meriwether Lewis hadn't died at Grinder's—and she said I was the second person to raise the issue. She wanted to know if I was working with the original caller, since we were both from Louisiana."

"Jesus," I whispered. "But she remembers it was a man?"

"Oh, yes. And he was asking about records of the Grinder family."

"The people who owned the inn where Lewis died?" I asked.

"Yes. He seemed especially interested in Robert Grinder, the absent husband of the woman who supposedly witnessed Lewis's death. And he asked several times what evidence there was that the body buried under the monument on the Trace is really Lewis's."

"So maybe we have our murderer," Pepper said.

"Maybe we have both of them," Esme corrected. "The person who killed Brady Flowers in 1998 and the person who killed Meriwether Lewis in 1809."

"Okay," I said, getting up again. "But what's the motive? The box? Is our present-day killer looking for the metal box because it may have the information he was looking for in Tennessee?"

"It makes sense," Esme said.

"Then why," I asked, "did he wait until we started our research to resume his? It doesn't make sense. The box, if it's there, has been there since 1861. Why did this person call the Drew woman in Tennessee and then never contact her again? Why is it that our visiting the plantation suddenly triggers his interest after so many years? And what about the piece of paper in Flowers's hand? Was that paper from the box? Does that mean the killer's found the box already?"

"I don't know," Esme said. "If we only knew more about him, whoever he is."

Shelby Deeds raised a hand.

"Isn't there one thing we can be pretty sure of?" he asked.

"What's that?" Esme asked, frowning.

Deeds looked from one of us to the other. "Our mysterious killer is almost certainly a historian."

I blinked and Esme said, "Of course."

Deeds scratched his cheek. "This sort of thing doesn't have any value to someone with no interest in history. If it were a question of buried treasure, this person wouldn't have called Dorcas in Columbia. No, this is someone who knows where to look and what to look for. Someone like . . ." he smiled over at Esme, the sad eyes suddenly coming alive, "you or me."

"Since it was a man," Esme said, "that only leaves you, Shelby."

"Yes, well, I suppose I'd better get my alibis together. But you see what I'm saying."

"He's right," I told Pepper. "This killer isn't just some thug. It's somebody who knows computers and knows research methods. Like a member of the history department."

Esme's dark brows arched. "My colleagues may be a bunch of pompous egomaniacs, but they're all too comfortably ensconced in their niches to exert the effort required to commit murder. This is more likely to be the work of some perpetual graduate student, who's been working on his dissertation for the last ten years and is scared somebody's going to publish before he can get his thesis approved. Believe me, a desperate graduate student is capable of anything."

I smiled. "Any students in your department fill the bill?"

Esme shrugged. "There're one or two who've made a career of finishing their dissertations. But one's a woman and the other, who really is a peculiar bird, is doing his on the economic history of rum production in the Indies."

"What about Nick DeLage?" Pepper asked. "He'd do anything for a dollar."

I nodded. "But somebody would have to put the idea in his head. He's not what I'd call an historian."

"In that case," Esme said, her face grave, "we have a very serious situation. It means we haven't met the killer yet."

"Or," Shelby Deeds said, "it's someone we *have* met but would never associate with this."

"Whatever the case," I said, "we need to decide how we're going to work from here. We need to decide who's going to do what and we need to take precautions."

"Agreed," Deeds said. He picked up a yellow legal pad and began to write. "Here," he said, holding it up for us to see. "I've written down a few of the things that need to be done, if everybody agrees."

I looked at the precise, almost calligraphic handwriting.

"First," he said, "I've made arrangements to drive up to Columbia and talk to Dorcas Drew. I can make the drive in a day, but it means I'll have to get on the road as soon as we finish here, because there're some things I need to do at home before I leave in the morning."

"I'll go with you, then," Esme volunteered, but Deeds shook his head.

"No. We need you to use your contacts here to get permission from the library to let our expert examine the will."

"Ummm," Esme said. "I do know the archives people pretty well and if you'll give me a letter, I know your reputation—"

"I'll type one up on your computer before I leave," Deeds said, then turned to Pepper and me. "The other thing is the journals. You have to get permission for our expert to take them for analysis. I understand Miss Fabré has let you borrow them once already.''

Pepper exhaled. ''What do we do about Nick?''

''I don't know,'' I said. ''Once he sniffs something big, he'll be looking for money.''

''Are we obligated to let him in on things?'' Esme asked.

''I don't see how we can hold it back,'' I said. ''He has control of the property and we'll need his cooperation if we do any more work there.''

''Well, I'll have to leave that to you,'' Deeds said. ''Of course, the examination of the documents is just a formality. But we need to be able to show they're genuine if we expect to take this any further.''

''But we still don't know what we're looking for exactly,'' Esme said. ''It's kind of like blundering around in the dark.''

''True,'' Deeds said. ''But our mysterious killer seems to know what *he's* looking for. So if we follow his lead, we may just blunder onto the answer.''

I couldn't think of a better strategy.

≡ SEVENTEEN

Nick DeLage agreed to see us at ten-thirty. His office was on Florida, a four-lane boulevard that leads east from the river all the way to the next parish. DeLage Insurance was in a one-story complex that included a firm of consulting engineers, a hypnotherapist, and a couple of dentists. A peroxide blond secretary in her late thirties sat in the midst of a computer array I envied—big-screen monitor, flatbed scanner, and printer, which was busy spewing out brightly colored pages. The secretary took my card and buzzed her boss, but he must have been waiting because he came right out.

"So where do we stand?" he asked pleasantly, after we all took our seats in his office. One wall was covered with certificates, intermingled with pictures of DeLage shaking hands with mostly forgotten politicians. A plaque in the center said he'd sold a million dollars' worth of insurance in 1995. Just under it, in a gold frame, was a fancy computer mockup of a thousand-dollar bill with DeLage's picture in the center, and the legend, OUR FIRST THOUSAND DOLLARS.

Nick DeLage smiled, but his eyes ate us alive.

I took a deep breath and told him where we stood.

When I was finished he whistled.

"Lewis, huh? Isn't he the man Louisiana's named for?"

"It was named for the king of France," Pepper said.

"Well, I never was any good at history." He picked up a paperweight that said U.S. SENATE and pretended to examine it.

"Does this make Désirée worth more?"

"I'm not sure," I said. "I don't know how you compute historical value."

"It's easy," he said. "Land that's laying there unused sells for whatever you can get from somebody. Land you can develop into a tourist attraction goes for a hell of a lot more."

"That's what you see this as?" I asked. "A tourist attraction?"

DeLage shrugged. "Why not? You told me this place in Tennessee where Lewis is supposed to be buried is a national park. You don't think the government got that land for nothing. Why not have a national park down here?" He leaned toward us. "Hey, there'd be plenty of archaeology work for you folks. We'd all do real good."

A vision of souvenir stands and hamburger stalls sprang into my mind.

"Only," DeLage went on, "I wouldn't want some half-assed little out-of-the-way park, like these state commemorative areas. I could get the tourist commission involved, maybe get some help from the gambling boats." His eyes were alight with enthusiasm. "Look, we could dress people up in the costumes they used to wear, see? Throw big parties. You say this Lewis was shot: We could stage that again, only right here."

"We aren't sure the man really is buried there at this point," I told him. "We need to do more study."

DeLage shrugged. "So do it." He squinted. "Or do you need some money? I might be able to get some backers."

"I think we can handle it at this point," I said. "But we'll need to look a little more closely at your aunt's journals."

"Why?"

"Because if we make a claim like this people will say it's all a forgery unless we have the original documents analyzed."

"Yeah, well, I know how that works. You get your expert, they get theirs, just like in court. The key's getting the right man." He looked at Pepper and grinned. "Or woman."

"We know somebody who can do it," I said. "He used to work for the FBI."

"Yeah?" He shook his head. "Never had much use for those guys. Traffic cops with law degrees. What else we got?"

"That's about it," I said. "But we'd like to borrow the journals."

The close-set eyes pinioned me.

"Soon as we have an agreement in writing," he said. "I'll have my lawyers draw one up."

I took a deep breath. It was what I'd been afraid of.

"You don't mind if we see your aunt," Pepper said then.

DeLage shrugged. "Why not? So long as she's feeling up to it."

I got up and he followed suit.

"Sounds like we may have something here, right?" he asked, trying to sound casual. "Hell, this could be a big deal. And I don't reckon it would hurt your reputation to find out where this guy is really buried. Maybe you could write a book. Then you wouldn't even have to do this kind of work anymore. That'd be okay, wouldn't it?"

"Depends," I said noncommittally.

He walked us to the door and stopped to put a hand on the blond secretary's shoulder. "By the way, heard anything more about who killed old Flowers?"

"No," I said.

"Me, either. Well, maybe it was a burglar, huh?"

"All things are possible," I said and hurried out of the office.

We were out of the parking lot before Pepper spoke.

"Disneyland on the River, huh?"

"Something like that."

"I think we ought to go see Miss Ouida right now and try to get the journals," she said. "I don't trust that bastard."

"I couldn't agree more."

It was eleven-thirty when we parked in the nursing home lot. We went to the reception desk and asked for Ouida Fabré, but the receptionist shook her head.

"Miss Ouida's having a bad day. It would be best to come another time."

"When would you suggest?" I asked.

"Some other time," the woman repeated.

There wasn't anything else to do but leave.

*   *   *

I picked the Blazer up at noon and Pepper followed me to a Lebanese restaurant about two miles south of the campus. We took a table in the corner, away from the other diners, and my skin tingled at the quiet intimacy of the setting.

Last night, after we'd finished at Esme's, she'd dropped me off for a couple of hours' sleep and gone home to her own place. When she'd swung by this morning to pick me up I was cursing myself for not having made my move.

"Pepper, about last night . . ."

"Shhhh." She reached over the table and squeezed my hand. "Let's order. Do you like taboulleh?"

"Love it," I said.

The waiter came.

"And a glass of wine?" she asked.

"Absolutely."

"There's not much more we can do at this point," I said as we ate. "I mean, we can't see Miss Ouida, and Esme's taking care of getting permission to look at the will. Shelby Deeds is on his way to Tennessee and I guess we're temporarily out of work."

"So what do you suggest?" she asked softly.

"We could drop by my place," I suggested and then felt deflated when she shook her head negatively.

"No." She took a sip from the wineglass. "My apartment is closer."

My heartbeat started to quicken again.

"Finish eating," I said.

It was a short drive from the restaurant to the Highland Road subdivision where she lived. She turned into the driveway ahead of me and I parked just behind her Integra. Like a guilty teenager, I looked around to see if anyone was watching from the house, but it appeared deserted.

Love in the Afternoon, I thought, remembering the old movie. Except that I wasn't Gary Cooper, she wasn't Audrey Hepburn, and there sure weren't any gypsies to play music. But who the hell needed them?

I floated up the steps after her, feeling eighteen again and as light on my feet as a dancer. I figured this must be a dream, but if it was I didn't want to wake up.

But I did wake up, and sooner than I expected.

It happened when she stopped in front of her door and gave a little cry.

"Alan, somebody's been here."

I reached the top of the landing and saw the door cracked open.

"Let me go in first," I said, gently pushing her to the side.

"Don't go in," she warned. "He might still be inside."

I pushed the door open slowly and looked in.

The room was a shambles, with books pulled onto the floor and stuffing from the sofa scattered in great heaps over the rug.

I turned around and put my arms around Pepper. There wasn't a lot to say.

The police came in twenty minutes, a patrolman in a marked car who looked inside, asked if anything was missing (how could you tell?), and wrote some notes. Probably kids, he said: There'd been other break-ins in the neighborhood. When I told him there was more to it and explained about Flowers, he squinted at me, said he'd pass it on to the detectives, and asked Pepper not to come back until the crime scene people had checked the premises. He handed her his card with the case number and asked where she'd be. I gave him my own card and told him to call us if they needed a statement. Then we drove to my office.

"It has to have happened this morning," she said, settling into the chair next to my desk. "But our killer wouldn't have risked it in broad daylight. A burglar, maybe, but not our killer."

I nodded as Marilyn appeared in the doorway.

"Is everything all right?" she asked, her eyes going from me to Pepper and back again.

"Fine," I said.

She looked at us a second longer and then went back into the outer room.

Pepper leaned forward: "She knows something," she whispered. "Did you see her eyes on us when we came in?"

"Marilyn's very protective," I said. "And jealous as hell."

"You don't mean she . . ."

"For me?" I laughed. "No. She's got a boyfriend. But she doesn't like to share my attention with other women."

"That's silly. It's so—"

"Female," I quipped and saw her go red. Then she saw me smiling and exhaled sharply.

"No wonder you're single."

Thank God the phone rang.

"It's Esme," I told her as I heard the historian's voice.

"Alan, I just wanted to check in and let you know I've got tentative approval to have our expert take the will out for examination. There are some papers that have to be signed and, as usual, it has to go through a herd of vice chancellors, but it seems pro forma, so long as our man has the right credentials."

"Good. Any word from Shelby?"

"Not yet. He left early this morning, though. He said he'll call when he gets to Columbia."

"Somebody ransacked Pepper's apartment."

"While you were at my place last night?"

"Or while we were running around this morning. We just found it."

"Was it a burglary or was it our killer?"

"I'd bet the latter," I said. "He was sending a message. He couldn't get into my place because of the alarm."

"Which means this person isn't a professional criminal," Esme pointed out. "They can always get around alarms, or so I hear."

"Be careful, Esme. You're the only one he hasn't gone after so far."

"Pooh. He knows better than to tangle with me. By the way, did he leave any kind of message this time?"

"Not that we saw."

"Hmmm. You might want to check again. This individual likes to leave calling cards." She tisked. "Well, keep me abreast. I assume you and Pepper will be together when I need you?"

"More or less," I said, and, when I'd disconnected, turned on my computer.

"What's the story?" Pepper asked.

"Esme wanted to know if we'd found a warning. I thought I'd check my E-mail."

"You don't think he'd try the same thing over again?"

"I doubt it. But you can't tell. He's been a step ahead so far."

I clicked the mouse several times, accessing the Internet and then calling up my E-mail.

A message from yesterday, from an ex-crewman who'd gone west to excavate at pueblo ruins and wanted to say hello and how were things in the great swamp?

A note from an archaeologist in Mississippi who was doing a study of Indian mounds and wanted a copy of a report we'd done a couple of years ago.

And finally:

YOU WON'T STOP.
I'VE KILLED ONCE.
DO YOU REALLY WANT ME TO KILL AGAIN?

▰ EIGHTEEN

"Damn," Pepper swore, staring down over my shoulder at the blue screen. "Sent this morning at ten-fifteen."

"Look at the address," I said.

After the sequence of letters listing the carrier were the telltale letters CRTASSOC.

"He sent it from my computer!" Pepper cried. "He just walked right in, in the middle of the morning, wrecked the place, and then sent you an E-mail letter from my computer."

"Which means he has your password," I said.

She shrugged. "That's no problem. I have it on a piece of paper taped to the wall over my desk."

"So the message may have been lagniappe," I said. "Just something he threw in when he saw your password."

"Could be," she allowed. "Bastard."

Her fists clenched.

"I'll print it out and give it to the police," I said. "For all the good it will do."

I went into the outer office, got the sheet out of the printer, put it into an envelope, and called for the patrolman who'd made the initial report.

"Well, it tells us *something*," I said, "but I'm not sure what that leaves."

"Oh?"

"It wasn't DeLage: We talked to him on the phone at nine and he'd have had to have wings to get back to his office at ten-thirty when we met with him."

"So we still have a faceless killer."

"Yeah," I said. "But it has to be somebody DeLage or Miss Ouida knows, or—"

My phone buzzed and I picked it up.

"I don't know who it is," Marilyn said, "but she's upset. Insists on talking to you personally."

I punched the button.

"Hello?"

"Mr. Graham?"

My breath caught: The voice belonged to Ouida Fabré.

"Miss Ouida?" I asked and pressed the button to put her on the speaker phone so Pepper could hear.

"Mr. Graham, I'm so scared. I can't talk for long. If they see me on the phone they'll get aggravated and they can be mean."

"What's wrong, Miss Ouida?"

"It's Nicholas," the old woman said, her voice quavering. "He took my books."

I muttered an epithet.

"They're the only thing I have." She sounded on the verge of tears.

"When did this happen?" I asked.

"Just a little while ago. That nurse, Ida Krogh, came here and took them away. They can't do that, can they? Those are mine. I just want to die."

Her voice died away in a moan.

"Don't give up, Miss Ouida," Pepper said. "We'll do everything we can."

"My nephew thinks I've lost my mind," Ouida moaned. "But that doctor you brought the other day doesn't think so, does he?"

"Of course not," Pepper said. "And we'll get you out, Miss Ouida. That's a promise."

"God bless you. I have to go now. They're coming."

The line went dead.

"We have to get her out of there," Pepper said.

I looked down at her hands, where she was supporting herself on the desk, and saw that her knuckles were white.

"How?" I asked quietly.

"I don't know. A court order. Whatever it takes."

I lifted the phone, punched in Dogbite's number, and turned on the speaker.

"So who's the lawyer for Ouida Fabré?" I asked. He gave me the name and I wrote it down: Stafford Oates.

"What do we do now?" I asked.

"We call him and make a case that Nick DeLage is trying to screw the old lady. If Oates agrees, he goes to the court to have the incompetency judgment reversed."

"Is that all?"

"Sure. The judge will ask for expert testimony or he may just interview her, and then he'll make a ruling."

"But in the meantime, what about any of her property DeLage has?"

"As curator he can dispose of it if it's a prudent thing to do."

"What the hell does that mean?"

"If she's got some bonds lying around and he thinks he can make more money for her by selling them and investing in something else, he can do it. Or he could conceivably sell land of hers if he thought the opportunity was too good to pass up. But he has to keep records and he can't profit by it, like selling it all to himself for a dollar."

"And if we have an expert tell her lawyer she's mentally competent?" Pepper asked.

Dogbite grunted. "He'll probably have to make a formal examination."

Pepper shrugged.

"And, of course," Dogbite went on, "you'll piss off Nick. So if you've got any notion of getting onto the property again before the end of the millennium, you better think about it first. Her lawyer will have to take into account the possibility that you and Alan may have an ulterior motive."

"Ulterior motive?" Pepper cried.

"He's right," I said. "He'd have to consider it."

"I don't care what Nick DeLage thinks," Pepper declared. "We can't let him keep that old lady in that place."

"Alan?" Dogbite asked.

I looked over at Pepper.

"Call her lawyer," I said. "We'll deal with Nick."

Pepper's look was almost reward enough. Almost . . . I got up and walked to my window as she punched in the number for Fitzhugh Griffin. We'd played it by the numbers and as a result Nick DeLage had the journals. Without the journals nobody would believe our story, regardless of the will. There had been clever forgeries before and without the journals to examine, historians would write it off as a curious *maybe*.

As for the metal box, we had even less chance of finding that now.

I turned back to my desk.

"Fitz says he'll talk to her lawyer," Pepper said. "He'll give her a full battery of tests if the lawyer will let him."

I nodded.

"I know what you're thinking," she said. "We may not ever get to work at Désirée now. But we can't let Nick do this."

"You're right," I said.

But being right was scant comfort.

The patrolman came half an hour later, picked up my printout of the threat, and told Pepper she could probably go back and straighten up her place now. I offered to go with her, but she insisted on going alone. I supposed that putting one's place back together after it's been ransacked demands privacy, like examining an intimate part of your body immediately after the surgeon's sewed it up. I waded through paperwork, took a call from La Bombast, who was amazingly congenial, and was just stuffing papers into my attaché case to take home when Freddie St. Ambrose called.

"Al, baby, how's it going?"

A call from Freddie was never good news.

"Busy, Freddie. What's up?"

"Even without the Désirée job."

I felt my blood pressure ratchet up. "What are you talking about?"

"That's why I'm calling. Professional courtesy. Nick DeLage said he'd call with the bad news, but I told him it was a matter between professionals and, I hope, old friends."

"DeLage?"

"Yes. Al, I don't know how to say this, but Mr. DeLage is some pissed. Feels like you went behind his back on some shit. Something about conniving against the best interests of his aunt. He's very protective of the old lady, I understand."

"Freddie, spit it out: Are you saying DeLage hired you?"

"Calm down, Al. Just business, what else can I say? I

didn't initiate the contact, he called me. Said he had an interesting project. Well, once he started to explain I knew exactly what it was, because I saw that little business on TV the other night. And I gotta say, I wondered then what my friends had gotten their asses into. That bitch on TV all but accused you of murder, for Christ's sakes. I'd of sued."

"You stole our job."

"That's a hell of a thing to say. I just told you, he called *us*. Said he was canning your asses. What am I gonna do, turn down work? And this is truly historically significant. *Somebody's* gotta do it."

"Don't make too much of a sacrifice, Freddie."

"Well, ta-ta, Al. Just letting you know my crew will be out at the plantation starting tomorrow and we don't really need to see any of your people, if you get my meaning."

"Screw you."

"Where's the professionalism, Al? Well, never mind. But answer one question before you go hit the wall with your fist."

I waited, tempted to disconnect before he asked.

"What?" I said finally.

"That man that was killed: You didn't *really* do it, did you?"

That was when I disconnected and slammed the wall.

I drove home in a foul mood. I cleaned the living room with a vengeance, throwing all the empty cans and bottles into a garbage bag, vacuuming the rug, and emptying the ashtray. I carried the empty dishes to the sink, put away the card table, and drowned the room with lemon scent.

Freddie St. Ambrose. That son-of-a-bitch was going to take his wrecking crew to Désirée and put holes every ten feet. He'd call it archaeology and, since it was private land and not under the jurisdiction of any regulatory agency, he could do as he pleased.

They'd probably even disinter the remains on top of the Indian mound. In the end, there was a good chance they'd destroy any hope we ever had of knowing who the man on the mound was.

Not that it would bother Nick DeLage: He'd promote Désirée as a private historical attraction. And he'd sell the diaries for what he could get. Later archaeologists would be left with Freddie's fallout, which meant not knowing the provenience of anything Freddie had found.

It made a train wreck look like a business plan.

I was standing in the garden, explaining it all to Digger, who seemed more interested in whether he would get his meal before or after his walk, when I heard the phone in the kitchen.

Pepper, probably. She'd be as angry as I was. But I had to tell her.

I went in and grabbed the receiver.

"Yes?"

"Alan?" It wasn't Pepper at all, but Esme, and there was something I didn't like in her tone.

"What's wrong?"

"Alan, it's Shelby. He never called like he promised, so I called his house, but there wasn't any answer."

"Well, there's probably an explanation."

"I hope so. I'm going to call the State Police."

"All right. Keep me abreast."

She was worried enough without my telling her about DeLage's little caper. And Shelby was probably all right.

At least, that's what I told myself as I opened a can of dog food for Digger and then called Pepper's number.

Much later, the phone beside my bed rang, and when I got it to my ear I heard Esme telling me they'd located Shelby Deeds.

"He's in the hospital in Hammond," Esme said. "The police found him late last night on the interstate. They said he'd been drinking and drove off the road. Alan, it sounds like he may die."

At almost midnight the hospital was quiet except for the soft slaps of our shoes in the hallway. Incandescent light painted the corridor and showed no mercy to the face of the weary nurse at the second-floor desk.

"He's been moved from intensive care to a regular room," she told us. "Are you family?"

"Yes," Esme said without hesitation. "We've just come in from Baton Rouge."

"He's in Room 253," the nurse said, "but I don't know if he's awake."

We followed her finger down the hallway, stopping in front of a door that was partly open.

Esme pushed it the rest of the way and stepped inside the darkened room.

"Shelby?" she whispered.

Someone inside answered with a moan.

Esme went in the rest of the way and we followed.

The sheet-covered form was a bare outline against the soft light spilling in through the doorway and it took a moment to make out the old man's face.

"Shelby, it's me. I came as soon as I heard. I brought Alan and Pepper."

"Esme?" His voice was little more than a whisper.

"What in the world happened to you?" Esme asked. "You don't know how worried we've been."

There was a silence, punctuated only by the beep of the monitor at the side of the bed. I looked up at the jagged lines tumbling in disorganized fashion across the screen.

"I don't know," Shelby said finally. "I was on the way back home. I stopped for some coffee at a McDonald's before I got on the interstate."

We waited.

"I remember—I must've been somewhere near Ponchatoula. Lights in the mirror, coming up behind me, blinding."

"You ran off the road," Esme said.

"Yes."

"Do you remember anything after that?" Esme asked.

The head on the pillow moved slowly from side to side.

"Lights. I think there were police. But that was after. I must've been there a long time."

Esme looked over at me and I knew she was trying to make up her mind whether to say anything about the liquor.

"Coffee," she said finally. "That's what you were drinking?"

"Yes, of course. Why?"

She shook her head. "Nothing."

"Were they saying something different?" he asked, trying to raise his head from the pillow. "Were they saying . . . ?" His head fell back and he groaned.

"Don't worry about anything," Esme reassured him. "The important thing is for you to get better."

"No." His head moved slowly from side to side. "Important thing is . . . find out who."

"What are you talking about?" Esme asked. "Right now you're all that matters, you silly man."

"Not so," he protested and a hand came out from under the covers to catch her own.

"I'm old. I could just as easily die of a stroke as a little bump on the head. But I don't want to go not knowing."

Esme shook her own head and sighed. "We'll finish this when you're better."

"No. Finish it . . . now."

"Shelby, I really don't think there's any reason to continue this conversation. I don't see taking you out of here and packing you into a car, and I certainly don't see loading your bed into a trailer and hauling it up to Tennessee, so—"

"Don't understand," he whispered, as if all the strength had been drained out of him by the argument. "The longer . . . wait . . . the more chances for whoever—"

"But we'll make them put a guard outside your door," Esme protested.

"Nobody . . . safe," he breathed and I leaned forward to hear his words. "Have to go."

"Go?" she asked, frowning.

His head shifted and I felt his eyes on Pepper and me.

"To Tennessee," he wheezed. "To see Dorcas Drew."

▰ NINETEEN

We stayed over at a motel in Hammond and took off just before eight in the morning, after a quick check of the hospital room. We'd found Esme asleep on the couch and Shelby Deeds staring morosely at a hospital breakfast of poached eggs and dry toast. He gave us Dorcas Drew's telephone number and then, ominously, told us not to be put off by her manner.

"It's the librarian in her," he said cryptically.

Once on I-55, headed north, I called the office on the cell phone and informed Marilyn I would be in Tennessee for a day or two and told her the transmission was breaking up when she started to protest. Then I handed the phone to Pepper.

"Maybe you ought to talk to this Dorcas woman," I suggested.

"Me? Why not you?"

"She may respond better to another woman," I said quickly.

"Or she may hate other women and only respond to men," Pepper countered.

"I'm driving?" I asked.

She smiled. "You poor man, can't do but one thing at a time." She punched in the number and waited, her eyes laughing at me. I reached over and took the phone.

"Yes?" The voice on the other end was sharp, even through the static, and I had the feeling I'd interrupted something.

"Miss Dorcas Drew?" I asked. "My name is Alan Graham. I'm a friend of Shelby Deeds."

131

"Then why isn't he calling?"

"Shelby's in the hospital," I said. "He was hurt in an accident."

"You're telling me he won't be coming," she said.

"No, ma'am. But he asked me to come in his place."

Silence, punctuated by the crackling of static. Then: "Are you his student?"

"Not exactly. We're working together on a project. I'm an archaeologist and—"

"It doesn't matter. Well, I'll have to rearrange my schedule. I'd planned for him to be here by noon."

It felt like an accusation.

"I'm sorry. Right now we're on I-55 just north of Hammond, Louisiana, so—"

"We?"

"I have my, er, colleague with me. A woman." I looked over at Pepper, silently willing her help.

"Humph," Dorcas Drew said.

"Pardon?"

"You don't really want to take that route," she said finally.

"We don't?"

"It takes you to Memphis. You don't want to go to Memphis. I'm closer to Nashville."

"Well, I thought we'd just take the interstate from Memphis east and—"

"You'll miss everything."

"Oh."

"You are trying to understand the last journey of Governor Lewis along the Natchez Trace, am I correct?" Her tone was impatient, as if she were instructing a child.

"Yes," I admitted, feeling like I'd been caught bringing the wrong homework to history class.

"Well, the governor did not go from Memphis to Nashville. Not the way you're going. He started in Memphis, but there was no direct road between the two cities. The only route was down a trail from Fort Pickering—today's Memphis—to Houston, Mississippi, just south of Tupelo. That's where the Fort Pickering trail met the Natchez Trace."

I took the outer lane, passing a Winnebago with a NO JOB, NO WORRIES sticker on the back.

"If you're going to drive all the way up here to talk to me

about the governor, then you should, at the very least, take advantage of the situation. Unless, of course, you've already made this trip in the past."

I'd been to Nashville a couple of times, but I knew that would hardly satisfy.

"What would you recommend, Miss Drew?" I asked meekly.

When she spoke again her voice was notably softer. "When you leave Jackson, take the interstate up to Canton, Mississippi. After Canton there'll be signs directing you to the Natchez Trace Parkway. Stay on the parkway all the way to Dogwood Mudhole, in Tennessee."

Two hours later we reached Jackson, an urban sprawl in the gently rolling pine forests. I'd put on a Pete Fountain tape five miles back and the tones of "A Closer Walk" were floating out from the speakers. I stole a glance at Pepper, still unable to believe all that had happened between us.

Maybe, I told myself, I'd dreamed it.

Nah. Because she was smiling back at me and even reached over to squeeze my hand.

Caught out.

"I've been thinking," I began.

"You want me to come into Moundmasters," she said.

My mouth dropped open. "How did you know what I was going to say?"

She shrugged. "Just figured it."

"That's scary."

"I have to think about it. I don't know what David would say. And Marilyn hates me."

"No, she doesn't. She's just protective. And David knows we're weak when it comes to historic archaeology."

"I don't know if it would work," she said.

"Probably not," I agreed.

"So let's keep it the way it is now."

"Right."

"For the time being."

By the time we crossed into Alabama it was almost three. We were passing limestone outcrops now, jutting out from where the road had been carved from the sides of the hills, and I tried to imagine what it had been like for the fevered rider that October 1809. What were pleasantly rolling hills to us must have been incredible obstacles to him. And the multicolored leaves—had he had time to appreciate their beauty, or had his imagination given them a more sinister significance?

"Almost there," Pepper said and I opened my eyes.

I looked down at my watch. Four-twenty. My God, I'd been asleep almost an hour and a half.

Pepper held up the Park Service map.

"We're almost at Dogwood Mudhole," she said.

I straightened in my seat and looked out the window.

Hills, exposed limestone, gray sky.

I rolled down my window and breathed in the air from outside. It was cool, with the first nip of fall.

"Did she say why she picked this place for us to meet?" Pepper asked.

"No. But there's probably a reason," I said. "She sounds like somebody with firm ideas."

"Crazy, in other words."

"I didn't say that."

I checked the map. "We seem to be following the old Trace exactly now," I said. "The Dogwood Mudhole ought to be right up here in a mile or two."

"I hope she's there."

"It is a long way to come," I admitted.

A Park Service sign advised us that the Dogwood Mudhole stop was just ahead and Pepper slowed and pulled into a semicircular turnoff on the left. A two-year old gray Mazda with Tennessee plates was parked against the curb. It looked empty.

We stopped and got out.

A sign advised us that the real Dogwood Mudhole was an impassable mire located a mile to the south on a part of the old Trace that was off the modern parkway, and that this was as close as the parkway got. For all the Park Service signage, there was nothing to see but trees and a barbed-wire fence.

I edged over to the Mazda to see if there was someone sleeping inside, but our first impression had been correct, and there was nothing on the seat or the dash that gave a clue as to who its owner might be.

"You think this is her car?" Pepper asked.

I shrugged. "Beats me. But if it is, I don't know where she is."

In answer there was a crunching of leaves and we turned to the wall of trees in front of us.

A few seconds later a tiny figure appeared, mottled with shadow. It kept coming, stepping deliberately over a log, and then emerged into the failing sunlight.

"I assume you are the people Shelby sent?" the figure asked in a waspish voice and I knew we had met Dorcas Drew.

I offered a hand, which she took quickly and then released.

"We weren't sure if this was your car—" I began but she cut me off.

"I don't know who else you think would be out here at this time of day. I was doing some exploring. Walking around. As the sign says, this is really just a faux reference point. The real mudhole is a mile away."

I saw Pepper smile.

"And you . . . ?" Dorcas Drew asked, turning to my companion.

Pepper introduced herself and our guide nodded. I gave her a closer look: Her short gray hair was clipped as closely as a boy's and the gold rings in her ears touched her shoulders. Her blue jeans were clean and pressed but were hardly new, as if she used them often, and her blouse was a simple gray slip-over shirt with a pocket. Hiking boots, dark glasses, and a fanny pack completed her wardrobe, giving the impression of someone who was as comfortable in the woods as in library stacks.

"Well," Dorcas Drew said. "I suppose you want to know why I asked you to meet me here instead of at the monument."

"We figured you had reasons," I said and knew I'd made the right response.

"Indeed. Dogwood Mudhole—the real one, south of here—was a stopping point on the Trace, because it was so hard to cross in the rainy times. Of course, it would have been relatively dry when the governor and his companions arrived, but they stopped, nevertheless. The mudhole"—she swept the woods with her hand—"is where the governor and the others camped the night before the governor died at Grinder's Stand.''

"Ahhh," Pepper and I said together.

"That is," our informant told us, "if you believe Major Neelly."

"The Indian agent," Pepper said.

Dorcas Drew jerked her head. "Yes. The man who so conveniently appeared at Fort Pickering and agreed to accompany the governor over the Trace all the way to Nashville."

"You don't seem to hold him in high regard," I said.

"I neither hold him in high nor low regard," Dorcas said. "I can only report what information we have: He appeared fortuitously, but such things happen. In Neely's case one must wonder, but no one can ever know."

"You mean there's something more to it?" Pepper asked.

Dorcas Drew's little mouth twisted as if she'd tasted something sour.

"Neelly had only been Indian agent since August. His first important assignment was to transport a prisoner to Nashville for trial. This man, George Lanehart by name, had committed a robbery in a Chickasaw village. The man he'd robbed was an influential Englishman who owned a nearby plantation. But Neelly, instead of taking this Lanehart in hand, paid ninety dollars to a second party to transport Lanehart for him and, instead, headed for Fort Pickering, a hundred miles to the northwest." The little woman's mouth was puckered with visible disgust now. "Neelly only made eighty-three dollars a month as Indian agent."

"That *is* a little odd," I admitted.

"No odder," she said, "than the refusal by General Wilkinson to grant Captain Russell leave from Fort Pickering to accompany the governor to Nashville."

"Wilkinson again," I said.

"Yes. The man who nominated James Neelly for his job as Indian agent to the Chickasaws."

"Then you think—" Pepper began but Dorcas held up a hand.

"What I think is unimportant. Now that you have come here, it is more important that you try to put yourself in the governor's place and see things through his eyes. Try to forget this modern highway and these ridiculous Park Service signs and imagine things as they were then, when the governor passed this way.''

''Must've been pretty lonely,'' Pepper said.

''Yes, but not as much as you might think by reading some of the drivel that's been written about this place. In the early days, when the governor came this way, the stands were about every day's ride. But the land above the Duck River was ceded by the Chickasaws in 1805 and the whites moved in very quickly. Homesteads were spread through the valley every five miles or so. Grinder's was a little below that, on Little Swan Creek, in the Indian lands, but that hadn't stopped settlers from coming into the area. So you could reach a neighbor in a couple of hours by horseback. That's important to remember.''

She turned abruptly and started to unlock her car door.

''Now we'll take the last journey.''

Pepper and I looked at each other.

''I mean we will take the parkway to Grinder's Stand and the governor's grave. Needless to say, it isn't exactly the route the governor followed, but there is one point where a section of the old Trace leaves the highway and we'll follow that. I'll go ahead of you slowly. When we go into the woods, try to envision that evening almost two hundred years ago.''

Pepper slipped back behind the wheel and started the engine.

''She's really into this, isn't she?''

I nodded, but before I could say anything, Dorcas Drew had backed out her car and was heading onto the parkway.

We came to the old Trace detour in about eight miles and she pulled up at the side of the road and rolled down her window.

''You should take this part of the road alone. One car is bad enough, two will absolutely ruin the effect. It's only two miles and I'll meet you at the end of the detour.''

Without waiting for a reply she raised her window and wheeled back onto the highway.

Pepper turned right, onto a narrow one-lane track that led into the forest.

The foliage closed around us and I felt isolated from the modern world. The trail rose slowly and then curved along the top of a ridge. It was five now and the shadows had merged, forming a twilight broken only by occasional glimpses of a gray sky.

"It *is* kind of eerie," Pepper said as we crept along the dirt path, our tires crunching gravel and sticks. I ran my window down and scanned the depths of the forest, where I felt eyes staring out at me.

"I can imagine how it would have been if you were feverish," she said. "Lewis might have seen all sorts of things."

We came to an overlook, where the valley spread before us. The sky was a ruddy color, as if the sun had been plunged into an ocean.

"He would have been hurrying," I said. "He wouldn't have wanted to pitch camp in the dark."

We started downward, with a dropoff on our right. Five minutes later we reemerged onto the tar top. The gray Mazda was parked on the side of the road, waiting for us. Without so much as an acknowledgment, it pulled onto the parkway as we approached and Pepper followed.

We drove without speaking for five miles, each of us immersed in our thoughts, and then we saw the sign at the same time, advertising the Meriwether Lewis National Monument.

The Mazda gave a left turn signal and disappeared, and Pepper turned after it.

For some reason I felt my heart thumping, as if I were on the way to a funeral.

But why? It had all happened so long ago. The man Dorcas Drew so primly referred to as the governor was dead, and regardless of where he was buried, he wasn't likely to come back to haunt anybody.

Besides, this was a national monument, controlled by the National Park Service. It had probably been so rearranged and sanitized by the government the governor had served that there would be little left to remind the visitor of his presence.

Then we swerved left and I saw it in the twilight, a single cabin in a clearing, and my heart started to pound faster.

The clearing was totally deserted, the parking area vacant.

Two hundred yards beyond the cabin an obelisk pointed a single granite finger at the darkening sky. And as I watched, a rider materialized from the forest, plodding toward us along the path.

▰TWENTY

We stared, mesmerized, the motor still running, until Dorcas Drew got out of her car and walked over to where we had stopped.

"I wish those yahoos down in the valley would show some respect," she complained, nodding at the man on horseback. "This *is* sacred ground."

I saw now that the horseman wore jeans and a plaid shirt. He continued around the track, past the flagpole with its drooping colors, and nodded a greeting as he passed us, heading in the direction from which we'd come.

When he was gone, the place was deserted except for ourselves.

"So this is it," Pepper said, looking over at the log cabin to our left.

"That?" Dorcas laughed. "Hardly. What you see here is a modern replica. The central breezeway—the dogtrot—has been filled in and the building is oriented toward the parking area instead of toward the old Trace path." She shook her head disapprovingly. "Everything is wrong."

I stared over at the cabin. A sign said the room on the left side was the ranger's office and the right room was a museum.

"I wouldn't bother looking in there," Dorcas said. "They don't have anything a sixth grader doesn't already know. The real Grinder cabin was over here." She pointed, and we got out and followed her to a spot a few feet north of the replica building. Here, a sign said, were the remains of the Grinders' original building and when we looked I could see stone foundations, almost covered by grass.

"The cabin," Dorcas explained, "would have faced the other way, because the old Trace was on the other side, about a hundred feet away, in the direction we're facing. It ran roughly north and south, just along the west edge of the clearing, and passed just beyond the monolith over there."

She marched over to one of the foundation stones and nudged at it with her foot.

"The stable or barn was probably about a hundred yards to the south, about where we turned in from the road. We're standing roughly where Mrs. Grinder stood that day when she saw the governor come out of the woods and ask for a place to stay."

Pepper crossed her hands over her body and I could see she was shivering. I put my arm around her. Dorcas checked us out of the corner of her eye and I thought I saw the hint of a smile.

"So we're standing right about where it happened," Pepper said.

"Yes," Dorcas said. "We are standing in the very place where the governor was shot."

She pointed ahead of us, into the gloom. "According to one account, he crawled all the way back to the road and was found there the next morning by a post rider named Robert Smith."

"I haven't heard that version," I said.

"No. There are local versions that our Major Neely and Mrs. Priscilla Grinder somehow omitted."

"You sound as if you suspect their account," Pepper said.

"Accounts—plural. Priscilla Grinder gave three different versions over the years. The first was to Neely, the next morning. The second was to a friend of the governor's, Alexander Wilson, who visited Grinder's Stand a year later and paid Mr. Grinder to take care of the grave."

"And the third?" I asked.

"To an unknown teacher who published it in a newspaper in 1845."

"What are the differences?" Pepper asked.

"In the first version, the one Neely reported to Jefferson, Lewis is restless, hardly touches his food, paces back and forth talking to himself, and then goes into the sleeping cabin alone. Mrs. Grinder has given him the family cabin and taken herself, her children, and her servants to the kitchen cabin, across the breezeway. Lewis's man Pernier and Neely's servant retire to the stable, a hundred yards behind the house. Priscilla is then awakened in the early hours by two pistol shots. Pernier and Neely's man come running from the stable and they and Mrs. Grinder find the governor on the floorboard, in agony. He tells Pernier he's shot himself and asks for water. The servant gives the governor water from a gourd, but the governor expires soon afterward and some time after that Neely arrives and sees to his burial."

I nodded. "And the second version?"

Dorcas folded her arms. "That's the one Priscilla Grinder gave to Alexander Wilson in 1811. In this one, when the two servants ride up shortly after the governor arrived, he asks Pernier where his gunpowder is, but whatever Pernier replies, Priscilla doesn't understand. The governor is restless and when he goes to his cabin, he paces for several hours, talking to himself as if he's reciting a speech he plans to make—which may, indeed, have been the case. Then, all at once, she hears a pistol report, the governor cries out, and she hears another shot."

I looked down at the little scatter of stones that were all that marked the Grinder dwelling.

"The next thing she hears is the governor scratching at her door, begging for water. The logs were unplastered so she could see between them, into the yard. There, the poor man has fallen against a tree stump. Then he crawls over to a bucket and scrapes in it for water, but the bucket is dry."

"You mean she didn't give him any?" Pepper asked, amazed.

"In this account, Priscilla is too afraid to leave her quarters and waits until daybreak to send her children to the barn for the servants. The servants run in and find the governor with a wound in the side and with his brains exposed from a head wound. He begs them to take his rifle and finish the job, but, of course, they don't. He dies at sunup."

Pepper muttered something under her breath. "And this woman lived on the frontier?"

"You aren't the first to have commented on Priscilla Grinder's timidity," Dorcas declared.

"And the third version?" I asked.

"Stranger still. In this one, reported almost forty years after the event, she says that the governor had no sooner arrived that evening than two or three men rode up. The governor pulled out his pistols and the men turned and rode away."

"Bizarre," Pepper said.

"It gets stranger still," Dorcas said. "In this version, the governor and the two servants retire to the same room. The governor has been acting so strangely that Priscilla asks Pernier to take away his pistols, but Pernier tells her it doesn't matter, because the governor has no powder for them. Priscilla and her children go to sleep in the kitchen and in the early hours hear three shots."

"*Three* shots?" I asked.

"Three. And she hears someone fall and cry, 'Oh, Lord. Congress relieve me.' "

"Congress?" I snorted. "I'd want doctors, not politicians."

"Precisely," Dorcas said. "Once more, she sees the governor crawling around, searching for water, and once more the servants arrive: It turns out they haven't been with him after all, but in the stable, as in the other versions. Pernier, the governor's servant, is wearing the governor's gold watch and the governor's clothes, and the dying governor is wearing old and tattered clothes."

"Jeez," Pepper said. "You mean Pernier stole—"

But Dorcas held up a hand. "The governor is brought to the cabin and when Priscilla asks why he did it, he says, 'If I had not done it someone else would.' He lingers long enough to be seen alive by some of the neighbors. Apparently he revives enough to try to cut his throat but is prevented. And finally, that morning, he dies—all before Major Neelly appears."

"This Neelly sounds pretty shady," Pepper said. "All that business about having to round up horses that strayed. Wasn't he supposed to stick with Lewis and guard him?"

"Yes, he was. And there are some very strange things about Neelly. Shall we drive over to the grave?"

We got back into the Blazer and followed the Mazda two hundred yards along a circular drive to the big obelisk. Dorcas stopped her car and got out again.

"The sign here gives the details of the inscription," she

explained, pointing to a metal sign in front of us. I strained to read the inscription in the gloom:

MERIWETHER LEWIS
1774–1809

Beneath this monument erected under legislative Act by the state of Tennessee, A.D. 1848, reposes the dust of Meriwether Lewis, a captain in the United States Army, private secretary to President Jefferson, senior commander of the Lewis and Clark expedition, and governor of the Territory of Louisiana.

In the Grinder house, the ruins of which are still discernible, 230 yards from this spot, his life of romantic endeavor and lasting achievement came tragically to its close on the night of Oct 11, 1809.

Great care was taken to identify the grave. George Nixon, Esq., an old surveyor, had become very early acquainted with the locality. He pointed out the place; but to make doubly sure, the grave was reopened and the upper portion of the skeleton examined and such evidence found as to leave no doubt of the place of interment.

"It's from the report by the Tennessee legislature's committee, which was commissioned to investigate and establish the monument," Dorcas said. "They didn't even get the date right: The governor died the morning of the eleventh, not that night."

"How was the skeleton identified?" I asked.

"He was buried in his Army uniform, which he must have had in his pack. They found a brass button from his uniform coat," she said. "There was a hole in the back of the skull, although the skull itself was said to be in a state of decay. And the blacksmith who made the nails for the coffin identified them."

"So there was time to make a coffin?" Pepper asked.

"Oh, yes. The blacksmith lived fifteen miles away, and the accounts say a coffin was made from an oak tree on the Grinder place, so there was obviously a period of several days before the governor was put into the ground. Time for the tree to be hewn into planks, time for nails to be made, and time for the justice of the peace to assemble a jury for the inquest.''

I looked up at the obelisk. The twenty-foot-high plinth, set on a square granite base, had been broken off near the top, giving the impression of something unfinished.

"It symbolizes the governor's life,'' Dorcas explained. "That's why the sculptor, Lemuel Kirby, truncated the obelisk.''

"What about the inquest?'' Pepper said. "Are the records in the courthouse?''

Dorcas shook her head. "In the early days of Maury County, coroner's juries didn't record their findings with the county clerk. The records of this case would have been kept in the private docket book of the jury foreman, Samuel Whitesides. They probably still exist.''

"You've seen them?'' Pepper asked.

Dorcas looked away. "Not personally. They're valuable family heirlooms. I'm not sure which member of the family has them now. But I can assure you, they say nothing surprising. The jury was unable to come to any certain conclusion, given the circumstances.''

I walked forward, across the closely mowed grass and halted in surprise.

"There are other graves here,'' I said, staring down at the little square of granite under my foot.

"Of course,'' Dorcas said, as if I should have known. "Fifty or sixty. Including the grave of the post rider, Robert Smith, though his is one of those marked UNKNOWN.''

I looked closely at the ground and, true enough, several of the little squares in the grass had the word UNKNOWN in place of a name. None, however, bore a date.

"Why aren't there any upright stones, with dates and inscriptions?'' I asked.

Dorcas snorted.

"Ask the Park Service. They took them all down a few years ago and stored them in the equipment shed.'' She jerked her head toward the entrance to the park. "One more example of our glorious federal bureaucracy that knows better than anybody else how to deal with history.''

It was my turn to smile. I was starting to like the little woman.

"Just look," she cried indignantly. "The American flag: It's pitch-dark now, or close to it, and the flag is still up. They don't even send anybody here to take it down. And the ranger isn't on duty but half a day. At the grave of one of Americas's greatest heroes!"

"Must be money," I mumbled.

"Money? They have plenty for a whole corps of archaeologists to sit on their dignity over in Atlanta. I've talked to other researchers. The National Park Service is a top-heavy disgrace, in my opinion."

I was beginning to love the little lady.

"Then I suppose," Pepper ventured, "the governor would feel right at home."

Dorcas shot her an angry look and then realized what she was saying and nodded.

"You are right, my dear. He suffered in his lifetime due to bureaucratic government bungling. It's just a pity it has to continue after his death."

"These graves," I began, "do they all postdate the Lewis burial?"

Dorcas shrugged. "So far as I know. The place was pretty much deserted until the 1840s. Then there developed some sentiment to properly commemorate the governor's life and an attempt was made to relocate his resting place and erect a suitable monument."

I stared up again at the lonely granite finger. "But I guess by that time most of the old-timers who remembered the event were gone."

"Yes, mostly," she said. "Plus, there was a move to take land away from Maury County and create a new county and name it after the governor—as if we in Maury hadn't done enough."

"So this isn't Maury anymore," Pepper said.

"That is correct," Dorcas said. "It is now Lewis County, which was formed in 1843. We have all the original courthouse records in Columbia. But in Lewis County, they'd like to think they have a monopoly on any investigation of the governor's death. You should have seen them last year when they held that silly inquest in the county seat."

"A new inquest?" Pepper and I said together.

Dorcas Drew gave a little laugh.

"Of course. Did you think you were the only people interested in the way the governor died?"

As if in confirmation, a single white car emerged from the direction of the parkway and sat, motor running, in front of the replica cabin.

"You can find the story in the Lewis County newspaper," she said vaguely. "It's in the Hohenwald Library. That's the county seat. It's only about eight miles from here, on Highway 20."

"Do you remember what prompted this?" I asked.

"The usual," she said. "Someone from the outside who wanted publicity."

Pepper and I looked at each other.

"Pringle," I said and Pepper nodded.

"I think that was the name," Dorcas confirmed. "You know him?"

"He's a retired dentist who runs around exhuming famous people," Pepper told her. "He gets a lot of press attention."

"This one fizzled," Dorcas said. "The Park Service wasn't interested."

She checked her wristwatch. "Well, it's dark now . . ."

"Yes, we appreciate your time," I said. "Just a couple more questions before you go."

The little woman cocked her head. "Yes?"

"What do you think about Lewis's state of mind when he reached Grinder's? Was he mentally unstable or was there some organic cause?"

Dorcas Drew stared at me for a second, as if trying to decide her answer, and her brows went up a fraction of an inch.

"So many people have written about that I'm sure I couldn't say. Thomas Jefferson later claimed that he had detected a moodiness in the governor as a young man, but this was entirely after the fact, and we simply *must* distrust Mr. Jefferson's motives. And even if the governor was moody, so what?"

We waited and Dorcas sighed.

"There are a number of theories. Some say the governor was driven to drink by his problems with the War Department. They use the fact that he was court-martialed while in the Army on a charge of berating a superior officer while he was drunk. They seldom remind us that he was acquitted, or that even his worst enemy, Frederick Bates, never accused him of insobriety. On the other hand, Captain Russell, at Fort Pickering, mentions that he restricted the governor to wine and later accuses Neelly of encouraging him to drink hard liquor on the trail.''

"Well," Pepper said, "there are lots of organic conditions that could cause a person to drink to get relief.''

"Precisely," Dorcas said. "And here's where the trail grows murky."

"There are a lot of contenders for a likely illness," I surmised.

Dorcas nodded. "Too many, and he would quite likely have drunk alcohol to relieve the symptoms of any one of them.''

I had my notebook out then, but in the darkness the page was a white blur.

"One theory is that he suffered from malaria," Dorcas began. "An eminent physician has traced his symptoms and declared that the culprit. Well, a lot of people suffered from malaria back then and he did have bouts of chills and fever. I can only say it's plausible.''

"Next candidate?" I asked.

"Less flattering, I'm afraid. A second medical expert declares it was the last stage of syphilis, and he even points to the night the governor allegedly contracted the disease. It was in August of 1805, in the Rocky Mountains, from a Shoshone woman.''

"Really," Pepper said. "You mean there's proof?"

"Of the entirely negative type," Dorcas sniffed. "We know the men of the expedition made free with the Indian women, because the captains noted it. But the captains never indicated in their journals that they themselves indulged.''

"Well, they wouldn't, would they?" Pepper ventured.

"Negative evidence," Dorcas huffed. "Our expert's sole proof is that the governor was away from his men with some Indians and thus had an *opportunity* to become infected. I hardly think it would stand in a court of law.''

"Other theories?" I asked.

"Mercury," Dorcas offered. "It was one of the standard treatments for syphilis in those days. Ingestion of too much mercury produces symptoms of mental derangement. The governor and Lieutenant Clark routinely treated their infected men with mercury. Presumably, if the governor was infected, he might have treated himself. Or he might have ingested the chemical accidentally, from handling it."

I scribbled *Mercury* across my pad and hoped I'd be able to read it when I transcribed my notes.

"And then there're all the various poisons," Dorcas said airily. "If some enemy in St. Louis was trying to kill him, they might have put something in his food."

"Like his servant Pernier?" Pepper said.

"It's a possibility."

"What happened to Pernier afterward?" Pepper asked.

"Nobody knows," Dorcas said. "He visited Thomas Jefferson at Monticello, presumably to collect some money Lewis owed him, and then he drops out of history. Some members of the Lewis family claimed that he went to see the governor's mother and she accused him of killing her son, and that Pernier cut his own throat afterward, but there's no proof."

"Tell me," Pepper asked, "what did this legislative committee think about his death? They were a lot closer to it than we were."

"Oh, they thought he was murdered. But they didn't know by whom. As you are aware, there's no shortage of candidates. But around here . . ." she leaned closer, as if the stones might overhear, "people have always thought it was a local and that the motive was robbery."

"Somebody like Grinder?" Pepper asked.

"He was a prime suspect. It was so convenient for him not to have been there when it happened. Or so his wife claimed. He had a bad reputation."

"I still like Neelly," Pepper said.

"Yes, a good many people do. After the burial, he took the governor's pistols and rifle and tomahawk, and the governor's brother had to made a special trip down a year later to reclaim them from Neelly's wife. Neelly was fired as Indian agent the next year. But we'll never know the truth." She sighed again. "The governor will remain buried beneath this stone and his spirit will never rest."

The white car by the cabin hadn't moved for five minutes

and I could still hear the low hum of its engine.

"Because," she went on, turning on me like an angry bird protecting its nest, "there is not the slightest possibility that the governor survived Grinder's Stand and made his way downriver to Baton Rouge. So if that's why you're here, you're both wasting your time. I told Shelby that yesterday and I told that other man the same thing when he called before, asking all those questions about Robert Grinder and whether the body buried here was the governor's."

"This other man," I said. "Do you remember anything about him?"

"No," she snapped. "It's been five years or more. I suppose he gave his name, but I didn't pay any attention. He said he was from Louisiana and he was interested in the Grinder family records. He had some far-fetched notion such as the one Shelby mentioned, about the governor not being buried here. I told him he was quite mistaken."

"That's all?"

"He said he wanted to come look through the courthouse records and private genealogical records some of the members of the historical society have. I told him that would be fine. But I never heard from him again."

"Did he say anything about himself?" I persisted. "Maybe that he was on a faculty, or what city he was from?"

"All I remember is that he said he was calling from Louisiana and suggested the governor was buried near Baton Rouge. It was so absurd I didn't pay much attention after that."

"I see." I turned to Pepper to see if she had anything else to ask, but she only shrugged.

"Miss Drew," I asked, "do you think there's any chance at all you can find the docket book with the inquest records?"

For an instant I thought she was going to launch into a tirade, but instead her brows just arched up a fraction.

"I can try. But even if I find it I don't think there'll be anything in it that surprises anyone."

"Thank you," I said, handing her one of my cards. "You can call me collect."

"How far is it to Columbia?" Pepper asked then.

"Half an hour," Dorcas said. "But if you're looking for a

motel, there's a place, the Deerfield, in Hohenwald. That's only eight miles."

"We appreciate your help," I told her. "Would you like us to follow you back? It's dark and you're alone and—"

"I'm not alone," Dorcas said, unzipping her fanny pack and revealing the butt of a revolver. "Believe me."

We started back toward our cars and as we walked I saw the white vehicle by the cabin back slowly into the road and then start slowly away, out of the park area. Only when it was almost to the main road did I see its lights go on.

"You know it's a crime, don't you?" Dorcas asked, wheeling on us as she reached her Mazda.

"Pardon?"

"The way the government has treated him. Hounding the poor man to death, and then leaving this place in such a disgraceful state."

I looked at the outline of the monolith, a milky shape against the night.

"He made the greatest exploration in American history, and thanks to some clerks in the War Department he died a virtual pauper."

She sighed.

"It seems like somebody could have done something," Pepper offered.

"Oh, they did," Dorcas said. "Three years after he died all his vouchers were approved and the government paid. Generous of them, don't you think?"

Fifteen minutes later, after a ride down a narrow blacktop that threaded its way through the valley, we reached the motel. I thought how cozy a single warm room would be but settled for two, adjoining.

Once I heard Pepper's shower running in the next room I called Esme and, surprisingly, got her.

"Alan, how wonderful to hear your voice. You're in . . ."

"Hohenwald, Tennessee," I told her and then recounted our conversation with Dorcas Drew. "She doesn't have much time for our theory," I said.

"Yes, well, it wouldn't be quite as nice to have the place where Meriwether Lewis was *almost* buried, would it?"

"So how is Shelby?"

"That old reprobate. He checked out of the hospital an hour after you left this morning. I pleaded and threatened, but he wouldn't hear of it. He said he had a documents expert to meet at the airport."

"So you got permission from the university?"

"With my legendary charm. The examiner is making a preliminary examination of the will tomorrow. I got the physics department to agree to let him use some of their facilities. Then, if necessary, he'll take it somewhere else for the other tests."

"Where is Shelby?" I asked.

There was a silence. "He really wasn't fit to go back to his house by himself."

"You mean . . ."

"I was a nurse a long time ago. At least, I took a first-aid course."

"He's staying with you."

"Alan, it isn't like it's something *immoral*."

"Not at all. I'm very happy for you both."

"I'll pretend I didn't hear that."

I gave her the motel's telephone number and my room.

"We'll probably be back tomorrow night," I said.

When I'd finished with Esme I called Marilyn at home.

"Any disasters?" I asked. "And has Digger been fed?"

"I fed him," Marilyn reported in her usual clipped tones. "As for disasters, I've handled them all. That television woman called and wanted a comment from you about our being fired by Nick DeLage. She wanted to know if the police had talked to you any more about that killing across the river: Seems like they haven't made any progress. Anyway, I hung up on her."

"Good."

"And that woman whose class you talked to brought arrow points for you to identify. Said her school kids had dug 'em up over the years. I told her you'd be glad to look at them and get back to her. She has a thing for you, in case you didn't notice."

Poor Rosemary Amadie.

Finally, I called my home phone, but there were no messages, for which I was just as glad.

*　　*　　*

We found a tiny café that served chicken-fried steaks and catfish.

"I was thinking," Pepper said, cutting into her fish filet. "Considering what Dorcas told us—"

"You think it was Neelly," I said.

"You're doing it, too," she told me.

"What?"

"Reading my train of thought."

"Sorry."

She jabbed me gently with a finger. "Listen to what I'm saying: Neelly is the only logical one. He turned up at Fort Pickering when he had no business being there. According to Dorcas, Neelly owed General Wilkinson for his job. And don't forget that Captain Russell, the commander at Pickering, wanted to escort Lewis himself, but Wilkinson wouldn't give him leave."

I shrugged. "They didn't have a telegraph. Russell would have to have sent a rider south, or send someone downstream in a boat. It would have taken days to communicate with Wilkinson and Lewis wasn't there all that long."

"It was long enough for Russell to ask and be denied," she said. "And if Russell sent such a request, it would have alerted Wilkinson to exactly where Lewis was."

"There's another possibility," I said. "He may just have sent a rider to Fort Adams. That was closer, between Natchez and Baton Rouge. We don't really know the chain of command at this point."

"Pooh. I guess you think it was Pernier."

"Lewis's servant? He had opportunity and, if Mrs. G.'s last story has any weight, motive. A lonely cabin is a good place for a robbery."

"He could have stolen Lewis's clothes after the fact. After somebody else did him in."

"Neelly wasn't even there," I reminded her.

"That's what he said. And maybe he wasn't. But he could have arranged it with somebody else and then, to cover himself, conveniently stayed away until it was over."

"Grinder," I said.

"*Grinder,*" she repeated. "Remember what Dorcas said? That the locals suspected him? I put more weight on what local people think than by what historians say years later."

"Hearsay," I countered. "They could probably tell you where he buried his treasure."

"Skeptic."

"Absolutely."

That night I stared at the ceiling and tried to make sense of it all. The room was cozy and warm and had a safety chain. There were people in some of the other rooms and the courthouse with the sheriff's office was just a few blocks away. Such a contrast to the lonely clearing, and the woman with a couple of squalling brats and two servant children, that night when the man in a blue-striped duster had ridden up. In his cabin, the logs had been unchinked and anyone could look inside.

So what had the Grinder woman seen?

As I drifted off, the tall finger of the monument hovered in my dreams like an exclamation point. I was walking across the cold, gray stones set in the earth, and I was staring at one that said UNKNOWN.

I heard someone calling my name then, but when I turned around there was no one there.

▰ TWENTY-ONE

The next morning, after a breakfast of hotcakes and eggs, we drove over to the one-story red brick library just north of the courthouse. The attractive, gray-haired librarian listened when we told her what Dorcas Drew had said about the recent inquest and nodded.

"I'll have to find the newspaper story," she said. "I'll bring it to you in the reading room."

She indicated a doorway just to the left of the main desk. I followed Pepper to the entrance and then bumped into her when she halted suddenly.

"Look."

He was on the wall, in full color: Meriwether Lewis, in a copy of the famous painting by Charles Willson Peale. The same painting that I'd seen in black and white, in the frontispiece of the book Shelby Deeds had shown us. Only in color, Lewis looked alive, as if he were posing for an artist in this very room.

A table occupied the center of the room, but the wall just left of the portrait was covered by a shelf filled with volumes.

"These are all on local history," Pepper said. "A history of Lewis County, a genealogy—"

"Here you are." The librarian swept back into the room with a newspaper. "The *County Herald,* June of last year."

I stared down at the story on the front page.

**CORONER'S JURY REQUESTS EXHUMATION OF
LEWIS' BODY**

One column, near the top, was devoted to a display of artifacts and photographs associated with the Lewis case and at the bottom was a photo of the coroner's jury itself, eight local men and women, with the coroner in the middle.

I read the story:

After almost two days of testimony, a coroner's jury meeting at the National Guard Armory ruled that it is not known what caused the death of Meriwether Lewis. At the request of internationally known forensic scientist Dr. Marcus Pringle, who assembled a team of experts, the jury voted to issue an order for the exhumation of the explorer's body. The order will be forwarded to the National Park Service, as part of a petition.

I skimmed the rest of the story, which outlined what was and was not known about Lewis's death and listed the members of Pringle's team. It was an impressive crew, with credentials from prestigious universities and laboratories.

I took the newspaper out to the main desk and asked the librarian to copy it.

"Any chance they'll exhume Lewis's remains?" I asked.

She smiled sardonically. "Lewis's descendants were for it. They hate the idea that he may have committed suicide. But the National Park Service wouldn't agree."

I got my copy, paid the fee, and returned to the reading room.

"You need to see this," Pepper said, pointing to a book open before her on the table. "This is a county history. Look what it says about the Lewis grave . . ."

I sat down and read where she was pointing:

There must have been some kind of settlement at this point where Swann Creek crosses the Trace, because a discussion arose at the time the state of Tennessee appropriated money to build a monument to Meriwether Lewis, as to whether or not Lewis' grave was at this place or a mile south on top of the ridge near the site of Grinder's Stand. At this time there were a number of graves at this point. And this is why the graves were entered and parts of the skeleton of Meriwether Lewis were identified. Further precautions were taken and the blacksmith who made the nails that went into the coffin, identified the nails.

"So you see?" she said, excited. "It's not really certain the monument marks the grave of Lewis. And with unknown graves near his, they could easily have dug up another skeleton by mistake. It was forty years later. The skull was in bad condition."

"But the uniform buttons?"

"Half the male population had uniforms. And as far as a blacksmith identifying his own nails after forty years, that sounds pretty questionable: You've seen iron nails after a few years in the ground. They rust to the point where all you can make out is their general shape and the heads." She shook her head. "My God, Alan, they weren't even sure they were within a *mile* of the right grave site."

We leafed through the volume, marking relevant pages. There was a report by the Park Service, giving the dimensions of the Grinder house, and several excerpts from newspapers and history texts. When we were finished, the librarian made our copies and we thanked her and wandered back out into the sunlight.

"Where now?" Pepper asked.

"I think we have all we're likely to get from around here," I said. "But you know . . ."

"I do, too," she said, finishing my thought. "I'd like to see it in daylight."

The air was crisp when we got out in front of the cabin. A handful of motorcyclists had pulled up in front of the monolith, two hundred yards to the north, and I heard a raucous laugh.

"I wonder what the governor would have thought," Pepper mused.

I shook my head.

The ranger's office was closed and, just as Dorcas had told us, the little display in the "museum" side of the cabin added little. We walked over to the ring of stones that marked the real Grinder house.

"From what I read, it was oriented north-south, like the replica," Pepper said. "Lewis would have slept in the south cabin, and the kitchen, where Mrs. G. slept, would have been in the north half."

I looked south, in the direction that the stable would have been. The stable where the servants either did or didn't sleep.

I tried to imagine Mrs. Grinder sending a child to get them, tried to imagine the wounded Lewis crawling on this very ground and falling against a now-gone stump. Tried to imagine . . .

But it was no good. The daylight, the closely cropped grass, the paved parking area . . . it wasn't the same, and might never be, except just at twilight or right before dawn.

We walked over to the plinth and I counted my paces.

"The figures we read are about right, as far as the distance from the grave to the house," I said, as the bikers watched curiously. We walked through the cemetery, looking down at the graves and reading the inscriptions on the sides of the monument.

"You think they'll be willing to move this to Désirée?" Pepper joked.

I smiled. "Where Nick DeLage can charge tourists for a look?"

In answer, Pepper brought out her camera and I stood by the obelisk while she snapped pictures.

As she put the camera away, the motorcycle engines roared into life and the cyclists thundered off.

When the last echo had died away, Pepper turned to me.

"The Park Service will *have* to agree now, won't they? I mean, if our evidence shows that he isn't buried here, they'll have trouble not agreeing to help settle the issue."

I nodded. "I think you're right."

She gave a wistful little smile. "It's a pity, in a way."

"How's that?"

"Sometimes I get the feeling there are some questions that aren't meant to be answered."

We took Highway 64 to Memphis and then headed south on I-55, arriving in Baton Rouge just after eight. During the trip back I sensed Pepper's mood changing so that by the time we reached home she'd withdrawn into herself. I wasn't sure if it was a strange empathy with the hero whose death we were trying to unravel or whether the questions surrounding Lewis's death had reminded her of the mystery in her own life—a brother she'd traced to Louisiana and then never seen again. Though she seldom spoke of it, her brother's disappearance had done things to her she didn't like to admit. They'd been close, she told me once, and when he'd vanished she'd felt abandoned for the second time. The first time was when her father had died.

I knew how she felt because I'd fought the same battle. So, despite wanting her insanely, I knew that the best thing was to let her work through the mood.

There were no messages of importance on my machine and Esme didn't answer, so I placed a quick call to Marilyn.

"David called in and said he'd need an extra week in the field," she reported, "which means another twenty-five hundred dollars out of the project."

"But it was budgeted," I said.

"It was budgeted in case it was needed. It would have been nice if it hadn't been. To defray some of the unbudgeted trips some people take."

There wasn't much I could say to that.

"Nothing else?"

"Not unless you count the doings of the competition."

"Oh?"

"Freddie called up and demanded that his person, whoever that is, look at this will he claims you're examining. I told him to talk to you. He was all sugar and cream at first, but when I told him no, he got ugly."

"That's Freddie."

"And your friend DeLage had a story in the paper. He's bringing in a big name to exhume the remains at Désirée."

I felt a sinking feeling. "Let me guess. It wouldn't be—"

"Dr. Marcus Pringle," Marilyn said with disgust. "He's scheduled a news conference tomorrow at twelve-fifteen."

There was a silence while I took a couple of deep breaths.

"Alan, are you still there?"

"Yeah."

"Tomorrow's Friday. You *will* be in, won't you?"

"Yeah. Tomorrow. Thanks."

*   *   *

I had trouble sleeping, and only partly because Digger had a loud dispute with the possum. For, as if to taunt me, the images of Nick DeLage and Freddie St. Ambrose leaped into my mind and I once more had to confront the bitter realization that, no matter what we found out with our investigations along the periphery, the important aspects of the Lewis investigation were out of our hands now. Freddie would work with Pringle to exhume whatever remained of the burial atop the Indian mound at Désirée, and together they would pressure the Park Service to allow the grave in Tennessee to be reopened. They would smile from newspaper feature stories and give interviews on the *Today* show. Publishers would bid for the rights to their book and they would publish learned papers about the solution to the Meriwether Lewis mystery. Fifty years from now, textbooks would have their names in the footnotes and people would trickle in through the gates of the restored plantation and pay their fee to see where a great American had finally come to rest.

It made me a bad person to be around the next morning.

So much for the archaeologist as cold, objective scientist.

I watched the clock tick toward twelve like Gary Cooper in *High Noon*.

According to the morning paper, the news conference was to be held at Désirée.

Just before noon I turned on the small black and white TV that I kept on a shelf in my office and Marilyn, Gator, Frank, and the Mahatma crowded around it as I sat back in my chair, gritting my teeth.

"Maybe it won't be on," Gator suggested. "Some murder may have bumped it."

Marilyn skewered him with her gaze: "They scheduled it at twelve-fifteen so they could get any other stories out of the way first."

Usually I didn't hope for murders or other tragedies, but this time the petty part of me was hoping a juicy shooting or, better, the arrest of a politician, would pop out to preempt DeLage's production.

But it wasn't to be. After three minutes devoted to complaints about interstate highway repairs in the middle of the city, and stories on a scam by a group of traveling con artists, the Peale portrait of Meriwether Lewis flashed on the screen and I heard the male commentator giving a not-too-scrambled version of Lewis's last trip along the Trace.

"And now," he proclaimed, "a local businessman is funding a project to determine if the famous explorer survived that night on the Natchez Trace and managed to live out his life on a plantation in West Baton Rouge Parish."

I held my breath, waiting for Sarah Goforth, but instead I saw a tall blond woman with closely set eyes who explained that she was at the Désirée Plantation and a news conference was just starting.

The camera panned to a small group of men standing in the center of the cemetery. I recognized Nick DeLage, looking self-confident; a smug Freddie, adorned in a safari outfit he must have bought yesterday; and a lank, bald man with a beak nose, bow tie, and nervous smile who I knew was Marcus Pringle.

DeLage began by reading from a prepared paper that I was sure he'd already handed out:

"DeLage Insurance has contracted with Pyramid Consulting to make historical and archaeological investigations at Désirée Plantation. Because there is reason to believe that the famous explorer, Meriwether Lewis, may be interred on the grounds, and that he may have thus escaped assassination at Grinder's Stand in Tennessee, it will be necessary to exhume the remains at Désirée and a petition will also be sent to the National Park Service to allow exhumation of the remains now located at Meriwether Lewis National Monument and said to be those of Lewis." DeLage paused to lick his lips and then started to read again:

"Pyramid Consultants is owned by Dr. H. Frederick St. Ambrose, who is well-known and respected in the field of historic archaeology. Dr. St. Ambrose has hired the world-renowned forensic scientist Dr. Marcus Pringle to assist with the actual disinterment and analysis of the remains." DeLage looked up, his eyes radiating sincerity. "DeLage and Associates will sponsor this vital work and take it wherever it leads. Pending the outcome of the investigation, we plan to develop the site as a park commemorating the life of the explorer Meriwether Lewis, the man who explored the Louisiana Territory."

That was bad enough, but when he described Freddie St.

Ambrose as a widely respected archaeologist I felt my gorge
rise. And when he introduced a smiling Marcus Pringle it was
all I could do to stay in my chair.

Then Nick added the *coup de grace*:

"As you probably know; one of my employees died here
last week, and the authorities are still investigating. We've
terminated the firm originally involved and are confident now
that Dr. St. Ambrose and his colleagues will allow us to obtain the maximum data."

"Son-of-a-bitch," Gator snarled. "He makes it sound like
we had something to do—"

"Calm down," I said. But I was hardly feeling calm myself, as Pringle described what an honor it was to be associated with a man of Dr. St. Ambrose's stature.

But it finally ended and as the camera went back to the
blond reporter I stood and switched off the television.

"They won't have any luck with the Park Service," Gator
opined.

"The Park Service," Marilyn corrected, "responds to political pressure. I'll bet DeLage has already called both our
senators and that idiot we have for a congressman."

Gator's toothless mouth opened in shock. "But—"

"She's probably right," I said. "Well, there isn't anything
we can do about it."

"I could break Freddie's legs," Gator volunteered.

"I don't think so."

"Slash his tires?"

"Nice thought, but we'll pass."

"Boss—"

I patted him on the back and caught Frank Hill's smirk.

"And don't hack into his damn computer," I told Frank.
"That's just as bad."

"Whatever." Frank shrugged.

I went back into my office and flopped back into my chair.
Broken legs. Slashed tires. A deadly computer virus . . .

To tell the truth, none of them sounded so bad.

■ TWENTY-TWO

I called Pepper in midafternoon. She wasn't at her office and so I tried the apartment. She answered on the fourth ring.

"Did I wake you up?"

"Not really. I was just listening to some music and thinking."

"You okay?"

"Sure. And you?"

"I'm fine," I lied. "Just reading reports."

"I know about Pringle," she said. "Esme called me."

"Oh."

"There ought to be something . . ." She stopped in midsentence.

"It's okay," I told her. "We'll both live. We just have to cut our losses."

"Yes."

"You're safe?" I asked her. "I mean—"

"I'm fine. The killer'll go after Freddie now." She gave a bitter little laugh. "Anyway, I'll keep myself locked in tonight."

Silence. Then, "Alan . . ."

My heart thumped. "Yes?"

"Thanks for understanding."

"No problem," I lied.

I was still brooding at just after four when the phone rang and Marilyn told me it was Esme.

"Don't tell me Freddie's been badgering you, too," I said.

"My dear, I don't worry about that man," Esme declared. "Though, actually, he *has* caused some problems."

"Oh?"

"He called the chancellor's office and claimed we were interfering with a legitimate project and that the university was going to look bad, helping a company that had been fired by the client."

"That bastard. I ought to sue—"

"I'm sure Stanley would love the business."

I took a deep breath. She was right: Our lawyer would make money, Freddie's lawyer would make money, and the battery of attorneys the university employed would make money. The rest of us would lose.

"So what's the university going to do?"

"I spent most of the day with the vice chancellor for research. He's willing to let us have another day and then he says, in fairness, we ought to let Freddie's expert look at the document. His suggestion was that we all work in harmony."

"Of course it was. So we have, what? Twenty-four hours?"

"That's why I was calling, Alan. We may not need it."

"What?"

"Shelby's with our man right now. He just called me. They want us over there as soon as we can make it."

"You talked to Shelby?"

"I was out. There was a message on my machine. He just said to come, that his man, Flinders Mott, wanted to discuss things."

"Where are they?"

"The Life Science Building." She read the room number. "I'll be there in fifteen minutes," I said.

I took the elevator to the third floor, sharing the space with a couple of students and a white-coated professor with a clipboard. I took the hallway right, passing a series of open doors that revealed lab rooms with sinks and fume hoods. The one I wanted was on the end and when I walked in I saw two men hunched over a microscope. One of them looked up and I recognized a thinner Shelby Deeds, his face looking more gaunt than the last time I'd seen him. We shook hands and he introduced me to the other man, who raised his head slowly and took me in as if he were appraising a rare document.

"This is Flinders Mott," Shelby explained. "He retired from the FBI a few years ago, and since his hobby was history, he does a lot of business examining questioned documents."

Flinders Mott was small, graying, and wore thick, rimless glasses. A thin black mustache divided the space between his nose and upper lip. His handshake was limp, as if he didn't want to spare the time, and I was surprised at the cold dryness of his skin until I realized he was wearing latex gloves.

"I hear you've got some news," I said.

Shelby stuck his hands down into his pockets and looked at the floor. "I'll let Flinders do the talking."

Flinders Mott shoved back his chair and got up slowly, hiking his pants as he stood.

"I've been examining the document in question," he said in a reedy voice. "And I've brought several other mid–nineteenth century documents for comparison."

He opened a folder and carefully removed a yellowed sheet of paper, which he laid beside a document I realized must be the will.

"This is a handwritten letter dating from 1849. A woman's letter to her niece in Boston. Unquestionably authentic and unquestionably trivial, as a historic document. Please tell me what you see."

I looked down at the paper. The handwriting was a pleasantly sloping cursive that had gone brown over the years.

"The handwriting is different from the will," I said, shrugging. "Other than that . . ."

"Paper quality?" he asked. "A document should be written on paper that was available at the time."

He handed me a magnifying glass and I scanned the letter, and then the will.

"See any differences?" he asked.

"Should I?"

Flinders Mott allowed himself a small smile.

"No. The paper of both is clearly nineteenth century foolscap. Now let's put it under the microscope." He moved the letter onto the viewing platform and then bent to peer through the eyepiece and adjust the focus. "Do you see the handwriting?"

I took off my glasses and squinted into the instrument.

What I saw was a slightly raised strip of brown ink.

"Yes."

"The ink used in the nineteenth century turned brown over the years," he explained. "It's oxidation or rust caused by the iron in the ink itself. So if you have a document that purports to be nineteenth century but the ink is still black or blue, you have cause to be suspicious."

He removed the letter, replaced it in the folder, and then held up the Lewis will. Its ink was brown.

"Now let's examine the will under high power." He slid it under the scope, adjusted the eyepiece, and motioned for me to look.

"Tell me what you see now."

I saw another raised brown line, textured with tiny cracks.

"Looks the same," I said.

"Exactly?"

"There are some small cracks. From age, I guess."

Another tight little smile.

"No."

I looked up from the eyepiece to his face and then over at Shelby, who looked away.

"Then what do the cracks mean?" I asked, my throat dry.

"Ever hear of the Mormon letters?"

"It sounds familiar."

"Famous case a few years back. Fellow named Hoffman tried to sell some letters purportedly written by Joseph Smith, the founder of the church."

I was getting a very queasy feeling.

"When the Smith letters were examined, they showed the same pattern of cracks in the ink that this document has. It was very puzzling to the examiners. The ink appeared to be the same in chemical composition as other nineteenth century inks and the paper was undeniably old. They had to consider whether the letters were genuine and whether the cracks were the result of some environmental effect, such as humidity, or whether they indicated that the document was a modern forgery."

With the word *forgery* my throat tightened.

"The two examiners, Throckmorton and Flynn, did a number of experiments, mixing their own inks, using the ingredients that would have been used at the time the letters were supposed to have been written. They were able to duplicate the inks, of course, but the modern ink they mixed was clearly distinguishable from the early ink because of its color: The modern ink was black and the older, as you've seen, is brown.''

I had an urge to tell him to cut to the chase, but I knew I had to hear him out.

"So they set about to try to see if there was a way to turn an ink brown quickly and thus mimic the effects of age.''

"And they succeeded,'' I suggested.

"After many experiments. They found that they could make the ink turn brown by spraying the document with ammonia.''

Ammonia . . .

"But there was just one drawback,'' he continued. "When the spray dried and the ink was brown, something else happened.''

"Cracks,'' I said, my throat dry.

"Tiny cracks like you see here. Because ammonia is alkaline and nineteenth century inks contained gum arabic, a sugar, which is—''

"Acid,'' I said. "The cracks are the result of a chemical reaction.''

"Exactly.''

"So the will—''

"Is a very clever production, done by someone who managed to mix the right kind of ink and who was able to find some blank paper from the last century, and then was able to copy the real Meriwether Lewis's handwriting very convincingly.'' He gave a tight little smile. "Yes, very impressive. But, without a doubt, I can say that this will is a fraud.''

TWENTY-THREE

I am too old to drink myself into a stupor. That night I made an exception. Esme had arrived at the lab a few minutes after I had and listened to the same lecture from Flinders Mott. She'd asked a lot of questions and then, in the face of the little man's reasoning, wilted and admitted defeat.

"I'll have to tell the vice chancellor," she warned.

I shrugged.

They invited me to dinner, but I had no taste for wakes, and elected to go home instead, where I got out a bottle of Elmer T. Lee I'd been saving for a special occasion.

No sense calling Pepper: Why ruin her evening? She'd probably feel sorry for me and come running over. Well, I could do all right feeling sorry for myself.

I'm a slow drinker and by nine-thirty the bottle was still half full, but what I'd drunk was more than enough.

After all, the governor had been a drinking man. Captain Russell had taken away his hard liquor and put him on wine.

"Not exactly cold turkey," I told Digger, who looked at me with infinite sympathy. "But it probably beat the water."

His eyes told me he agreed.

"So we're back to square one," I explained. "Somebody fabricated this whole business. And that means the governor really is buried under that granite block and Pringle still isn't going to be able to dig him up. At least Freddie'll look like a fool, and DeLage won't make money from his tourist park."

The phone rang and I stared at it. I didn't want to talk to anyone in this condition, with my words jumbled and my

167

thoughts five seconds behind. The recorded message said to leave a number and then fell silent.

"Can't be important," I told Digger and he nuzzled me.

Then I heard a familiar voice: "Al, you son-of-a-bitch, what are you trying to pull? The vice chancellor called Nick and told him about the forgery. Is that your work? You trying to make us look stupid? You trying to screw up this whole deal?" By now the voice had grown to a shout. "My lawyer's gonna have your ass. That's a promise."

"Fuck you, Freddie," I said, and erased the recording.

I looked down at my confidant.

"Who, Digger? Who would do something like this?" I hiccuped. "Nick doesn't know enough. Sure, he could've hired somebody. But does he think nobody would catch it?"

I reached for the bottle and poured another swallow into my glass.

"But, then, why should they? Nick's cheap. He probably hired some half-assed amateur historian who thought he was too bright to get caught."

The whiskey went down warm and smooth.

"But does that mean our forger is the killer?"

Digger cocked his head.

"But what about Miss Ouida's journals? How could they be forged? But they have to be, Digger, 'cause, like Lincoln said, this onion can't endure half forged and half free." I shook my head. "Well, you know what I mean."

I wasn't sure he did, but the whiskey hit the bottom of my already inflamed stomach then and a sudden urge to heave overwhelmed me. I raced for the bathroom and the rest of the night was a kaleidoscope of retchings and tortured dreams of the governor, heading for Grinder's and telling someone (probably me), "I'm on my way to die. Don't look for me anywhere else."

The next morning I lay awake for an unknown time, wishing my stomach would disassociate itself from the rest of my body. My head hurt, but I couldn't bear to move, for fear it would set off my stomach again. My mouth felt like I'd gargled with cotton balls and the room stank with a sourness.

I had to get in to work or they'd be worrying about me.

And then I remembered it was Saturday.

Last night I dreamed Freddie called me, raving.

Except that as I lay there, sorting out memory from imagining, I realized it hadn't been a dream.

I reached over for Pepper and felt a furry body.

When I turned my head that way I saw two soulful eyes and a long snout.

"Go find that possum," I moaned.

Half an hour later I forced myself up and headed for the shower. The unshaven specter who stared at me from the mirror with bloodshot eyes was someone I barely recognized.

What was wrong with me? I was acting like a kid. Grownups didn't take their disappointments this way. After all, the only thing that had happened was that the company had lost a couple of grand and missed being involved in a scandal that could have ruined our reputation.

Or was it really the Lewis business I was disappointed about?

I showered, fed Digger, put on some coffee, and pulled out some frozen waffles. As I ate, I tried to make sense of it all. Someone had concocted this business, but the size of the fraud was what astounded me: He'd had to know about the burial of Louis, and he'd had to also know the story of the mysterious death of Lewis. That pointed to a historian, or at least a very well read amateur. But not just any amateur had access to Désirée. Ergo, we were looking for someone with connections to the Fabré family, and that led back to Nick.

But he didn't know enough history, so the idea had to have originated with the person who put him up to it.

I was back where I'd started last night. And the pieces still didn't fit.

I swallowed the last of the coffee and tried to jump-start my mind. Charlie Fabré had probably gotten a tax break by donating his family papers to the university. But someone had been needed to put the collection in order. Maybe Fabré had employed an archivist.

Who? Would the university have a record? Maybe . . . but the rare book room would be closed until Monday.

I cleaned up the dishes and tried to think what to do next. I wanted to call Pepper, although I didn't want to be the bearer of bad news. But Esme had probably already talked to her. Still, I couldn't be sure and I wanted to know she was all right.

She answered on the first ring.

"You talk to Esme?" I asked.

"Yes. It's a bitch, isn't it?"

"It was too good to be true," I said. "We should've known."

"Sometimes you have to take a chance."

"I guess."

"Alan, you're such a pessimist."

"Sorry."

"I mean, I won't let it go. I refuse."

"Pepper . . ."

"There's a poor old lady Nick DeLage has taken advantage of. I don't think for a minute she had anything to do with this."

"You're going to see her, then."

"Yes."

"Good for you. But watch out for that nurse, Krogh. I don't trust her."

"Me either. And Alan . . ."

"Yeah?"

A pause. "Nothing. We'll talk later."

"Right."

The rest of the day oozed away. I straightened up the house, and when my headache was gone, I took Digger for a mid-afternoon walk. It was a pleasant day, with a home football game tonight, and cars rushed past me along Park Boulevard with their purple banners rippling in the wind. In the big stadium parking lot, campers would be almost bumper to bumper, with people cooking chicken, sausages, and steaks on small grills. A few would even have prepared pots of jam-balaya, feeding all comers in a spirit of general benevolence. And, of course, regardless of university rules, there would be plenty of beer.

I had to get my mind off Pepper and back to the real prob-lem, which was the death of Meriwether Lewis.

Or was it?

The only death that could be effectively investigated was the murder of Brady Flowers.

Monday morning I would go to the rare book collection myself and see if I could find out who had catalogued the

Hardin collection, if such records, in fact, existed.

I went back to the house, put Digger in the backyard, disconnected the upstairs phone, and took a long, fitful nap. When I got up it was nearly dark. I went downstairs, checked my answering machine, and saw, to my chagrin, that there were no messages. I watched an old movie and then flipped to the five o'clock local news.

After a story about a three-car pileup at Whiskey Bay, I poured myself a glass of milk. When I came back I was looking at Sarah Goforth, standing outside the now locked gate of Désirée.

Oh, shit.

"Today, a story we brought you yesterday has taken a strange and unexpected twist. We reported that a local businessman, Nicholas DeLage, was sponsoring an investigation to determine if the final resting place of the famous explorer Meriwether Lewis is located at Désirée Plantation, just across the river from Baton Rouge. DeLage had hired a local archaeological consultant and had even brought in famed forensics scientist Marcus Pringle to study the bones buried at Désirée. But now, according to a high official at Louisiana State University, the documentation that purported to prove that the bones were those of Lewis has been shown to be a forgery. Dr. Pringle is unavailable for comment, but we have learned that he has returned to his university in Michigan. We called Nicholas DeLage, but he has not returned our calls. And according to the consulting firm chosen, the project has been canceled. A spokesman for Pyramid Consultants, Dr. Frederick St. Ambrose, blamed DeLage's previous consultant. According to St. Ambrose, the first archaeologists involved in the project 'failed to perform the most elementary research to verify that these documents were genuine.' "

I switched off the television.

It really wouldn't help to kick anything.

I went to sit in the backyard, away from the telephone. I didn't really want to have to commiserate with Esme or Marilyn or David, and I was afraid that the one person I wanted to talk to wouldn't call.

Digger's barking shook me out of my thoughts.

I turned my head: He was staring at the back door, which meant he'd heard somebody was at the front.

Pepper.

I let him in and he rushed to the front, still barking. I stopped in front of the big front door, took a deep breath, and looked through the peephole.

A pug face, black curls, square figure. And my spirits fell. Sarah Goforth.

TWENTY-FOUR

I started to leave her on the doorstep, but curiosity finally got the better of me and I opened the door.

"What do you want?" I asked.

"I don't blame you for being pissed," she said and I smelled alcohol. "Can I come in? Don't worry, I don't have a hidden camera."

I scanned the street, then shrugged and stepped aside.

"Nice place," she said and plumped onto the sofa.

"So why did you come?" I asked.

"I came to say I'm sorry."

"Really." I stared at her. "What's this about?"

"It's about the goddamn story, of course. Meriwether Lewis and all that."

"I saw the five o'clock news," I told her. "It doesn't sound like there's any more to say."

"That's what the damn station manager said." She screwed up her face. " 'There isn't any more to it.' Cut. Finis. End."

"Well, he's right."

"You don't understand," she said. "He just fired me."

I frowned. "Oh?"

"He said I drink." She looked around. "You got a bottle here somewhere?"

"Forget it and tell me what all this has got to do with me."

"What it's got to do with you is that you're saying all you know. I asked around about you, Dr. Alan Graham. And there's a couple things hit me in the eye. First, you've got a doctorate from Arizona State and excavation of a major site in Central America. You know your shit. Second, you've been involved in murders before. There was that Tunica business last year. You managed to solve that one. Third, you have a reputation.''

"A reputation?"

"You don't ever back down when you think you're right and there's an important issue at stake. You've taken some big risks. You turned in a bunch of developers who were wrecking an Indian Mound in Iberville Parish, even though they were putting pressure on every politician in the state. You've turned down bribes and you've ignored threats.''

"Nobody's perfect."

"Go on and joke, but you know it's true. Finally, you come from here and you feel like you've got a special interest in seeing things are done right.''

I shrugged. "Or seeing they aren't screwed up worse than usual, maybe.''

"Ha!'' She smirked.

"What's your point?"

"If somebody pulled the wool over your eyes with this will and these journals, there's a hell of a big story there for the right reporter. That's the point.''

"Who told you about the journals?"

"Nick DeLage showed 'em to me. Before things fell apart. He's got a few other family books and papers, but he doesn't know what they mean.''

"Original papers?" I asked.

"No, the usual published stuff. They're on his shelf where they can impress people.''

"You've been to his house?"

She smirked. "Once or twice. You have to put people at ease if they're going to work with you. The man's a letch.''

"Is that what you're doing here?"

"I'm here to explore. Don't you have any ideas?"

"I only know that whoever put all this together went to a lot of trouble.''

"That's what I figure, too. So why don't we find out together?''

"I don't think so.''

"My press pass can get me into places you can't go.''

"You said you just got fired.''

"I kept the pass.''

"You want your job back," I said. "Well, I can't help you."

"Damn it, I need that job. And if I can get a good story, a new slant, show 'em they were wrong, I'll get another job. And if this really is Meriwether Lewis buried over there, I want to be the one that breaks the story."

"I'm sorry," I said.

"Damn it, I'm *begging* . . ."

"I wish I could help."

She gave me a dark look, then wobbled to her feet.

"You overeducated males are all the same. Just like my husband. Just because he had a doctorate he thought he could lord it over the rest of the world. And you're no different. Look at this place: It looks like a damn museum. You don't even have a woman, do you? Well, enjoy your pitiful little life."

She wheeled and bolted through the door, weaving her way down the sidewalk to the street. She got into a dark blue Subaru and shot into the street, nearly hitting a minivan and driving up onto the boulevard divider.

When she'd blundered into my office I'd been angry with her, but now I only felt pity. People under pressure could be driven to do a lot of things.

The ringing phone brought me out of my thoughts.

Please let it be . . .

"Alan?" My heart jumped: It was Pepper's voice.

"Are you all right?" I asked, breathless.

"Fine. Why shouldn't I be?"

"Well, your place *was* ransacked . . ."

"I got the door fixed. I'm okay, really. And I've got good news: Fitz talked to the lawyer the court appointed for Miss Ouida and the lawyer called DeLage about getting the journals back. Fitz is over here now and we were going over things."

"Oh."

"Nick was pissed, but he said he didn't care at this point. It was all a hoax and he didn't want anything to do with it."

"Have you and Fitz eaten?" I asked hopefully. "I could bring a pizza."

"Not in this football traffic."

"Oh. I forgot. You're boxed in."

"Sorry."

"Look, when the game's over—"

"I'm turning in," she said. "But I have an idea. Can you come by tomorrow at about nine? I thought maybe if we drove down to New Orleans for the day . . ."

I shrugged to myself.

It was better than a sharp stick in the eye.

"Sure," I said. "New Orleans it is."

≡ TWENTY-FIVE

I picked her up at nine Sunday morning and we drove to New Orleans.

A good change of scene, she'd convinced me. We'd take the day for ourselves and forget everything that had happened.

It didn't work, though, because we both kept thinking of the man buried at Désirée. So we made the rounds of the zoo and the Quarter and got back to Baton Rouge at just after five. Pepper rushed off to visit Miss Ouida with the news about her journals. I went home and saw my message light blinking on the answering machine.

I groaned. What else could go wrong? I pressed the playback button and heard a woman's voice.

"Dr. Graham, this is Dorcas Drew. There's something you may be interested in. Would you give me a call?"

Dorcas Drew? The naysayer of the Natchez Trace? What could she have found out that would interest anybody now?

I wasn't sure I wanted to hear it at this stage, but she'd taken the time to call me, so it was only polite to call back.

There was no answer. I took Digger for a walk, and when we were done I showered and called Pepper.

"So how's Ouida?" I asked.

"Better. She's excited at the idea of having the journals back. But I don't like that Krogh woman. She kept hovering around, like she was trying to listen in on everything."

"She probably was. She's Nick's pipeline."

"Alan, listen, there's something I have to tell you."

My chest tightened. I didn't like the tone of her voice. "What?"

"You remember I told you last year that the final postcard I got from my brother came from Monroe, Louisiana?"

"I remember."

"Well, it was from the Holiday Inn there, one of those house postcards they put in every room. When I first came to Louisiana I went to the Holiday Inn and showed them the card and my brother's picture and one of the clerks remembered him. He promised to call me if he ever saw him again."

"And he called?"

"A half hour ago. Alan, I've got to go."

"I'll go with you. That's a five-hour drive and it's pitch-dark."

"No. I appreciate it, but I've got to do this myself."

"But you're tired. You're not in any state to drive on those two-lane roads."

"I've got to do it. I'll be okay, believe me."

"Is your brother staying there now?"

"I don't know. The clerk just said he'd seen him in a restaurant this morning. He was sure it was the same man. That means he may be staying somewhere in the area at one of the motels. I checked at the Holiday Inn and there's nobody registered there by his name. But if he's in the area, somebody might know something about him, whether he's a truck driver, what line or route, or whatever."

There was an almost manic tone in her voice now, something I hadn't heard before. I didn't like it. It was telling me that there were facets to her life that had been so totally hidden from me that anything might jump out.

"I'd promise to stay out of the way," I said lamely.

"No, thanks. I'll call from Monroe. I promise."

"Holiday Inn?"

"If they have space."

Silence while I groped for words. And in the end all I could come up with was, "Be careful."

"Don't worry."

"Pepper . . ." I'd better say it now.

"Tomorrow," she said, and the line went dead.

I stared at the phone, helpless. There was nothing in the world I could do to change her mind. Her brother was her only link to her past. It was important to her that she find him, or at least make the effort. And I was only a spectator.

But I couldn't just stand and wait. So I tried Dorcas Drew again and this time I got her.

"I've done a little more research," she told me. For some reason I thought her voice sounded a little less sure than it had before.

"I appreciate it," I said. "But I'd better tell you there've been some developments on this end, too." I explained about the forged will. "So it looks like the whole thing was a scheme, and who this Louis really was, I don't know, but it seems less likely he was Meriwether Lewis, the explorer." I took a deep breath. "In other words, you were right."

But instead of a cluck of triumph there was a moment of silence.

"Someone went to a great deal of trouble," she said finally.

"I know."

"I wonder . . ."

"Yes?"

"No. It's impossible." I could imagine her shaking her head in decision.

"What is it, Miss Drew?"

"It's a letter I found in the state archives. I thought it was genuine, but now . . ."

"What does the letter say?" I asked.

"I've copied it. It was from a schoolteacher in Maury County, to a judge living in Columbia. It's dated 1825 and it has to do with the history of the removal of the Chickasaw Indians to Oklahoma after their lands were ceded to the United States. Of course, the Indians had been moved out by that time."

"Go on."

"The writer, an Isaiah King, says, and I'll quote, 'There were, living among the Indians, certain half-breeds, who cause trouble, and until recent years there was a white man, reputed to be deranged, who was cared for by one of the chiefs, because the Indians are very sensible regarding such infirmities, and this man, whom the Indians had cared for since he had been brought to them wounded some years before, was regarded as an object of religious awe. It is said he vanished several years ago, and it is commonly thought he died of his wounds or was murdered by other Indians. I got this story from a half-breed man named Joshua Kettle who lived in a village about two days' journey from the Swan River and, in his youth, remembered seeing this red-haired man in the Indian camp.' '' She coughed. "He goes on to talk about other things then."

A red-haired man, wounded . . .

"Of course," she continued, "it could have been anybody. And this hardly counts as historical evidence. It's the rankest kind of hearsay. But I thought you might find it interesting, because it's the only thing remotely akin to evidence that I've been able to find that would substantiate your theory."

"Except that now the theory is bogus," I said.

"Yes. Which leads me to wonder whether this letter, too, has been planted."

"Planted for somebody to find," I surmised.

"Exactly." Another silence. "But this really is all very hard to understand. The amount of forgery, the sheer complexity of it . . ."

"I know. But, like you said, your letter may not really have anything to do with Lewis at all."

"No. But what I thought was interesting was that it developed a mechanism."

"A mechanism?"

"I mean that one of the main drawbacks of your theory was explaining how Lewis would have dropped out of sight after Grinder's Stand and then reappeared in your state. From this letter, it appears possible that someone could have been hidden out with the Indians. I don't say it happened. I simply state that the letter raises an interesting possibility I hadn't thought about."

"Nor had I." I considered for a few seconds. "So what now, Miss Drew?"

"I'm a friend of the state archivist. I intend to have this letter examined for authenticity. And I also plan to see if there are records on anyone else who may have looked at these particular archives in the last few years."

"Will you let me know what you find out?"

No answer.

"Miss Drew?"

"I'm sorry. I thought I heard . . . Well, no matter. What was it?"

There was a clear tone of distraction in her voice.

"Is something wrong?"

"No. I heard a noise in the next room. Silly. I'm alone and the door is locked. It must be Trifle."

"Trifle?"

"My cat."

"I'll call you tomorrow night if I don't hear from you first," I said.

"That will be fine. Dr. Graham . . ."

"Yes?"

"Nothing."

The line went dead.

I didn't like it. Her voice had been different, preoccupied. Or was it just that I was on edge myself and was projecting my own anxiety onto her?

The only way to ease my mind was to call her again. If things were all right, she'd answer. And I'd think of some question I'd forgotten to ask.

But this time there was no answer, even after the phone had rung ten times.

Calm down: She probably just stepped outside, I thought. *The cat was knocking things over and she put it out. Sure. No need to panic.*

But the tone in her voice . . .

An old lady who carries a gun is probably scared of lots of things. She heard the cat, the cat scared her . . .

Dorcas Drew didn't seem like the kind of woman to jump at shadows. And if there was a prowler, that big magnum of hers is a lot of protection. Anyway, it's really Pepper you're worried about. Give her ten minutes and then call again. She'll probably answer then.

I paced for five minutes and then called after six.

This time the line was busy.

She's there. Everything is cool. Case closed.

≡ TWENTY-SIX

On Monday morning I made my way into the office nearly an hour late after waiting around to see if Pepper would call. When she didn't I called the Holiday Inn in Monroe, but they didn't have any record of her.

Maybe she was staying somewhere else.

She'd be okay. At least she was far away from killings and forgeries. I should be glad she was safe.

I took a sympathetic call from Marvin Ghecko, clucking that he knew I'd had nothing to do with any forgeries, and he wanted me to know this wouldn't affect his esteem for me. I thanked him and was glad to get off the phone. He wasn't a bad guy, and, since being confirmed as State Archaeologist last year, he'd been a whirlwind of activity, but knowing that didn't help. When he was finished I got the long-awaited call from La Bombast, and this one made me cringe.

"Do you mean you've been working on this thing, even made a trip to Tennessee, on project funds, and didn't tell me?"

"None of that trip was charged to the project. You always tell us to get background. That's what I was doing, Bertha."

"And didn't tell me."

I took a blind leap of faith and crossed my fingers: "I called and they told me at the office you were sick."

Silence. "Well, I was, as a matter of fact. Vertigo. I was on my back for three days." Her tone had softened appreciably. "So you really called, Alan?"

"Cross my heart."

"Have you ever had vertigo?"

"No."

"It's horrible. Everything spins." She sighed. "And I had to come back and hear about this fraud."

"It didn't do much for me, either, if that's any help."

"Not much." Another sigh. "Well, stay out of it. That's a direct order. Finish the work on the report and leave this trash alone. It's already gotten us more bad publicity than the Comite Diversion Canal. And when the next contract comes up for bid—"

"It'll be a black mark."

"Yes." She sounded surprised. "Of course."

I told her goodbye and gratefully replaced the receiver.

"*Marilyn* . . ."

She came in with her head a fraction less jaunty than usual.

"What is it, Alan?"

"I wonder how Bertha found out I went to Tennessee."

She blushed and looked at the floor.

"I forgot to tell you. She called while you were in Tennessee."

"And?"

When she spoke again I could barely hear her voice: "I guess I let it slip."

"Jesus."

"Sorry. It was a bad day. The Mahatma hadn't shown up for work and my computer crashed and—"

"Okay." My turn to sigh.

"By the way, Rosemary Amadie called before you came in. She wanted to know if you'd looked at the arrow points she brought in."

I blinked. I hadn't thought about the point collection since she'd brought them.

"What did you tell her?"

"I said you'd have them classified for her and something written up by the end of the day."

"You didn't."

"The Mahatma is on one of his lemonade fasts, so he can't work in the field. I thought he could go through them quickly. She'll be happy and—"

"Get him on it," I said.

She smiled. "I'll tell him when he comes in."

"He isn't here?"

"He called and said he'd be a little late. There was a ceremony at the ashram last night and he stayed up chanting."

"Call him again and tell him his next incarnation may be something even lower than an archaeologist if I don't see him here in half an hour."

"Yes, Alan."

That settled, I called James Fellows, the archivist at the Hill Memorial Library.

"Do you remember anything much about the Fabré Collection?"

"Jesus, Alan, everybody is asking about that these days. This is horrible. To think that we had forgeries in here. Now I have to reexamine the entire body of documents."

"You won't be the first archive that's been hoodwinked, James. But I was interested in anything you could remember about who might have catalogued the collection for old man Fabré before he donated it to the university."

"I've been wondering the same thing. Because that's the person who would have been in the best position to commit the fraud. But, you see, that was before my time. Humphrey Elliott was the archivist then. And he died two years ago."

"Great."

"But I've been looking at the collection and the catalogue notes and I'll say one thing."

"What's that, James?"

"Whoever did it was extremely meticulous and very knowledgeable. His—or her—notes are excellent and everything is in order."

"Handwriting?"

"Typed. I'd say on a manual typewriter of some kind. One that needed work. The *e*'s barely hit the paper and the letters needed cleaning. I guess an expert could figure out which brand."

I thanked him and rang off.

Somebody had typed the archiving notes, on a manual typewriter. And then, just a few years later, had developed sufficient computer literacy to be sending E-mail.

Not impossible by any means. Except that the archivist had almost certainly been a middle-aged person, to have developed the kind of historical background information necessary to impress a stickler like James Fellows. And a middle-aged person who wrote with a manual typewriter wasn't likely to have suddenly abandoned it for a computer.

So where was this going?

I was still staring at the phone when it rang again and Marilyn told me it was "that woman."

Thank God.

"Pepper . . ."

"Who?" I didn't recognize the voice.

"Who's this?" I asked, confused.

"Alan? This is Sarah Goforth. I wanted to apologize."

My spirits fell as quickly as they'd risen.

"Oh."

"I know. I'm probably the last person you want to talk to. And I understand. Really."

"Forget it."

"I said some things I didn't mean."

"We all do sometimes." I was trying to think of a way to hang up without being rude.

"The fact is, I was in a rotten marriage for ten years. A professor-type who thought I didn't know anything and knocked me around when I tried to act like something besides a doting wife."

I waited for the punch line.

"I guess I took some of my frustration out on you."

"It happens. Well, thanks for calling and—"

"But I didn't just call to apologize. We need to talk."

Of course.

"I thought maybe if it was on the phone, you'd feel more comfortable. I know I shouldn't have come by your home."

"If it's about the Lewis thing—"

"It is, but before you hang up, listen to me. Please. Just give me two minutes of your time."

"All right."

"First, I'm cold sober right now. I want you to know that."

"Go on."

"Well, I'll try to cut to the chase: I think I can say who's behind all this."

"You mean . . . ?"

"The murder of the caretaker, Flowers, and the forgeries. They're the same person. We both know that."

"It seems logical."

"He's scared of being exposed. That's the only thing that makes sense. He put this whole fraud together, over years, and now it's coming to pieces, and he's trying to protect himself."

"I'd thought about that."

"The will is a forgery, right? But there's more than just the will: Now there're the journals. When they're disproved, the whole business will come tumbling down around this person's head. Because there aren't that many people who could have done something so elaborate."

"I agree."

"So it's important to get the journals, right?"

"Nick DeLage said he didn't need 'em anymore. I assume he'll send them back to his aunt."

"Wrong."

I didn't like the sound of the last word.

"Why not?" I asked.

"Because Nick is a money-grubber: As soon as somebody else says they want 'em, there'll be a price, whether they're forgeries or not. And second, there's the killer."

"You mean—"

"I mean even if Nick wanted to give them back, there's somebody out there who won't want it to happen. The journals have to be loaded with evidence against him."

There was no refuting her logic there.

"The will was just a few lines long," she went on. "It would have been a major project to forge, but nothing compared with the journals."

"I don't disagree."

"The will required just some paper and ink. But for the journals the forger had to find the kinds of notebooks they were written in. Those books either had to be totally unused or else he had to find some way to erase what was already in them. I think he would have had to use blanks, because erasing would be messy and leave traces."

"I'm still listening."

"Since they don't make daybooks like those anymore, it means this person had to search all over the country to find three similar ones dating from the same period. Now, he could have gone to antique shops, but it's more likely he sent for some specialty catalogue, the kind that advertises antique letters, memorabilia, and famous signatures. And if he did that, somebody knows about it and may even have a record of the purchase."

"Don't forget: That was years ago."

"Granted. And that's a difficulty. It may not pan out. There may be nothing. But if somebody *did* order these books, he may also have ordered other things over the years. We could try the different places that sell this sort of thing and ask for any Louisiana customers."

"And if it's a blank wall?"

"Then we have to look at the journals themselves. This person has to have left some evidence of himself. It has to be almost impossible to forge three notebooks, pretending to cover over thirty years, and not make some slips."

A terrible suspicion was beginning to dawn . . .

"You sound as if you've actually looked at these journals."

"I was wondering when you were going to get around to that," she said. "The fact is, Alan, I *have* them."

Someone laughed in the lab room and I heard a chair scrape.

"You what?"

"I have the journals of John Clay Hardin."

I exhaled.

"How in the hell . . . ?"

"I told you Nick's a lech. Now how about lunch?"

"Where?"

"You know the Alligator, on Bayou Manchac?"

"That's a bar."

"It's dark and there won't be anybody around at noon."

"I'll be there."

I sat frozen in my chair for a few seconds, trying to gather my thoughts. I called Esme and told her about Goforth. After she'd snorted a little about the woman's morals I asked the question that was really on my mind. "Have you talked to Pepper lately? She had some personal business to take care of," I said, my chest tightening as I thought of it.

"Her brother. I know. She called me right after she talked to you the other night. She was so afraid you'd take it the wrong way. But I told her you'd understand."

"Did you."

"Alan, it's very important to her. This is something she has to resolve. Be patient."

"Do I have any choice?"

"Not if you love her."

I started to object and then shut my mouth.

"It was a long way to drive at night," I said finally. "I was worried."

"I understand. But she can handle herself. You have to trust her on that."

"Yeah."

When I hung up I got up from my desk and walked into the sorting room.

The Mahatma was seated at the head of the sorting table with Rosemary Amadie's collection in front of him.

"Nice points," he said, smiling. "Wanna lay your hand on one? You can feel the aura of the man who made it five hundred years ago."

"The only aura I want is from the handbook of types," I said. "This afternoon. Done. Finished. Okay?"

"No problem." The Mahatma beamed his holy man smile.

I was walking back into my office when the phone rang again.

"Alan, it's for you."

I went back into my office.

Let it be Pepper. Please . . .

I lifted the receiver.

"Hello?"

"Dr. Graham? This is Dorcas Drew."

Dorcas Drew. I'd forgotten.

"Miss Drew. Are you all right?"

"Perfectly. Why shouldn't I be?"

"Oh, nothing."

"Actually, I'm not. I'm very distressed."

"About what?"

"What I'm going to tell you has to remain between us."

"I'll do my best. What's this about?"

When she spoke again her voice was a whisper. "I spoke to the state archivist about the people who had access to the letter I mentioned."

"And?"

"A great many people use the state archives. But this particular collection hasn't seen that many visitors and the archivist remembers them all. Especially the ones who came back at least once.''

My breath caught.

"Came back?" I asked.

"First they had to go through the collections and find a good document to switch, because the documents in the collection are numbered and described. You couldn't just sneak in an extra one."

"I see."

"Once they'd found the right document to switch, they'd have to prepare a substitute, with the right paper and ink and handwriting."

"So they had to spend some time in the archives just to find a candidate."

"Exactly. And presumably to photograph it while no one was looking. I assume there was originally an innocuous letter by this Isaiah King. The forger would have gone home, developed his film, and rewritten the letter to include the business about the white man who lived with the Indians. Then he would have had to go back to the archives and substitute the false document for the original when no one was looking."

"A lot of trouble to go to for a document that isn't exactly conclusive," I said.

"That's the beauty of it: Seldom in history is one piece of evidence conclusive. It's the weight of evidence. Bits here and there."

"Who looked at this collection more than once?" I asked.

"Just two names," she said crisply. "And you know them both."

My breath caught.

"The first was Melville Freeman. Distinguished research professor at Harvard University. An authority on pre–Civil War America."

"I know the name."

"But I don't think he's the one we want."

"Why?"

"He was working on a new biography of James Polk. Polk grew up in Columbia, as you may know. The archivist said he was looking for letters that might have mentioned Polk as a youth. That was his reason for looking at that particular set of documents. But there's another reason, too.''

"Oh?''

"He died two years ago, quite suddenly. I understand his manuscript was in a very rough stage.''

"And the other historian?''

"The other historian,'' she said in a level voice, "was Dr. Shelby Deeds.''

≡ TWENTY-SEVEN

It took a long time for me to answer.

"Shelby Deeds?"

"I know. It's hard to believe."

"But Shelby was almost killed the other night. Someone tried to run him off the road."

"I can't speak to that issue," Dorcas pronounced. "But I do know that Shelby is an alcoholic. I'd thought he'd overcome the problem, but one can't ever know."

"But why would he pull such an elaborate hoax? What's the motive? Surely he knew he'd get caught."

"I couldn't say. But alcoholics often don't think coherently. They don't always see the consequences of their actions. I was married to one for more years than I should have been."

"You?"

"Does that surprise you, Dr. Graham?"

"No, of course not. I just—"

"Would it surprise you more to learn it was to Shelby Deeds?"

I grabbed the arm of my chair.

"*What?*"

"I wondered if he told you. Well, it wasn't a happy time, at least not the last years. I couldn't take it anymore, so I left. That was ten years ago. I came back here, where I was born. I cared for Shelby, but you can't live with two different people."

"And you think he's relapsed?"

"It wouldn't be the first time. But I don't know." She

191

sighed. "All I can do is tell you what I found out and see that this document is examined for authenticity. Beyond that, the matter is out of my hands."

I thanked her and sat motionless for a long time.

There was no chance of doing more work this morning. I would be stewing as I waited for Pepper to call, and stewing as I thought about the possibility that Shelby Deeds was behind this business. No, I couldn't stay in the office. So I took a long drive on the River Road, wishing Sam was back, and knowing as I passed his house and saw it still closed up that he wasn't.

I took the long way back, following the bends of the River Road, asking myself what question I should be concerned with. I was within a mile of the campus when I glanced at my watch and realized it was twelve-thirty.

Christ. I'd agreed to meet Sarah Goforth at the Alligator Bar at noon.

I turned on my flip phone and called the office.

"She called three times," Marilyn told me. "She sounded upset."

"Damn. Well, if she calls again, tell her I'm on my way. I don't guess there were any other calls?"

"Just that woman," Marilyn said. "She said to tell you she was all right."

Pepper.

"Did she say when she'd be back?"

"No."

"And you didn't ask."

"I thought if she wanted me to know she'd have told me."

"Right."

I pushed the disconnect button and turned right, away from the river and alongside the veterinary medicine complex and the baseball stadium. I headed south on Nicholson, leaving the city behind and passing fields of soybeans and cane until I came to the parish line, about five miles south of the city. I knew the Alligator, of course. Years ago it had been a decrepit, wooden-frame hovel where beer was sold to the fishermen who used the landing at Alligator Bayou to go down to Spanish Lake, in the swamp. Generations of college kids had made their way to the Alligator as an excursion in local color. But a few years ago an environmentalist had bought the old bar, built a pavilion out back, and started to run boat tours as a way of publicizing the natural beauty of the swamp. They hosted weekend parties and had bands, but the decor hadn't changed.

It was on a gravel road outside the city, but there were enough people around to keep a lone woman from feeling too uneasy.

I slid around the bend and straightened out a foot from where the road sloughed into the bayou.

It was just ahead.

Five minutes later I saw it, a boat landing on the right, and just beyond that a frame shack with a beer sign.

There was only a dented blue Ford Ranger out front.

I pulled in beside it, got out, and hurried up the steps to the door.

It took a few seconds for my eyes to adjust to the light. To my right was a wooden counter, but the stools were all empty. To the left were a pair of pool tables, where a lone man in a checkered shirt and a red baseball cap played against himself. The ceiling was papered with dollar bills, from past patrons who'd left their names and messages.

It was no good. I'd missed her.

"Help you?" The bartender, an elderly man with bifocals, appeared from the kitchen area, towel in hand.

"I was supposed to meet a woman here," I said. "She called half an hour ago."

"She left," the barkeep said and went to work wiping the top of the counter.

"A short woman, curly black hair, fortiesh," I said.

The barman gave a little nod.

"She's gone. You want something to drink?"

"A Dr Pepper," I said.

Maybe if I waited a few minutes she'd come back.

The barkeep went to a refrigerator, took out a red can, and handed it to me. I gave him a five-dollar bill and pocketed my change. He vanished from where he'd come and left me alone with the pool player.

"Your girlfriend?" the pool player asked, a cigarette bobbing between his lips as he lined up a shot.

"Not exactly. Did you see her?"

"I seen her," he said with a thick Cajun accent. "She was nervous."

I got up and went over to the pool table.

"Buy you a beer?"

"No, thanks." His hands moved a fraction and the cue stick hit the white ball and sent it caroming against the far side of the table and then spinning back at an angle to collide with the nine ball, which disappeared into a corner pocket.

"Nice shot," I said.

The man straightened. "She was in here two times, that woman."

"Two times?"

He walked around the table, scoping out his next shot.

"First time she sat at the bar, drank three vodkas. Straight. That was when she made the call."

"And then she left?"

"Yeah, but she wasn't too steady. I thought maybe she'd end up in the bayou. But she come back ten minutes later."

"What happened then?"

"She was scared. Something scared her. Don't know what it was. Didn't ask. Figured it was a man. Husband, maybe. She was running away. Figured that out from the big suitcase."

"She had a suitcase?"

He nodded and then squinted at me with brown eyes.

"You not her husband, then?"

"Not her husband, not her lover. Just a friend she called to meet her here."

He bent over, went through the motions of his next shot, and then thought better of it.

"That woman, she's in trouble."

"What did she do then?"

"She made another call and went back to the bar, but this time she didn't order nothing. That's when I went outside."

"You left?"

"Just outside," he said, jerking his head at the parking lot. "Somebody was after that girl. I wanted to see if they was out there."

"And did you see anything?"

"Couple niggers fishing."

"Then what?"

"She left again."

"While you were standing outside?"

"That's right. She come out, got into this little car, and took off like she was a race car driver. I thought she was going into the bayou, but she straightened out."

"Which way was she headed?"

"Left. Down the Bayou Paul Road."

The way I'd come. And yet I hadn't passed her.

"Thanks."

The man nodded and went back to his pool game.

What now? There were a couple of turnoffs where she could have left the bayou road and headed south. Maybe if I retraced my route . . .

I'd gone four miles on the gravel when I saw the sheriff's car ahead. It was blocking the gravel road, its flashers on, and a man in jeans and a T-shirt was pointing down into the bayou as a deputy stood beside him.

I stopped and got out.

"Trouble?" I asked.

"Car went in the bayou," the deputy said. "You can get around me."

That was when I saw the car roof. Blue. A small car, like a Subaru.

I felt sick.

The deputy's eyes were on me now.

"We got an ambulance on the way. You know this car, mister?"

"I don't know. I was supposed to meet a woman at the Alligator."

"She drive a car like this?"

"Same color," I said.

It was downhill from then on, mainly because the Subaru's windshield had been shattered and the same shotgun blast had virtually erased Sarah's face.

They took me to across the river to Plaquemine and questioned me for two hours.

It was seven-thirty before Dogbite made it down from Baton Rouge and convinced them that they didn't have enough for an arrest.

"Why does this shit keep happening to you?" he demanded, walking me to where they'd impounded my car.

"It's the patron saint of lawyers, making work for you," I said.

"St. Yves," he said. "Every once in a while he comes through."

I thanked him and got into my car.

A smart person would have driven back to Baton Rouge and let the law take its uncertain course.

But I wasn't feeling that smart. I drove back to the Alligator.

The place was alive this time, with a couple of Cherokees and a Stingray outside on the gravel. Inside, six or seven college kids crowded around the pool tables. Frat boys with their dates.

The man I'd talked to earlier hadn't said anything about her having the suitcase when she left. It was a long shot but worth the try.

But where would you hide a suitcase in here?

Two women walked out of the restroom then.

"Excuse me," I said, "but did you notice a suitcase in there?"

The pair giggled and one, who was barely more than a girl, gave me a strange look.

"That thing is yours?"

"My wife left it," I said. "Would you mind . . . ?"

"Sure. It's in the way." She looked at her friend and giggled some more. "You can't even get to the toilet."

She went back through the door and returned a few seconds later lugging an old-fashioned tan suitcase with three stripes.

"This it?"

"That's it," I said. "Thanks."

"Funny place to leave it," the girl said and the pair started giggling again.

I carried it outside and thrust it into my Blazer, then headed right, toward the interstate. But before I got there I pulled off onto the side of the road and opened the piece of luggage.

They were there, all three of them: The journals of John Clay Hardin.

I was probably breaking all sorts of laws. But the journals didn't belong to the police, or to me, or even to Nick Fabré. They belonged to Ouida Fabré and I was sure I was doing what she would want.

It was the kind of decision that made Dogbite gnash his teeth.

I took the suitcase home and there, in the privacy of my study, with Digger on guard in the hallway, opened it again and took out the journals.

They looked the same as before, which didn't surprise me. I hadn't really expected that anyone had pulled a switch. I placed them on the little antique desk left me by my father and leafed through them, page by page.

I went through the early years, my eyes stopping, inevitably, at some of the more interesting entries.

Whoever had forged the journal had done a masterful job of reconstructing the daily life of a plantation owner in the first half of the last century. There was nothing so spectacular, on the one hand, or so glaringly out of place, on the other, that anyone but the most competent document examiner would suspect a fraud.

But, then, maybe that was because it *wasn't*. Maybe it was because what I was reading in the first journal and even the second was genuine—the thoughts and observations of John Clay Hardin.

Why forge three journals if you already had two? Maybe the mysterious forger had stumbled on the journals and realized their potential. All he—or she—would have to have done was forge a third volume. And the third volume was the one with the least amount of material.

I turned to the third book and opened it, staring hard for some evidence that my theory was right. I took a magnifying glass out of my desk drawer and, under my desk lamp, searched for the telltale cracks in the faded brown handwriting.

There were none.

Well, maybe I needed a microscope. I could take the journals to the office and examine them there with one of the scopes we used for looking at artifacts.

Then caution asserted itself: I wasn't an expert on questioned documents. I was an archaeologist. This was something best left to an expert.

But what expert? It was Shelby Deeds's expert who had said the will was forged, and everyone had gone along with it. But now Shelby was under suspicion, and if he was suspect, what did that say about his expert witness? The man had been introduced to me as Flinders Mott, an authority on forgeries. But what did I really know about him? I, as well as everyone else, had been taking Shelby's word that the man was who he said he was.

Then sanity grabbed me back from the edge of the abyss: Flinders Mott hadn't invented those cracks in the brown letters. And the document he'd showed us for comparison hadn't had them.

But the comparison document had been one he'd provided.

There was only one way to know: I would have to send the journals away.

I called Dorcas Drew.

"I need to send you something," I said and explained about the journals, leaving out the death of Sarah Goforth. "Whoever is going to look at the letter you found in the archives can probably make a determination of the journals. The owner is okay with this. But I have to know if these journals are forgeries."

"Send them to me in the morning," she said. "I'll get back to you as soon as I know something."

I hung up and turned back to the last journal.

I remember Father said he had papers in an oilskin when he was found by the river & how he looked at them & made no sense, so left them & afterwards the papers disapered.

We were back to the mysterious lock box.

Why would someone fabricate the story about the lock box? To increase the value of the land itself? But all that was in the box were some papers and the elder Hardin had been unable to read them.

Unless the journals—or this portion of them—had been forged to deliberately mislead. What if the box contained something of intrinsic value, like gold or a treasure map? What if the real journal had been doctored somehow to make the contents of the box seem unintelligible?

It was necessary to find the box, if it existed. But that required knowing more about the plantation itself and its original layout, and Esme had already dug through all the known archival material.

Then my eye fell on a little book perched on the edge of

my bookshelf. I'd forgotten about it ever since bringing it home from the office. It was Adrian Prescott's *Great Homes on the River: Sketches of the Plantation Past.*

I thumbed through it and found the selection on Désirée. It was concise but well written. I checked the publication date: 1987. I didn't know who Adrian Prescott was, though the flyleaf listed him as a native of East Baton Rouge Parish whose avocation was history. Maybe tomorrow I could find him, if he was still alive, and see if he could offer any suggestions.

Anything was better than standing still.

▰▰TWENTY-EIGHT

The next morning I went to the office early and, after wrapping the journals in brown paper, put them in a mailing box. Then I secured the box with plastic tape, addressed it to Dorcas Drew, and drove to the post office, where I sent it by Express Mail. I checked our box and found, to my relief, a brown government envelope of the kind checks come in.

I got back to the office just in time to be at my desk when Marilyn arrived.

Before she could begin I handed her the brown government envelope, like a cat presenting its master with a bird.

Her little face relaxed and she actually smiled.

"I was starting to get my résumé together," she said.

"So is there anything pressing?" I asked.

"Is that a way of saying you're taking off again?"

I told her about the murder of Sarah Goforth, leaving out any mention of the journals.

"Oh, God," she groaned. "Alan, how do you get involved in these things? Do you mean there may be policemen here today? What will I tell them?"

"Tell them I'm out on business but I'll be back."

"And if the murderer comes instead?"

"Keep the doors locked."

"Thanks."

I reached into my pocket for my keys. None of the lab crew had shown up yet, but I saw Rosemary Amadie's projectile point collection arrayed on the sorting table, a small card next to each item, with the type of point, geographical area, and dates.

The Mahatma could do good work when he focused on his current incarnation.

"And if that woman calls?" Marilyn asked.

"Tell Pepper I'm fine and to hurry back," I said. "But you don't need to say anything about the murder."

I left quickly, because I knew that it was only a few minutes before the cops or the media or both came for more details. And I couldn't make any progress if I was sitting in an interrogation room.

I went home, circling the block to make sure nobody in an unmarked car was waiting for me, and finally parked out front and went inside. I retrieved the little book by Adrian Prescott and checked the phone directory for a listing.

Seventeen Prescotts, but not an *A.* or an *Adrian.*

I drove to a shopping center not far from my house, where the publisher had offices. It was a local company that specialized in subsidy works on local themes, and once in a while a really valuable reference work resulted. I went up a narrow set of stairs between a pet store and a pharmacy and found myself in an office overflowing with books of all kinds.

A woman with graying hair and bifocals looked up at me from her desk beside the stairwell and asked if she could help.

"Do you know Adrian Prescott?" I asked, showing her the little book.

She examined the volume carefully, as if she were evaluating its construction, then laid it down on her desk, face up.

"This was published before I came here," she said. "Mr. Herman may know about it, though. Did you want to order copies?"

I told her I was looking for the author, and she got up without another word and disappeared into the back.

There was a morning paper on her desk, and I wondered if she'd gotten to the part about the body found in Bayou Manchac, or the local man questioned about the crime.

The woman reappeared two minutes later, leading a giant with gray, tousled hair. Wearing blue jeans and a red-checkered shirt with suspenders, the giant reminded me of a clean-shaven Paul Bunyan with rimless glasses.

"Herman Dugas," the giant said, smiling and sticking out a huge hand. "You're interested in Adrian Prescott's book?"

I mumbled my own name quickly, hoping nobody read the

paper that closely, and told him I was more interested in the author.

Herman Dugas scratched his chin.

"Mr. Prescott. Nice old gent. Seemed to know his stuff, but what do I know?" He chuckled.

"I wanted to talk to him about one of the plantations he wrote about," I explained. "But there wasn't a listing in the phone book."

The giant nodded.

"He was in bad health. He may have passed away."

The woman's head jerked up, as if she'd known the author.

"Then that's the end of that," I said, chagrined. I turned to leave.

"Too bad. He was gonna write another book."

"Oh?"

"Yeah. He was having trouble finding the money, though. I think he was trying to get some kind of grant."

"A grant?"

"That's what I remember."

"What was the book going to be about?"

He shook his head. "I don't remember. It was history, of course. That was his thing. But he wasn't a professional historian. I remember he was upset about that: He said you practically had to be a university professor to get any kind of research grant, no matter how good you were."

"And he wasn't a professor."

"No. He was retired from the state. Used to be an accountant. He hated it."

"Do you remember what agency?"

"Nah. He'd been retired five or six years when we did his book. I think he retired when his wife died."

"Did he have other family?"

"Some kids, I think. But I never met 'em."

"Could you do me a favor?"

"What's that?"

"Could you check your records and see what address he left?"

The woman looked offended. "We can't—"

But the giant was unfazed. "Don't see why not. Haven't heard from him for a long time, but we ought to have something." He folded his big arms across his chest.

"Come back just before four-thirty. I got a few other things to do, but I ought to have time to look it up by then."

"Thanks," I said. "I appreciate it."

I left the office, got into my Blazer, and headed back down Stanford toward the office.

An idea was taking shape. I didn't know its full implications or how it would emerge, but my unconscious was telling me to pursue the lead. If Adrian Prescott was working on another book, and if he'd wanted to get a grant for research, then maybe he was the man who'd archived the Fabré papers. And that meant that maybe he was the man behind the fraud.

My chain of thought was shattered by the wail of a siren and I looked into my mirror to see flashing blue lights.

Oh, Christ. What had I done, forgotten to signal when I'd turned onto Morning Glory?

I pulled to the side and fished for my driver's license, but before I could get it out a voice on a loudspeaker was telling me to get out of my car and keep my hands in sight.

"You could've waited for me to get back to my office," I complained, but the policeman, a black hulk with a beer belly, wasn't interested in anything I had to say.

Half an hour later, after six other police cars had come speeding up like sharks after blood and half the neighborhood had had the opportunity to see the criminal sitting shackled in the rear of his captor's unit, I was driven downtown. But instead of going to the police station on Mayflower, I was taken instead to the district attorney's office on St. Louis. I was shown into a long conference room and the hulk behind me released my handcuffs as four men, seated at chairs near the head of a conference table, looked on, scowling.

"That all, sir?" the cop asked, and the man at the head of the table nodded.

"Thanks."

The door closed, leaving me with the four men.

"Sit down," the man at the head of the table ordered.

I pulled out a chair and sat, aware of their eyes on me.

For the first time I noted the camcorder on a tripod in the corner, and the tape recorder on the conference table.

"Mr. Graham," the man at the head began, "my name is John Kech. This is Chief Deputy Comeaux of West Baton Rouge Parish, Lieutenant DeSoto from Iberville Parish, and

Lieutenant Crane from the Baton Rouge Police Department.
I'm an assistant district attorney for East Baton Rouge.''

If they were watching for a reaction they may have seen
me blush. I didn't like the looks of this at all.

''Mr. Graham,'' Kech went on, ''I have a paper here for
you to read. I'm going to go over it with you. It explains your
rights.''

He slid a piece of paper toward me over the table.

''What the paper says is that you have the right to remain
silent . . .''

I blotted out the rest of the litany, my eyes fixed on the
line at the bottom where I was supposed to sign. When Kech
had finished he paused for a moment. I looked back at him.
His eyes, behind the rimless glasses, were cold gray.

''Do you understand what I've just read?''

I pushed the piece of paper away from me as if it were
contaminated by a virus.

''I want my lawyer.''

The men at the head of the table heaved a collective sigh.

''*Fils putain*,'' the cop from Iberville mumbled.

''Is there some reason you need a lawyer?'' Comeaux
asked, but Kech held up a hand.

''Can't talk to him anymore without his lawyer,'' he said.

We stared at one another for another hour until Dogbite
came.

He breezed into the room with a briefcase that looked sus-
piciously light, shook hands with Kech, whom he called
Jackie, and asked him how he'd done in the football pool.
Then he asked if he'd dumped his shares of some stock I'd
never heard of, laughed at one of Kech's jokes, and finally
turned to me and said, ''Not again.''

''I didn't do anything,'' I protested.

''He didn't do anything,'' Dogbite cried, wheeling to face
the others. ''Why is my client here?''

''Big problem for us, Stan,'' Kech told him with false con-
cern. ''One, your client was on the scene when a man named
Flowers was murdered in West Baton Rouge. His only alibi
witness is a woman nobody can find.''

''What else?'' Dogbite demanded.

''Your client is implicated in a swindle. Forged documents,
claims about famous dead people, a real first-rate scam.'' He

tapped a thick folder I hadn't noticed before. "A man named Nick DeLage says your client's been trying to worm his way into the confidence of his poor old aunt. And he thinks your client even sent a woman named Sarah Goforth to steal some documents from him."

"What else?" Dogbite said, biting a fingernail.

"We talked to Goforth's supervisor at the TV station. *Ex*-supervisor, because he fired her a few days ago. Said Goforth made a trip to Tennessee, trying to follow up this story."

The white car in the parking lot at the Lewis monument . . .

"Then said Goforth turned up dead in Bayou Manchac, without enough of a face for her nearest and dearest to identify. And your client here admits he was in the immediate area, even went to meet her."

Dogbite turned to face me. "Sounds like a strong case," he accused.

"Goddamn it, Stanley, who are you representing?" I yelled.

He blinked and turned back to the accusers. "My client is innocent," he declared with all the conviction of someone reading a detergent label.

"Then he won't mind answering some questions," the Baton Rouge detective said.

"I'm not answering any questions unless I'm charged," I said, hoping I sounded confident.

"He's absolutely right," Dogbite seconded, and then looked over at me. "Are you sure?"

"You're goddamn right I'm sure," I said. "Whose side are you on?"

"Yours," Dogbite said, biting another nail. Then he leaned over and whispered, "You sure you don't want to cut a deal?"

"Am I under arrest?" I demanded.

"Let's keep this informal," Kech said smoothly. "Just answer a few questions. What's wrong with that?"

The Iberville deputy, DeSoto, jumped in then.

"Do you have any property of Mr. Nicholas DeLage?" he croaked.

"No."

"What about these journals that were stolen from him?"

Kech asked. "Maybe you thought you were doing his aunt a favor by taking them, right?"

His attempt to be personable failed.

"I don't have any journals," I said.

"We can get a warrant to search your house and business," he said pleasantly. "Do you know how much time a business loses when records are subpoenaed? When whole walls are torn out?"

"You're going too far," Dogbite said finally. "My client said he doesn't have the things, and you don't have probable cause for a warrant. My client has been threatened himself on several occasions. His girlfr—associate has even had her apartment broken into and he's had his car vandalized."

Kech shrugged. "*Somebody* broke into her apartment and *somebody* trashed his car. But we only have his word it wasn't him.

"Speaking of this associate," Kech said, leaning forward, "where is she just now?"

"Out of town," I said. "In Monroe."

"Monroe?" The D.A.'s brows went up a fraction. "What's in Monroe?"

"Her brother," I said and explained Pepper's search.

The lawmen exchanged glances and I could see I'd opened a small chink of doubt.

"Look," I said quickly, trying to exploit the opening, "I think the person who forged the Lewis will is the same person who annotated the Fabré documents when they were given to the library. I don't know who the person is, but I think finding them is the key to this thing."

Kech folded his arms. "So this person, whoever he or she is, is killing people because he knows about this colossal scam?"

"Something like that. I think we stumbled on it by accident, as part of our work for the Corps of Engineers, and the killings are to keep us from finding out something incriminating."

The policemen's faces showed confusion, boredom, and hostility, but Kech was maintaining a pretense of interest.

"And there isn't any record of who this annotator is."

"There probably is somewhere, but it has to be ferreted out."

"This is crap," Chief Deputy Comeaux growled. "I say charge him now."

But Kech held up a hand. "There's time for that."

"Plenty of time," Dogbite chimed in. "Dr. Graham is an upstanding, well-respected archaeologist with an international reputation, a responsible citizen who runs a business vital to the community, who has assets—"

"Yeah, we know all about that," Kech said. He sighed and looked at his colleagues. "Okay. We're going to hold off for now. But only for now. You," the prosecutor declared, spearing me with the cold gray eyes, "stay in this parish. You got that? No playing cops and robbers. And if I find you've concealed any evidence or hindered our investigation—"

"You'll be looking for dinosaurs in Angola," Lieutenant Crane pronounced.

"Paleontologists look for dinosaurs," I said. "I'm an archaeologist. We look for—"

But Dogbite was already hurrying me out of the room.

"Right, whatever, thanks, Jackie." He was shoving me toward the door with one hand and grabbing at his briefcase with the other. "Lemme know if you need tickets for the next Kingfish season. I've got a friend who knows the assistant trainer and . . ."

He didn't speak again until we were on the street.

"Jesus, Alan, don't wise off to those guys. It was all I could do to—"

"All *you* could do? Goddamn it, Stanley, what's your idea of defending somebody? Giving them the option of suicide?"

"There's no need to talk that way, Alan," he huffed. "I left a very important client to come here. You wouldn't get in these spots if you'd leave law enforcement to the authorities."

"Oh, sure, like the three stooges and their handler in there."

"That kind of talk will only get you convicted."

"Apparently it doesn't take much."

"I'll bill you for my time."

I called the office on my cell phone, was told there were no emergencies, and no, that woman hadn't called back. But

Rosemary Amadie was coming to pick up her projectile point collection and was bringing a pecan pie.

A pie was just what I needed.

I picked up a hamburger and made my way back to the publisher's. It was only three-thirty, but what the hell? I needed to see sane people.

This time the woman at the desk scurried into the back when she saw me and a few seconds later Herman the giant lumbered out with a battered manila file under one arm.

"Think I got what you want," he said, dropping the file on the table. He extracted a piece of paper.

"This is the last letter I got from him. From 1992. Haven't heard a word since."

He handed me the letter:

Dear Mr. Dugas:

I am still working on the matter we discussed. My health has not been good lately so has delayed our work. I will talk to you when things improve.

> Sincerely,
> A. Prescott

But it wasn't the words that got my attention, it was the print: The letter had been typed on a machine with an almost nonfunctional *e*, and the *o*'s and *p*'s were almost filled in from lack of cleaning.

What had James Fellows, the archivist, said?

. . . a manual typewriter of some kind. One that needed work. The e*'s barely hit the paper and the letters needed cleaning . . .*

Adrian Prescott was the man hired by Charles Fabré to prepare his documents for donation to the university.

I copied the address at the top of the letter. It was in Broadmoor, a subdivision that had developed right after World War II, on the east side of Airline Highway, which at that time had curved along the outskirts of the city.

"Thanks. You've been a big help."

I shook hands with Mr. Dugas and the receptionist and went back out into the sunlight.

The address was six years old. Adrian Prescott might have moved. The house might have been sold. Prescott might even have died.

The house was a one-story brick structure with a carport on the right side and a neatly tended lawn. There were no cars in the drive, but a child's plastic scooter was on the front walk. I had the feeling that Adrian Prescott hadn't lived here for several years. Next door, an elderly man was raking leaves and I walked over and introduced myself.

"I hear Adrian Prescott was your neighbor," I said.

"Adrian?" The old man cleared his throat. "Adrian hasn't lived there since '91 or '92. He was in bad health. Had a stroke while he was hunting. Put an end to that. Pretty much had to stay inside afterward." He shook his head. "The Newtons live there now."

"You have any idea where Mr. Prescott went?" I asked.

"He had some kids. Adrian, Junior. Junior, we called him. I think he's in some kind of investments. Little girl, the youngest, married when she was in high school and moved away. Haven't read any obituary in the paper, so I expect Adrian's living with Junior. Anyway, Junior would know where he is." He leaned on his rake. "But I told all this to that woman."

"Woman?"

"The one from the TV station. She came by here a couple of days ago. What's everybody looking for Adrian for?"

"A rich relative died," I said and thanked him.

I left knowing I was on the right track. Sarah Goforth had come to the same conclusion I had. But how? Had she found out something from Nick DeLage? Or had she just run across the same little book I had and followed up the lead?

But how had she gotten Prescott's last address? The phone book didn't list an Adrian or an A. Prescott. Then I told myself to think it through: There were other Prescotts and she may have called all the names listed until she found a relative. Or maybe she'd gone to old phone books in the library, which is what I'd have done if the publisher hadn't been able to help.

It didn't matter; the fact was that she'd been looking for Prescott and now she was dead.

And the police in three parishes wanted to charge me with the crime.

*   *   *

When I got back to the office I found Rosemary Amadie admiring the Mahatma's work. A foil-covered dish was on the table beside her.

"Of course," the Mahatma was explaining, "I think when you feel the vibes from these points, you can open a channel to the Indian who made 'em. This one in the middle, with the serrated edge, the Palmer point? Touch it and see if you don't feel something, a kind of energy . . ."

Rosemary had a hand on it and her eyes were closed.

"It *does* feel warm . . ."

"It's the energy," the Mahatma said. "It's a nexus of cosmic forces . . ."

Rosemary opened her eyes then and blinked in surprise when she saw me standing to the side, a slightly disgusted look on my face.

"Oh, Dr. Graham," she said. "I didn't see you there."

"Rosemary," I acknowledged, ignoring the Mahatma's smile.

She put a hand on my arm.

"I hope you're all right," she said in a barely audible voice. "I saw that business in the paper. It said they were questioning you. Then I came here and saw a hearse outside . . ."

"It was all a mistake," I said.

"I'm glad to hear that. I brought a pie, but I was so scared you'd be in jail . . ."

"Never happen," I told her.

That was when footsteps stampeded across the front porch and Lieutenant Crane burst in with three blue-clad SWAT-team members at his back.

"Search warrant," he sneered. "We have one for your office and one for your house. Want to stand aside?"

◼ TWENTY-NINE

I watched Crane and his three stooges tear the office apart, drawing yelps of outrage from Marilyn and a growl from Gator. Only the Mahatma seemed unfazed, but I knew it was only a matter of time before I lost what little composure I had. My call to Dogbite elicited the information that he was arguing a motion on the ninth hole at the country club. I watched the team of professional wreckers root through our files and turned to Rosemary Amadie.

"I'll walk you to your car," I told her, bagging the point collection and handing the bags to her.

"We just came from your house," Crane called after me. "You're lucky the dog was outside."

I slammed the door in his face.

"I feel so badly for you," Rosemary said. "I wish there was something I could do."

"Me, too," I said and watched her walk away.

I didn't want to go back inside, but it wouldn't be right to let Marilyn and the others take the heat.

When I went in again, our file drawers gaped open, there was a heap of papers on the floor, and a slice of the new pie was missing.

Marilyn mouthed the word *bastards* and I nodded concurrence. They were in my office now, digging in my desk.

"If you'd tell me what you're looking for, maybe I can save you some trouble," I said but Crane slammed the door in my face.

Then, half an hour later, they left as quickly as they'd

come. I looked around at the ruin and flinched when I thought of what I'd find at home.

"Alan," Marilyn said coolly, "this has to stop."

"There ain't one of 'em whose asses I couldn't kick," Gator said.

The Mahatma alone was silent, seated at the sorting table with his eyes closed, mouthing a silent mantra.

I carried the pecan pie to the trash can and dumped it in. Too bad, but I didn't want any after this.

It was a long time before I went home. I couldn't nerve myself up to face the wreckage.

I went to a bar near the overpass on Perkins and had three beers. It was a place with big TV screens that blasted sports at you every second, but it was far enough away to make me feel halfway safe.

They'd taken swabs of my hands when I'd been brought to the sheriff's office in Plaquemine and I hadn't heard anything more. When the test showed no gunpowder residue on my hands maybe they'd ease up. Or did a shotgun leave residue? I wasn't sure; maybe the test only worked with handguns, in which case I was back where I started.

So what had they been looking for, the journals?

If that was the case, they'd come up empty. Even the copies were with Shelby Deeds.

Shelby.

I hadn't mentioned him to my inquisitors. Since I wasn't sure I understood what was going on, I couldn't hope that they would understand it, unless there was some homespun scholar on their staff.

It would have made no sense to tell them we were really looking at two sets of crimes, removed from each other by nearly two hundred years.

And it would have been like pulling teeth to get them to acknowledge that the earlier crime was the key.

Well, why should they? Most murders are simple. Dogbite had told me that a thousand times. Somebody gets shot in a crap game, a husband wants his wife's insurance money, a robber sees someone with a big roll and kills them to keep the victim quiet.

No history, no Sherlockian reasoning, no research. Grab

the closest person and if he doesn't confess in the first three hours, sit by the phone and wait for somebody who hates him to call. Twentieth century detection at work.

Not quite so simple this time. A famous American was dead, but it had never been clear how he died. Two hundred years later somebody had decided to capitalize on his death.

The lockbox had to be the key. I'd hoped that Adrian Prescott would have some idea where it might be hidden, but now I realized that if he did, he would have taken it himself. Provided he was the killer. No, there was a good chance it was still out there.

I thought of the big holes Pepper and I had seen when we'd been at the plantation when Flowers had found us down at the river. Somebody else had been looking, too. Flowers had let us know that.

What if it had been Flowers?

What if Brady Flowers had been an accomplice of the killer, and they'd had a falling out?

What if Flowers had already found the box?

I went to the pay phone and called Esme.

"Are you alone?" I asked her.

"Yes. Is everything all right?"

"You don't read the papers?"

"I just got back from Abita. I was with Shelby. We were, er, doing some research."

"You were with him all day and . . ."

"He came over yesterday evening. We met for dinner at Juban's. After that is none of your business."

"Right."

"Why, what happened?"

I told her about Sarah Goforth's murder. "Naturally, the cops would love to hang it around my neck. They've already torn up the office."

"Oh, Alan . . ."

I didn't want to tell her about Prescott. If, for some reason, Shelby was involved, and she mentioned the name, it could only put her in danger.

"Look, Esme, do you have any maps on historical land use at Désirée?"

"Of course. There are a couple of very good ones."

"Can I come to your place and look at them?"

"Right now?"

"If I can."

"I suppose so."

I was already parking in her drive when I realized how unen-
thusiastic her offer to see me had been. Well, too late now.

I went up the steps to her door and knocked.

When she opened the door her face wore a distracted expression.

"I hope I'm not interrupting you," I said and then . . . then
I saw Shelby Deeds seated on the couch.

"It's all right, Alan," Shelby said, rising to give me a
hand. "I hear you've had a bad time in the last day or so."

"You might say that," I agreed.

He shook his head. "This business gets curioser and curioser, doesn't it?"

"It does." I nodded at some rolled-up papers on the coffee
table. "Are these the maps?"

"Those are the ones," Esme said, spreading them out.
"This is an 1858 surveyor's plat. It shows the big house, where
the Hardin family lived, the sugar house, the slave quarters, the
overseer's house, the blacksmith's, and the commissary."

I turned my head to orient myself to the map and read the
numbers the surveyor had placed by his drawings of the
buildings, and the legend at the bottom of the chart.

"Mind saying what you're looking for?" Shelby asked.

"Land use," I said. "I'm looking for land use."

A plot just behind the big house and slightly to the south
was labeled *Garden*. Near it was another building, not much
larger than one of the slave cabins. The label said simply,
Mechanic's house.

I'd found the hut where Louis had lived.

"Here's a Mississippi River Commission map from 1878,"
Esme said, unrolling a blue sheet. "But it's hard to make out.
The best map after the 1858 one is another plat that the first
Fabré had made when he sold a piece of land on the south."

This time the garden was gone, as was the mechanic's
house. And where the mechanic's dwelling had been there
was now another rectangle, that read *Chapel*.

"Oh, I see . . ." Shelby intoned. "They tore down the mechanic's house and put the chapel on top of it."

Esme frowned. "Alan, where is all this going? If the papers are forgeries . . ."

"I'm not sure," I said.

"Nor am I," Shelby declared, taking out a cigarette. "Or do you have a notion, Alan?"

I tried to laugh. "Notions aren't evidence."

Shelby snorted and lit a match. "We aren't policemen here, Alan. You can try your ideas on us. We won't call you crazy."

"Okay, what if only part of the journal was forged?" I said. "The last part? What if there's really a box and it has something really valuable?"

Shelby sat up straight, the match burning toward his fingers. "What are you saying?"

"I'm saying maybe there's something at Désirée after all."

"But what?"

I shrugged. "There really was a man named Louis who lived there. We know that much from the gravestone. If most of the journal is genuine, then this Louis, whoever he was, did have something valuable in his possession when he died."

Esme frowned. "So you think that, even though Louis wasn't the famous explorer, he might have been somebody else with a secret of some kind."

"It makes sense," I said. "Or why would somebody be so determined to keep that secret from being found out?"

Shelby coughed and shook his head. "I don't know. A week ago I thought we were about to rewrite history. Then I find out somebody else has been trying to do it for us. Now we're back to rewriting history, but with a footnote."

"Something like that," I confirmed.

"But what could be in the box?" Esme asked.

"There's only one way to know," I said. "We have to find it."

Shelby got up slowly and exhaled a puff of gray smoke.

"Do you have any idea where it is, Alan?"

"I'm not sure," I told him. "But when I am, I'll call you."

I still didn't want to go home to the disaster zone. For a long time I drove around the city, finally ending up downtown, at the river. I parked on one of the side streets, walked to the levee, and watched the lights from the casino boat, moored just upstream.

It had been almost three hundred years since a Canadian named Iberville had come upriver from the Gulf and named this place after a red pole the Indians had stuck on the east bank. Almost two hundred years since another man had washed ashore a few miles upstream. Not half a century since a kid named Alan had raced along this very levee, between his parents, after Sunday mass at St. Joseph's. The Canadian was dead, the man who had washed ashore was dead, and little Alan was well into middle age. A feeling of helplessness descended over me and my limbs felt like lead.

Why did any of it matter? It was just a game historians played, and if it weren't for the game, two people would still be alive now. What I was turning over in my mind could only make things worse, even get someone else killed.

If I was smart I'd let it go.

If I was smart I'd never have decided to shovel dirt for a living.

I went home at last, as the sun began its western meltdown and darkness started to reach out of the east. I didn't want to confront what the law had done to my home, but Digger didn't deserve to go hungry.

The scene at home was even worse than I expected. Books were scattered on the floor and files of papers were strewn in every direction. File cabinets had been left open and pictures were crooked on the walls. About the only thing they hadn't done was break down the door; apparently they'd called a locksmith, as well as the alarm company.

I let Digger in and instead of jumping up on me he wagged his tail, head down, as if to say he was sorry he hadn't been able to do anything. I patted his head and opened a can of food for him, then called Dogbite again.

"Those bastards wrecked my office and my house," I complained.

"I know."

"And you didn't warn me?"

"I didn't find out about it until late this afternoon. I was with Judge Dear."

"How's his chip shot?"

"If you're going to be sarcastic, Alan, I'm going back to my supper."

"They wrecked the frigging place!"

"Of course they did." He was lecturing a backward child. "It's a good sign."

"What?"

"It's their way of trying to scare you into doing something stupid. If they had any evidence they wouldn't have done any of this."

"Stanley, that makes me feel really great."

I hung up and started for the refrigerator, but walking around all the books on the floor was too much effort.

Maybe I'd spend the night in a hotel.

Sure, and let those bastards run me out of my own house. No way.

I was still staring at it when the doorbell rang.

Oh, Jesus. Maybe they've come back . . .

I stood rooted, waiting to see if they'd go away.

But they didn't.

I wasn't in a mood for company, but I might as well see who it was.

I jerked the door open and saw her standing there, looking small and fragile.

"You probably hate me," she said.

I reached out and folded my arms around her.

"No," I said. "Not exactly."

"I know I left you at a terrible time. I don't deserve you." Her face was buried against my chest now and I felt her tears wet against my skin.

I brought her inside and closed the door behind us.

"It doesn't matter," I said and all of a sudden I began to tremble.

"Alan, what's wrong? You're shaking." She gave a little gasp. "My God, what happened in here?"

"The police," I said. "It's their way of scaring me. I guess they succeeded."

Now I was shivering like someone with a fever, ashamed of my weakness and yet unable to will my limbs to be still.

"Sit down," she said. "I'll fix you a drink."

"That would be good."

I watched her disappear into the kitchen, making her way around the heaps that were my possessions.

I'd been okay up to now, plotting how to deal with things.

All it had taken was seeing her again to trigger this reaction. Now I felt like I was falling apart.

Much later we lay in the bed upstairs, with her, still dressed, snuggled against me under the blanket. The shaking had stopped and a warmth brought on partly by a stiff glass of whiskey and partly by her body had chased away the shivers.

"I thought I was going to find him this time," she said. "It was so close. There was a motel where he'd stayed. He told the man he was coming back this week. I waited for two days. It was a real dump. I didn't feel safe. But I didn't care."

I let her talk, knowing she needed the release.

"He never came. I don't even think they ever saw him. It was some kind of setup."

"A setup?"

"A scam. This man came on the last day and said he could find him if I'd give him some money. He claimed to be with some kind of truck licensing company. It sounded bogus. I left in the middle of the night."

I ran my hand through her hair.

"They figured they'd get me up there and then build up my hopes. Then, the longer they let me wait, the more willing I'd be to pay."

"I'm sorry," I said.

"And meanwhile, you were down here, almost getting killed, because I was chasing ghosts . . ."

"He isn't a ghost. You'll find him."

"Yeah."

She nestled against me and slept.

The next day, after I checked in at the office, I made a call to Ivy Dupuy. Ivy was an artifact collector I'd met four years before, on a pipeline survey in Ascension Parish. Like many collectors, he was suspicious of professional archaeologists, but he'd trusted me enough to show me some sites that no one had ever reported. In return, I'd sent him some books on archaeology. I hadn't seen him for a year and a half, but he had an impish sense of humor and I thought what I was proposing would appeal.

It did, and once settled, he agreed to await my confirming call.

I drove home for lunch, gritting my teeth at the thought of the mess I was about to see.

Pepper, barefoot, with sleeves rolled up, turned around from where she was shelving books.

"Hi. It's almost back to normal."

I looked around at the restored room. "I can't believe it."

"I already did the upstairs and the study. I know I got a few things out of order, but—"

"But nothing," I said, sweeping her into my arms. "It looks great."

"It's the least I could do after what I put you through."

"You didn't put me through anything. It was important to you."

For a second she looked anguished and I thought she was going to crack, but the mood vanished as quickly as it had come.

"So what now?" she asked. "Have you thought of anything?"

"Sort of," I said and told her my plan.

"This is crazy," she said. "You could end up in even worse trouble."

"What are they going to do?" I asked. "Trash my house and office?"

Dogbite scowled at me from across his desk.

"What is this, Agatha Christie? You get everybody together in a room and then go around the circle one by one?"

"Not quite," I said.

He turned to Pepper. "Is he holding out on me?"

"I've never known Alan to lie," she said primly.

"Humor me, Stanley," I pleaded. "Just round up the usual suspects."

"It'll take some doing," he groused. "I don't know if I can arrange things like you want."

"You won't know if you don't try," I said.

Dogbite shook his head. "Get out of here." As I reached the door his voice followed me: "And remember, I don't work for nothing."

≡ THIRTY

It was just after seven when I tried Dorcas.

"I'm sorry I'm so early—"

"I've been up for two hours," she snapped. "Besides, I was going to call you this morning anyway."

"You got the journals."

"I got them," she said, "and my associate is looking them over now."

"Good."

"But he's sure about the letter."

"He is," I repeated, my pulse accelerating.

"Oh, yes. I know he thought I was crazy. But I told him it was your insistence."

"What does he think?"

"That it's genuine, of course. There are some additional tests, if you want to pay for them. But he did a microscopic examination and there are no reasons at this stage to doubt the age of it. The paper is old enough and the ink seems to be, too. There are no erasures or alterations."

Pepper was staring at me. "What is it?" she whispered.

"So there really was a white man living with the Indians in the years after Meriwether Lewis was supposed to have been killed."

"There were many," Dorcas corrected. "But this particular one was apparently special, if you recall."

I did recall.

"Of course," Dorcas went on, "this could have been almost any white man. There's no proof whatsoever that it was

Governor Lewis. Except that the letter mentions that this white man was red-haired.''

"Like Lewis."

"His nickname was the Red Stork. Of course, with so many Scots-Irish settlers, red hair wasn't *that* unusual.''

"When will your friend finish with the journals?''

"A few days. But from his first glance, and this is admittedly superficial . . .''

"Yes?''

"He doesn't see anything that strikes him as false.''

I thanked her and replaced the phone slowly. I was only vaguely aware of Pepper's tugging my arm.

"Alan, what is it? What's going on?''

I told her about the letter of Isaiah King.

"We assumed that since the will was forged, the letter and the journals must be phony, too.''

"It's a reasonable assumption,'' she said. "But if they aren't . . .''

"Then either Shelby's expert was wrong about the will, or somebody forged the will only.''

"But why?''

"I'm not sure. Except . . .''

"Yes?''

"The will is the only document that spells the old man's name as Lewis.''

"Meaning?''

"Meaning I guess it's time for me to wake up a certain lawyer.''

It took until that afternoon, of course. Pepper and I picked up Dogbite and drove over under a heavy sky. Esme and Shelby Deeds arrived five minutes later. The crime scene tape was still up, but by now it was faded and bedraggled, like the plantation house itself.

I was crazy. They were all humoring me. It would be a miracle if everything came together.

The October wind chased the leaves across the once stately lawn, riffling the maps under my arm, and Dogbite consulted his watch.

"I'll give it fifteen more minutes,'' he said.

A white Porsche wheeled into the drive then, spraying

rocks behind it, and skidded to a halt on the grass, as if to accentuate its owner's claims.

Nick DeLage got out and homed on us like a torpedo.

"You're Kirby?" he asked Dogbite, ignoring me.

"That's right," Dogbite said, fishing out a business card. "Thanks for coming, Mr. DeLage."

"I came here because I want to see what this man"—he jerked his head at me—"is trying to pull."

He turned to face me. "Bud, I'm about to bury your ass under a ton of lawsuits."

Dogbite bit a fingernail.

"Now, Mr. DeLage," he began, but was interrupted by a blue Ford Crown Victoria, followed by a marked West Baton Rouge sheriff's car.

John Kech got out of the Ford and I recognized my old friend Deputy Spano as he shut the door of the marked cruiser.

"Stanley," Kech said, shaking Dogbite's hand. He turned to me. "Lieutenant Crane wanted to be here but he has a stomach virus. I told him he wasn't missing a thing."

Dogbite shot me a nervous glance. "Just waiting for a couple more," he said, licking his lips. "Should be any second now."

"I hope so," Kech said. "I'm only here because it's you, Stan. I stopped going on field trips in the Boy Scouts."

"I know, and I appreciate it," Dogbite assured him. "I owe you big-time."

He gave me a meaningful glare, which, translated, meant my bill had just gone up an order of magnitude.

"So who else are we waiting for?" Kech asked.

"Yeah," DeLage said. "I don't have all day. And who are these people?" He nodded at Esme and Shelby.

"These are two professional historians," I said. "They've been involved in this from the beginning and I thought they should be available to answer any questions."

"Involved from the beginning?" Kech said. "And this is the first time I've heard about them? Graham, why don't you tell us a little about what's going on here."

I held up a hand. "I think Dr. Deeds is better qualified," I said. "Shelby?"

Kech snorted, but Shelby rose to the occasion. He was

almost finished with a colorful account of Désirée, the Natchez Trace, and the adventures of Meriwether Lewis when a muddy gray Dakota pickup turned into the drive and crept toward us, a blue Jeep Cherokee following just behind.

I exhaled relief.

The last two players in the drama had arrived.

Ivy Dupuy dismounted from the truck and ambled toward us, while a thin, sandy-haired man with glasses and a bow tie got out of the Cherokee.

"Alan," Ivy declared, spitting tobacco juice onto the ground. "You got a hell of a little crowd here."

"What is this?" DeLage demanded.

"Mr. Dupuy is a friend," I said. "And this . . ."

The sandy-haired man in the bow tie was already handing around his card.

"Stafford Oates," he said earnestly. "I represent Miss Ouida Fabré. How are you, Mr. DeLage?"

"Did you call him?" DeLage rounded on me. "I'll have your ass—"

"Excuse me, Mr. DeLage, but you don't have any standing here," Oates said pleasantly. "I represent your aunt, and she is the legal owner of this property."

"You . . ." DeLage's face flushed red.

"He's right," Dogbite said.

"Maybe," I said, "we need to walk over to the Indian mound so I can explain what this is all about."

I started forward and the others trailed after me, with the exception of Ivy Dupuy.

Pepper leaned toward me as we walked. "Alan, you never did tell me exactly what you're planning."

"Cross your fingers," I said.

I skirted the pond, with the old chapel on the right, and something clutched inside my chest. What if I was wrong? What if this turned into a waste of everybody's time? What if I was miles off base?

I trudged up the mound and stopped, panting, at the top.

Everything was as it had been a few weeks ago, when I'd first come here. I opened the iron gate and went through the enclosure to stand by the brick vault with the single name.

When everyone had reached the summit I pointed down at the tomb.

"This is the man who started all this," I said. "Shelby has given you the background. Briefly, the question is whether this is the grave of an unknown person, or whether this is the grave of Meriwether Lewis."

"We know all that," DeLage snarled. "And we know all those documents backing up your claim are a fraud."

"We know," I corrected calmly, "that the will in the university library is probably a fraud. But there are three other documents that I believe are perfectly genuine. The first is the journal, or three journals, actually, which Shelby's mentioned; the second is a fragment of paper found in Brady Flowers's hand when he was killed; and the last is a letter in the Tennessee State Archives."

There was sudden silence, except for Shelby clearing his throat.

"Tennessee Archives?" he asked.

"That's right." I explained then about the Isaiah King letter.

"So you see," I said, "there is a possibility that the Lewis theory was right from the beginning."

"But if that's so, why the forged will?" Esme asked.

"I'm not sure. But let's leave that for right now and consider the possibility that the theory really is correct."

DeLage's face had gone pale.

"The journals mention a metal box that the old man had and this box contained documents that the journal writer, John Clay Hardin, couldn't make anything of."

"A code?" Shelby asked.

"Or a cipher," I said. "With information that may have some bearing on this whole thing. The killer must already have at least one of the papers, because Flowers was holding the edge of a handwritten document when he died. But there must be other papers the killer didn't get, papers that may still be in the box where Flowers left them."

"Lost documents from the Lewis and Clark expedition!" Shelby cried. "That would be fantastic. Some of Lewis's journals are incomplete. A secret page from one of those journals would be incredible."

"And worth money," I said. "Quite a lot."

The prosecutor, Kech, stepped forward. "So you brought us here because you know where the box is. I have to warn you, hiding evidence is obstruction of justice, and there may be misprision of felony if—''

"Hold on," Dogbite said. "Let's hear him out." His look warned me my story had better be good.

"I don't *know* where the box is," I said. "So I'm not hiding *anything*."

"You don't know where it is and you brought us all here?" DeLage exploded. He turned on Kech. "You ought to arrest him anyway."

"I said I didn't *know*," I said. "But I may have an *idea* and I thought that if I was right, it would be a good idea if everybody concerned was here to witness its discovery."

Kech gave a short little nod.

"All right, so where do you *think* it is?"

From the right corner of my vision, down by the pond and out of view of the little gathering, a ghostly figure in white was making its way toward us.

"When the old man died," I said, "he was rambling about artichokes. He had a garden, right about where the pond is now, and we all assumed that he must have buried the box in his garden. If that were the case, the box would have been destroyed long ago when the area was excavated for the pond."

"So you're saying it was buried somewhere else," Esme asked.

"I think so, because when Pepper—Dr. Courtney—and I came out here just before Flowers was killed, somebody had dug holes in different parts of the grounds. My guess is they were using a metal detector and digging wherever it gave them a reading."

"And they found the box," DeLage said.

"Not with the metal detector," I said. "Because if I'm right, the box wasn't buried in any of those places."

I dropped the maps on the ground then and spread them across the grave. Stafford Oates leaned down to hold one edge and Pepper held the other.

"This is a surveyor's plat of the plantation just before the Civil War," I said. "It shows most of the important features and all the structures. It even shows the Indian mound we're standing on."

"So?" Kech asked.

"The area marked *Garden* corresponds approximately to the area that was excavated for the pond," I said and waited for them to crane their heads and satisfy themselves that this was so. "You'll note that the plantation house is right where it is now, but the workers' houses, the mechanic's house, and the commissary are all gone."

"Interesting," Oates said.

I placed the later map over the first one.

"This dates to just after the Civil War, when the plantation was bought by Pierre Fabré, the husband of Eleanor Hardin. Note the things that are the same: the big house, the workers' houses, the commissary—"

"The garden's gone," Stafford Oates said.

"But there wasn't any pond there then," Nick DeLage said. "That pond wasn't put in until this century."

"Right on both counts," I said. "Anything else?"

"Oh, I see," Oates said. "The chapel is where the other house was."

"The mechanic's house," I said. "You're right. And since the old man, Louis, was a fix-it type, it stands to reason that the mechanic's house was where he lived."

Oates looked up at me. "You're saying the chapel was built where his house used to be."

"That's what I believe," I said.

Below us, the white figure had passed the mound, was heading toward the river . . .

"Well, let's go dig the damn thing up," DeLage snorted, but before he could turn I stopped him.

"It isn't there anymore," I said. "Brady Flowers found it."

"Flowers?" Spano said then. "The man who was killed?"

"That's right," I said. "I think it was Flowers who dug all the holes. I think he was involved with whoever killed him and forged the will."

"Why did the person kill him?" Spano asked.

"Where's the damned box?" DeLage demanded. "Where did that old bastard hide it?"

Where, indeed? I thought. *Time to produce. Time to be David Copperfield. Time to materialize a box . . .*

"I think the box never left these grounds," I said.

"Talk plain," the deputy said.

I saw movement to the left, below the mound. The figure in white was moving among the bee boxes.

"Well," I stalled, "where would you have put it if you were Brady Flowers and you didn't trust your partner?"

"Goddamn it, he's just leading us on!" DeLage cried. "He doesn't know anything."

"Hey . . ." Kech had turned to his right, toward the river. "What's that buzzing?"

"Bees," Shelby said. "Something's stirring them up."

"There's somebody down there," Esme said. "It looks like he's collecting honey."

"Are those Flowers's bees?" Kech asked, and I saw that he was beginning to make the connection.

DeLage shrugged. "I told him he could keep his bees here."

"Then who's that?" Kech asked.

DeLage shrugged again. "Hell if I know. He's all wrapped up."

The figure left the boxes as we watched and trudged toward the mound. As it neared, we could make out the black veil hanging from the wide-brimmed hat, and the heavy gloves that covered the hands. It was carrying something in one hand, wrapped in a white cloth. A few bees still swirled around the white, long-sleeved torso, and when the figure halted at the top of the mound, DeLage jumped back.

"Keep those little bastards away from me," he cried. "I'm allergic."

"Lots of people are," I said. "But I think you're safe."

The figure reached up and jerked off the protective hat, revealing the round face of Ivy Dupuy.

"Hot in this suit," he said. "Even in October."

"Mr. Dupuy isn't just my friend," I said. "He's also a beekeeper."

Dupuy set the hat down on the mound, beside the white bag, and then delved in the bag for a second.

"This what you was after?" he asked and produced a metal box, covered with sticky honey.

"Holy Christ," DeLage said. "You mean it was there."

I nodded as if I'd never had any doubt, trying to hide my butterflies.

"Open it," DeLage cried. "Let's see what's inside."

But even from three feet away I could see it had already been opened.

Before I could say anything DeLage lunged forward and grabbed the box from Ivy's gloved hands. He snatched out a piece of paper and was about to open it when Spano's hand clamped his wrist.

"Not so fast, *cuzin*." He pried the paper from the other man's grip and then released DeLage's hand like he was dropping a dead mackerel.

We crowded around as he opened the yellowed piece of foolscap and laid it on top of one of the crypts.

"Careful," Shelby warned. "The paper may crumble."

I looked down, not sure what I expected to see.

"What the hell?" Kech muttered.

The paper was crossed with lines, some kind of sketch. I saw a square with smaller squares set inside, and, in the now familiar ancient script, I made out the words *palisade* and *commissary*.

"It's a map," Oates said softly.

Shelby reached down then and carefully lifted the paper by one edge.

"Yes. A sketch, probably by Lewis himself. But of what? Fort Mandan, where they spent the winter that first year of the expedition? One of the enclaves along the way?"

"How about Fort Clatsop, on the Pacific Coast?" Esme suggested. "That's where they stayed until they were ready to come back."

Deeds nodded. "It could be any one of those places. There's no way to know which one."

"Yes, there is," I said. "I suspect the explanation is in the piece of paper that was torn out of Flowers's hand by his killer."

"The one that talked about the law?" Spano asked.

"The one that had those letters, *L-A-W*," I said. "But I think it was in some kind of code."

"Why? Is it a treasure map?" Spano asked.

"To a historian," Shelby declared. "It may be a document that will help rewrite American history."

"And the murderer has it," Kech said. "Great. What do we do now?"

"Put the map in a safe place," I told him, "and wait."

I shook hands with Ivy and tried to pay him, but he refused any money. As he drove off, I watched DeLage talking earnestly to Kech and Spano in a low voice.

"He's trying like hell to find a way to make money out of this," Stafford Oates said, smiling. "But somehow I think he's going to fail."

I looked hard at Oates. He was the same thin young man I'd been introduced to earlier, but I saw now there was an undergirding of steel.

My turn to smile. "You know, Mr. Oates, I think you're right."

He nodded, started for his Cherokee, and then turned.

"Nice meeting you, Dr. Graham. I'm sure if you have anything else to contribute I'll hear from you."

Dogbite gnawed another fingernail. "Alan, what's he mean?"

I shrugged. "Ask him."

Pepper touched my arm.

"Let's go home," she said.

We drove back in silence. I pulled up in my driveway but when we got out she made no effort to walk toward her car, parked at the curb. We looked at each other for a long second and then I led the way in and closed the door behind us.

"I thought . . ." I began but she put a finger across my lips.

"Shhh. Do you have to explain everything?"

She came against me then, hugging me tightly, and when I bent down, her face was tilted up to mine and our lips met.

"Pepper—" I began, but she cut me off.

"Why don't we go upstairs?"

Afterward, exhausted by our passion, I lay beside her in the bed and stared at the ceiling. It really had happened. And it was better than I'd imagined.

I heard her deep breathing next to me and reached out to touch her hair. She turned her head toward me and cooed in her sleep.

I didn't want this moment to end.

After a time I, too, drifted into sleep.

Pepper was laughing, holding up an ancient scroll filled

with letters in an antique script. As I watched, the letters danced, shifted, and rearranged themselves into names.

Adrian Prescott, Shelby Deeds, Nick DeLage, Dorcas Drew . . .

Major James Neelly, Captain Gilbert Russell, John Pernier, Robert Grinder . . .

General James Wilkinson, President Thomas Jefferson, General William Clark, Governor Meriwether Lewis . . .

John Clay Hardin, Dr. Charles Franklin Hardin, Louis . . .

They were at a ball, held under the Désirée oaks—Wilkinson, plump and smiling in his uniform, with shifty, cunning eyes; Jefferson, awkward and slightly remote; the servant Pernier in the background, holding the bridle of a horse; Dr. Charles Franklin Hardin, greeting guests; and dismounting, a tired, pale man in a blue-striped duster with a leather saddlebag and two pistols in his belt . . .

The fiddler suddenly stopped and the eyes of everyone turned to the stranger as if he were a ghost. And I realized as I watched that it was because the man in the duster had no face. They watched him come on, but with every step he took, his figure became less distinct, until, just before he reached the president, he faded away entirely.

The fiddler started up again, playing "Possum in the Gum Tree." And General Wilkinson was grinning in his Boy Scout uniform.

I shot upright in bed.

I should have known. But it had taken a dream to hit me in the face with it.

Wilkinson. *Damn.*

≡ THIRTY-ONE

I got up early, careful not to wake Pepper, and went downstairs to my office, where I found the telephone directory.

The address I wanted was there.

Maybe I should have called Kech. Or at least Dogbite. But I had a feeling Kech would be coming to see me quickly enough. Something about tampering with evidence. I had to get to the address first.

I fed Digger and consulted my watch. Six-thirty. There should be time. I hoped Pepper would forgive me.

I took North 19th out of the Garden District, driving into a neighborhood inhabited by poor blacks. I passed the decaying Dufroque school and half a mile later crossed over the freeway. I curved down onto it then, and a quarter of a mile later exited at the governor's mansion. On my left was the old powder magazine, built in the 1830s when Baton Rouge still had a military garrison, and on my right was the polluted capitol lake, which had once been a bayou that fed the Mississippi. A thin, gray mist clung to the old Indian mound on my left and half hid the capitol building, which loomed in front of me as a thirty-four-story monument to Huey Long. I turned left before reaching the capitol and entered Spanish Town, an ancient part of the city that had thrived in the 1920s and early 1930s when the university was still located downtown.

The houses were a grab bag of two-story Victorians and wooden-frame bungalows. Some had been bought by young couples and renovated, but others needed paint. The house I

was looking for was in the latter category, not exactly dilapidated, but in need of a minor face-lift.

I verified the address by the brass numbers beside the door
and noted a brown Mercury wagon in the drive. If I'd had
any doubts before, now I was sure.

I circled the block and pulled in two houses away, where
I could watch.

It didn't take long. A beige Honda Accord whisked up the
street past me and screeched to a stop at the curb. A stocky
black woman in white got out, carrying a satchel, and hurried
up the steps to the front porch. She knocked and the door
opened and then shut behind her.

I hunched in my seat and waited.

The sound of a slow-moving car came from behind me and
a white police cruiser slid slowly past.

All I needed was for him to stop, ask for my license. Kech
might have a warrant out for me by now.

The cop car vanished into the mist and I heard a door close.
I looked toward the house. A figure was getting into the station wagon, but the angle made recognition difficult.

The station wagon pulled out of the drive and then drove
away up the street.

I took a deep breath and told myself it was time.

I opened my door and walked toward the house, dragging
an invisible ball and chain.

For a long time I stood in front of the big oak door. There
was a little peephole and I wondered if somebody inside was
watching me.

I knocked and waited.

Thirty seconds later I heard the sound of a bolt sliding free
and a chain being unfastened. The door swung halfway open,
revealing a black woman in nurse's white.

"I came to see Mr. Prescott," I said.

The nurse stared at me.

"Mr. Prescott don't see nobody," she said. "He sleeping."

"It's important," I persisted. "My name is Dr. Alan Graham."

"You're a doctor?"

I nodded. Sometimes a minor deception is required.

"Just a minute."

She closed the door and I waited.

Two minutes later the door opened again.

"Mr. Prescott say you can come on back."

I followed her through a darkened room that smelled of mothballs. In the gloom I could barely make out a couch, chairs, a coffee table, bookshelves, and an old-fashioned gas space heater.

We went down a hallway to a room at the end and the nurse stood aside.

The big bed was empty and at first I thought he'd disappeared into the bathroom. Then I saw the big chair in the corner and the shriveled figure, with a book in its lap.

"Dr. Graham," the figure said in a reedy voice. "You tricked my nurse, didn't you?"

"Guilty," I said.

"Guilty?" The word ended in a wheeze. "What a choice of words."

He must have been eighty, and the skin was drawn so tightly over his bones it was hard to see how his blood could circulate. Then I realized that he was fully dressed, with a rich scarlet vest and matching tie, and the book in his lap was a Bible.

"You're very persistent," he said.

I shrugged. "Somebody was threatening to kill me."

He sighed. "That was a mistake."

"There've been other mistakes, haven't there, Mr. Prescott?"

"Yes," he said. "How did you find out?"

"Luck. Intuition. The way things fit together. And I talked to a man at the printer's who remembered you."

Prescott closed his eyes as if he'd been struck by a sudden pain.

"Of course," he said finally, opening his eyes. "Herman Dugas. But that was before I moved. How did he know where to find me?"

"He didn't. But it's hard to disappear these days."

"Not like two hundred years ago. People could disappear completely then."

"Why don't you tell me about it?" I asked.

"Why not?" He put his hands over the Bible and his eyelids closed halfway. "Dr. Graham, do you know how lucky you are? You get to do exactly what you want. You studied to be an archaeologist and you *are* one. But what if you had to do something else? Sell shoes, or real estate?"

"I wouldn't be any good at it," I said.

"But if you had to support your family, you'd have to do it anyway."

"Is that what happened?"

When he spoke again it sounded like tearing parchment.

"I was an accountant with the state Agriculture Department. Thirty-five years. I kept track of swine and cattle. Thirty-five years. Swine and cattle. Do you know what that's like?

"Year in, year out. Swine and cattle and sometimes horses. How many tons of fertilizer were used in a year. Do you know how I kept sane?"

Somewhere in the house a board creaked.

"History. I had an active imagination. I went through the motions, I kept the books, I answered the audits, I went to the office parties and picnics. But I wasn't really there." He was looking through me now, as if I weren't in the room. "I was somewhere else, with all the things I was reading, about the famous people who came this way. William Bartram, the naturalist. John James Audubon. James Bowie and his brother Rezin. Mike Fink, the keelboat man. Andy Jackson, marching up and down the Natchez Trace. Old Jamie Wilkinson, the traitor."

I heard a soft rustle behind me and turned to see the nurse.

"Everything okay, Mr. P.?"

"Fine, Adele. You can go back to what you were doing. Dr. Graham and I were just talking."

The nurse vanished as quickly as she'd come.

"I always thought I could have done as good a job as the professors at the university," Prescott went on. "The only difference, besides their degrees, was that they had access to the sources. But nobody takes you seriously without credentials."

"How did you meet Charlie Hardin?" I asked.

"We both belonged to a hunting club up near Raccourci. Hunting was my other passion."

I nodded. "He told you he had some family papers."

"Exactly. I remember the day, the hour, the place. It was about fifteen years ago, a couple of days after Christmas. We were sitting under a big hickory tree, freezing, waiting for a couple of the others to leave their stands and come out of the woods. Charlie and I didn't know each other, but I passed him my bottle and we started talking. He was surprised I knew the history of the land we were hunting on. He invited me to his place and said he wanted to show me something. That was the first time I laid eyes on the journals. After I read them, he took me to the cemetery behind the house and showed me the graves. That's when he said he wanted me to get his collection in shape so he could donate it to the school.''

"How long did it take for you to figure out about Lewis?"

"Two months, well into my cataloguing. But even then there wasn't any proof."

"You saw the letter in the Tennessee archives," I said.

The old man looked puzzled. "What letter is that?"

I explained and he straightened in the chair, as if he wanted to get up.

"Imagine that! My God, what I would have given to know about that. But, you see, that was part of the problem. I didn't have the budget of a professional historian. I couldn't ask a university for travel funds to visit all the places where documents might be stored."

"Is that where the will comes in?"

"I know I shouldn't have done it. But I was desperate and it seemed like such a little thing, and so much good would come of it."

"So you forged it."

"It was to use as leverage. I knew no public foundation would give me money for research, but there are private donors out there." His hand came down on the arm of the chair with what little force he could muster. "I *knew* the man at Désirée was Meriwether Lewis, but I couldn't prove it without more evidence. If I showed them something that linked all the evidence, they'd be more likely to give me money for research into the true story of the death of Meriwether Lewis."

"It would have made you famous."

"Yes. Oh, I know the professional historians would've sneered. So what? I could have gotten a major publisher, once

I had everything documented. Once I'd hired an archaeologist to exhume the remains.''

"It was an excellent job," I said. "You must have spent a lot of time putting it together."

"It was hard. I made a lot of mistakes at first. But when I was satisfied, I just put it in with the other documents and gave it a number and briefly described it. Charlie never saw it." He sighed. "Charlie never knew what all he had."

"But someone would have discovered the will was a forgery."

"Would they?" The thin shoulders twitched. "Maybe. Or maybe it would have disappeared. Been stolen. A great loss. But once I had evidence from other sources, once I'd found the evidence I know is in other places—like the letter you mentioned—the will wouldn't be necessary, would it?"

"No," I said.

"Then, of course, Charlie died. I lost my access to the materials. And I had my first stroke. For a long time I couldn't move or speak. When I recovered, the materials were all in the library."

"Except for the journals," I said.

"Yes. His daughter claimed them." He looked away and seemed to shrink back into his chair. "It didn't matter. By that time I was too sick to do anything about it. My son moved me to a nursing home."

"Your son?"

"Junior. That's what we called him. Adrian, Junior." In another room a television went on. Good. I didn't want us to be interrupted again.

"He took care of you."

"Oh, yes." There was a hint of bitterness in the chuckle. "My wife died while we were still in Broadmoor. I only had the children. My daughter got sick. That only left Junior."

"Who took you out of the nursing home?"

"I didn't belong there." Another sigh. "I don't belong here, either. I belong with my wife. There's not anything I want anymore."

I didn't have anything to answer. When he spoke again I had to step closer to understand him.

"There's all kinds of ways to be sick, Dr. Graham. Look

at me: I'm just bones now, ready for the grave. But there're other kinds of sickness. People walking around. You wouldn't know to look at them.''

I wasn't sure where he was going, but all I could do was listen.

"They say it's a gene. I don't know. Or maybe it's something that happens to somebody when they're young. All I know is it's a sickness, just the same as my not being able to get out of this chair.''

"Who, Mr. Prescott?"

But he didn't hear me.

"You'd never have known, either. Such a happy child. So normal. Until that third year in high school. That was when it happened.''

"Your child, Mr. Prescott?"

"They called it paranoid schizophrenia. 'Throw us your insurance policy and we'll do a snake dance. Pay us a little more, and we'll sign something that says *cured*.' "

Two tears leaked down his face and he made no attempt to wipe them away.

"Of course, we told everybody it was boarding school. But they knew.''

Someone turned up the volume of the television and then, with a shock, I realized the voices didn't come from a television at all.

"You have to understand," the old man begged. "It isn't her fault.''

There was movement in the hall behind me and I turned.

Rosemary Amadie was standing behind me, an enigmatic smile on her face.

"Well, Alan. I didn't really expect you so soon.''

"Rose—'' the old man began but the woman cut him off.

"It's all right, Papa. I'll take care of it. I take care of everything. I've always taken care of everything, haven't I?''

"Please," Prescott wheezed. "She's not responsible.''

"Papa, you're getting excited.'' She shook her head sadly. "Alan, you really shouldn't have come here. This is too much of a strain for him.''

"I imagine he's been under a lot of strain after the murders.''

"Murders?" Prescott croaked. "Rose, what's he saying? You said there was just Flowers."

"Papa, don't worry. I did what I had to." Her fists clenched as she faced me. "Alan, you have no right to upset him."

"It sounds like you've already upset him, Rosemary."

"No! I've protected him. I spent all my life protecting him. I took him out of that nursing home where my brother dumped him when he moved to California. I brought him here, to live with me. And when Flowers called about what your people were doing at Désirée, I had to keep other people from getting the credit Papa deserved."

"That was why the E-mail threats, the break-in, and trashing my car," I said.

"I was hoping to make my point," she said.

"It must have been a shock when you found out the will was a fake," I said dryly.

"You don't know how hard it was to tell her," Prescott said. "But after that man died, I had to tell her, to keep it from getting worse."

"It doesn't matter," Rosemary said quickly. "My father was driven to it."

"And you were driven to kill Flowers because he knew about your father's research and was willing to sell what else he'd found to the highest bidder."

"He was there when I was working on the original collection," Adrian Prescott said. "When I figured out who old Louis really was and read about the box, I went out one night and did some digging. Flowers caught me. I told him I was looking for some buried money. I paid him off. But after that he knew there was something valuable out there."

"And when we started doing the levee survey, it triggered him," I said.

"Yes." The old head gave a half nod. "I'd kept in contact with him over the years: I told him I'd pay him if he ever found anything interesting. So he called me and said some other people were looking for things."

Rosemary walked past me to stand beside her father. "I never meant for him to die. He called again, said he had something. He said he'd found the box, and he wanted money for what was inside."

"The cipher."

"Yes. He figured it was directions to a treasure." Her mouth curved downward in disdain. "He wanted more money than we had and I told him so. I decided to go get it for myself. I had no idea he'd call you and the girl when I turned him down."

"You didn't expect to see us there."

"No. If it hadn't been for you, I would have gotten the rest of it. As it was, I left a piece of it in his hand. But it doesn't matter."

"You have the paper," I said.

"No," Prescott wheezed, clutching his Bible closer to his body.

"But you need the map, too," I said.

"Map?" he asked.

"We found the box," I said. "There was a map inside." The hand on the Bible jerked.

"You saw this map?"

"Yes."

"For God's sake, Dr. Graham, tell me what it showed."

I stared at him for a long time.

"You haven't broken the cipher, have you?" I asked.

"We will!" Rosemary cried. "It's a well-known type of cipher. It just takes knowing the key word or phrase."

"But you don't know it, do you?" I asked.

"No. But we're very close. If I can just—" The old man coughed and closed his eyes. For an instant I thought he was dead. But then the breathing resumed and he folded his hands over the Bible and pressed it to his midsection as if he were stanching a hemorrhage.

"Jefferson," he said. "It has to have been Jefferson's idea. He invented a cipher machine, you know."

"Did he? Well, I'm not surprised."

"But—"

"We'll solve it, Papa. You can solve it if anybody can."

"May I see the piece of paper?" I asked.

Prescott's knuckles were white now, as he clutched the book to him. Rosemary shook her head. "I don't think so, Alan."

"I just thought I'd ask," I said. "Tell me, why did you kill Sarah Goforth?"

Prescott's hand came out, grasped his daughter's arm, and she laid a hand on his own.

"Now, Papa, it was necessary. She came here looking for you. She'd been talking to Nicholas DeLage. She knew."

"And she had the journals," I said.

She turned her head slowly to look at me. "Did she? Well, that's one more reason. Papa was the one to recognize what those journals were. She had no business with them."

"You shot her."

"It was necessary, Alan. Surely you see that."

"What did you do, hide in her car?"

"I followed her to that bar. When she left I drove after her. She ran off the road and got stuck in the bayou. I just got out and shot her through the window. Then I put my bumper against hers and pushed her the rest of the way into the water."

"You're pretty handy with a shotgun," I said.

"Shotgun, pistol, rifle." She patted her father's arm. "Papa used to call me his little tomboy."

"Rose," the old man groaned. "My God—"

"It's all right, Papa. It was that old Remington twelve-gauge you haven't used in years. There's no record of it. I dropped it off the bridge afterward. There's no evidence at all."

"You have to understand," Prescott said. "She isn't responsible. Rose was always different. They told us she was cured, and I thought when she married it would be all right, she'd grown up . . ."

"Papa, you really can't know," Rosemary said. "Philip Amadie was a perfect Jekyll-and-Hyde. A gentleman on the outside, an animal once the doors were closed. I couldn't tolerate it. Thank heavens it didn't last."

"Where's Philip now?" I asked, almost holding my breath for the answer.

"Oh, he's safe enough," she said breezily, but I saw her father flinch.

"Rose, you know Philip is dead."

"Yes, well, I suppose that's true. He died of gastroenteritis. At least, that's what they said."

Suddenly I remembered what Dogbite had said about Crane having a stomach virus. Crane, who'd had a slice of the pecan pie. Why should anyone have suspected poison?

"Did Philip eat one of your pecan pies by any chance?"

"Oh, Philip was a big eater. Indiscriminate. And he loved my cooking. I think I *did* make him a pie, now that you mention it."

"Rose . . ." The old man's voice was a whimper now.

I took a step toward her. "Rosemary, you know it's over, don't you?"

She frowned as if I'd said something foolish and shook her head.

"Perhaps. But, you see, Alan, it's not a question of whether it's over but how it ends."

I saw the little nickel-plated .25 then, pointing at my midsection.

"Would you just step back, please? I won't hesitate to shoot. Thank you."

I stepped back against the wall, and as I watched she came back along the opposite side of the room and slowly closed the door and put her back to it.

"After all, Alan, everyone must die. It's merely a question of when and how."

She was reaching down now, and to my horror I saw she was turning on the gas space heater by the wall.

"Rosemary . . ."

"If I let you leave this room alive, my father's life will have been for nothing. His memory will be destroyed. All for one small indiscretion."

"People will come looking for me."

"They'll come looking for all of us. But not immediately. I told the sitter to go home. It's your bad luck, Alan, that I left something and came back to get it. That's when she said you were here. But she won't be back until tomorrow and when she comes in, we'll all be dead."

"All of us?"

"Look at Papa. Do you think he really wants to live like this? As for me, what would I do without him? No, it's better we all go together. A match and this will all be over. One glorious explosion. An accident. There's no reason anyone should ever know about Papa's little mistake."

The gas was a steady hiss now and I'd broken into a sweat.

"Mr. Prescott, is this what you want?"

But the old man was oblivious, staring ahead with glassy eyes as if he were already gone.

"Rosemary, you're not going to keep this quiet. My people know I'm here. Do you really think I'd come here without telling anybody? How do you think I figured out it was you?"

"How *did* you figure it was me, Alan?"

"Once I figured your father was the man who catalogued the Fabré papers it was easy. I knew he must be old now and probably too sick, so who else could it be but another family member?"

"And that led to me."

"That and other things. The poison ivy you said you had on your arm after I went to the school that day. You said you got it on a field trip. I didn't think anything about it consciously. I thought October was kind of a strange time for field trips; when I was in school, we usually did them in late spring. But that was a long time ago. And I was looking for an obvious burn from the fire that almost killed us. But I guess my unconscious started working on it. I had a strange dream: I saw a character dressed in a Boy Scout uniform, and it was the result of something somebody said about our trip to the plantation being like a scout field trip. And I guess from there my mind jumped to your mention of a field trip and the poison ivy." I shrugged. "And my dog treed a possum."

"What?"

"Most people don't think of possums as being fierce, but I remembered how hard they fight to protect their young. And I wondered if our killer was protecting somebody."

"Clever."

"And then there was the box itself. My best guess was that the killer hadn't found it. Why not?"

"And what did you decide?"

"That maybe it was hidden in a place the killer couldn't go."

"Such as?"

"A beehive. You'd said something once about being allergic to bee stings."

"Oh, I am. I loved the outdoors, but a bee sting could give me a terrible reaction."

"Anyway, it all just sort of floated around in my subconscious and then it congealed."

Her smile hardened. "Where is the box, Alan?"

I nodded. "The D.A. has it. Also the map."

Rosemary Amadie stared at me a second longer and I thought she was going to pull the trigger, but instead she turned to look at her father.

"Then there really isn't any reason to keep on."

I waited. My eyes were heavy and I felt tired.

"It isn't fair, Alan. You know that. He deserves the credit, not you. You people had all the money of the U.S. government. All he had was the few dollars Charles Fabré paid him to sort through his collection of old papers. And yet my father found the truth. He made the discovery. But you were going to take it away from him. It's theft, Alan. You and your people are thieves as surely as if you'd stolen his soul."

"I didn't know your father existed," I said. "What was I supposed to do?"

"You people never think about men like my father. Don't you think I know how you feel about amateurs?" She smiled. " 'Here comes Rosemary Amadie. She's such a pest. You know she doesn't have any credentials.' I can just see what you're all thinking. And it was worse for my father. He was a true scholar. But all the university intellectuals can think about is publishing, getting tenure, moving on to the next faculty position."

"I'm not with the university, Rosemary. I'm in private business."

"Don't argue, Alan. It doesn't matter." She yawned. "Nothing matters now."

Maybe, I thought, *it doesn't. Nothing matters except resting . . .*

I let my eyelids close, then forced them back open.

No. It can't end this way.

I started toward her.

The little gun came slowly back up and wavered.

"Alan, I'll shoot."

The spark inside the gas-filled room would send us all sky-high.

". . . not a bad person, Alan, a gentleman, not like Philip.

He was an animal. I dreamed about you, though. Did you know that?"

I looked around for somewhere to go. A window to dive through. As if I could summon up the strength.

". . . another life, maybe it would have been different."

She was rambling now. She was closer to the heater. Maybe she'd lose consciousness first. She was already slumping down, back against the door.

I didn't have the strength to pull her out of the way.

". . . maybe shoot anyway, one big blaze, nice way to end it."

Nice?

"Alan?"

Screw you, you crazy bitch. I'm not going to answer. I won't play your game.

"Alan, are you in there?"

Pepper?

I opened my mouth and forced out a croak. "Pepper."

The door moved, hit Rosemary's body, stopped.

"Alan?" Pepper's voice again.

Rosemary's head raised.

"What . . . ?" The little pistol came up.

There wouldn't be another chance.

I willed my legs to move, lurched forward.

". . . going to shoot . . ."

I fell toward her, grabbing the hand with the automatic, forcing it away from my body.

The floor slammed my elbow and numbness lanced up my arm. The woman under me stirred, protested. I felt her body turning.

Don't let go with my left hand . . .

The door came partly open, hit my head.

"Alan?"

"Pepper." I felt the room spinning and heard myself talking far away: "Get the cipher . . . the Bible . . ."

Rosemary was on top of me now, we were two swimmers doing a slow-motion stroke, except that there was something cool washing against my face. Air from the next room, saving air . . .

Reviving her.

Her gun hand came down and with a last desperate effort

I pushed it away, pushed her off me, and struggled to my feet. She rolled backward and I used my last ounce of strength to lurch through the door, away . . . The pistol fired and there was a crash of thunder as the room exploded. The door buckled toward me and the lights went out.

■ THIRTY-TWO

I awoke in a hospital room, with Pepper leaning over the bed.

"He's awake," she said, and I heard a familiar voice say, "Thank God."

Esme appeared on the other side of the bed, Shelby Deeds looking over her shoulder.

"You've had a nice sleep, young man," the old historian said. "About time to get up and get back to work."

The door flew open and Sam MacGregor barged in, trailing a protesting nurse.

"He's my son. You can't keep me away. It's a matter of life and—oh, hello, Shelby. Alan, I was in the Rockies and heard you were dead."

"Exaggeration."

"That's a relief." Sam reached under his jacket, brought out a bottle of J. W. Dant, unscrewed the cap, and took a long pull.

"Now I feel better."

"You can't bring that in here," the rotund nurse warned, but Sam shushed her. "Go away. You're interrupting a religious observance."

"Somebody want to tell me what happened?" I asked.

"There are people in the hallway," the nurse protested. "There's a man with long hair sitting cross-legged on the floor and there's somebody with tattoos and—"

"Call security," Sam ordered. "The situation sounds desperate."

"Alan, what's going on?" David Goldman was in the room now, his sweat-stained T-shirt emitting an aroma that sent all heads in his direction. "I just came up from the Basin. Marilyn said you were dead."

"I wish," I groaned.

"Here," Sam said, handing me the bottle. "This will help."

I pushed the bottle away.

"The missing page . . ."

Pepper held up a piece of paper. "Do you believe in divine intervention?"

"What?"

"It's her way of telling you the damn thing was in the Bible," Sam said. "Nothing divine about it."

"When the door to the bedroom opened I saw the Bible lying there," Pepper said, "and I remembered what you said about getting the Bible, so I picked it up. The paper was inside. This is a photocopy, of course."

I forced myself upright in the bed. "Let me see."

She held it in front of me and I looked at the jumble of letters:

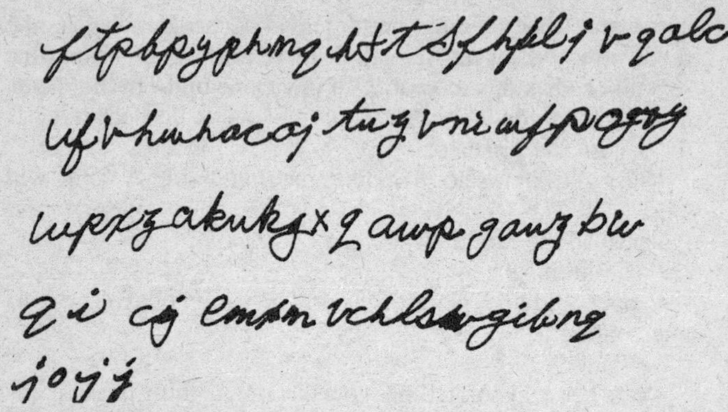

[handwritten cipher text]

"Anybody figured it out yet?" I asked.

Shelby cleared his throat. "We're working on it."

"Jefferson's cipher machine?" I asked.

"Jefferson, yes," Shelby confirmed. "Cipher machine, no."

"But it's the same principle," Esme said. "We think it has to be what they call a Vigenère cipher. It was invented four hundred years ago by a Frenchman named Blaise de Vigenère. It depends on a special word as the key to enciphering the message. Once the message is enciphered, the security is all but unbreakable."

"Or used to be," Sam said. "Nowadays, computers can break them. That's our next step."

"It will only work if you have a long enough text," Pepper said.

Esme put a hand on my shoulder.

"Poor Alan, we're wearing him out. Don't worry, we'll figure it out. You just get some sleep. All you need to know is we've found the documents and we know now who the old man was, and that's enough."

I slept. I dreamed. It was summer and the sweet smell of growing sugarcane cloyed the air. There was a thin thread of harpsichord music coming from the big house and as the old man toiled in the garden, the music brought back sharp images that startled and discomfited him. Like a kaleidoscope, they tumbled before him, until he fell over onto the ground, his head against the hard gumbo mud. Who were these girls, in their ball gowns? These men in carriages? What house was that, and in what distant place? Were these the shadows of his past or were they merely the intimation of approaching death?

He scrambled up onto his knees and shook his head to clear it.

Block away the hallucinations. Focus on what has to be done. Gather in the corn. The cabbages. The artichokes . . .

The next time I woke up the room was dark and only Pepper was there.

"They're gone," she said, "but it's nice to have friends."

"Yeah." I sighed. "The last thing I remember is trying to get the gun."

"The room blew up," Pepper said. "The door protected you, but Rosemary was still inside."

"Her father?"

"He didn't make it. I was out of the line of the blast. I managed to get you out. There isn't anything standing."

I shut my eyes. The memory was too strong to confront and I tried to block it out by focusing on something else. "How did you know where to find me?" I asked.

"It's complicated," she said vaguely. "We'll talk when you're better."

My head swam. I couldn't keep my train of thought. Then the strange message written by Meriwether Lewis crystallized in my mind and I tried to hold the focus.

". . . about the cipher . . . " I began.

Pepper smiled. "A man in the math department's working on it."

"Try artichokes," I said.

"What?"

"The key word. Try *artichokes*."

She shrugged. "Are you serious, or should I call the doctor?"

"Do you remember all the speculation about where the old man buried the box?"

"We thought at first he put it in his garden," she said.

"Because of his ramblings while he was dying," I told her.

"Right. He was talking about vegetables."

"Not just vegetables," I said. "One kind of vegetable."

"What?"

"Remember?" I prodded.

"Artichokes."

She came back hours later.

"It worked," she said, nodding. "*Artichokes* was the key."

I lay back against the pillow. "So simple."

She reached into her handbag, removed a sheet of paper, and handed it to me. I took it in one trembling hand and read the typed message:

Presdt. Thos. Jefferson

Dear Sir

I could not bring the documents with me for fear of Genl Ws spies. A full account of his acts I have buryd at the base of lrge oak tree 50 paces SE of blacksmiths cabn at Ft Pickrng. For sake of the Repub send Genl Clark for these papers as I may be done to death when you get this.

Wrttn on the 29th inst by Yr dvtd svt and friend, M. Lewis

"Of course," Pepper said, "I've added punctuation, but I've left his abbreviations the way he wrote them."

I reread the message and then let it fall onto my chest.

"So it was Wilkinson after all," I said.

"He thought so," Pepper said. "Shelby said Wilkinson was into all sorts of corrupt land deals when he was governor of Upper Louisiana, before Lewis came. He thinks Lewis may have found out some incriminating details. Maybe even had evidence of Wilkinson's treason, because there was a strong Spanish colony in St. Louis."

"And the map was Fort Pickering," I said.

"Right. And now it's part of Memphis."

"You mean . . ."

"I called an archaeologist up there," she said. "The old fort was pretty well demolished by Civil War breastworks and a moat a hundred and thirty-odd years ago. In fact, nobody's even sure just where it was."

"He encoded the message while he was at Pickering," I said. "Right after he buried the evidence. Something happened to make him fear for his life."

"Major Neelly appeared from nowhere and offered his services," Pepper said simply. "That's the only thing that makes sense."

Neelly, Russell, Grinder, Pernier . . .

The names swirled in my mind once more and whatever they'd given me to make me sleep was pressing my eyes shut. I felt her hand in mine and squeezed it to assure myself she was still there, but there was no holding off sleep. And as I slept I dreamed:

As the sun went down the man in the duster leaned back against the outer wall of the cabin, inhaled the smell of the wood fire, and took a sip of the whiskey the woman had provided. It was vile stuff, but it was what he was used to, and he needed it to keep his head level.

He was waiting for one man. He wasn't sure who it would be, but he knew that man would come.

Last night, at the camp near the mudhole, he hadn't slept: There was something about the Indian agent, Neelly, a restlessness. He'd fiddled with his gear, given the servants sidelong glances.

Are you the one? Well, you won't get me here.

Then, in the early hours of morning, the camp had been awakened by a halloa. The major was claiming two of the horses were loose, and in the morning he'd insisted on staying behind to find them. But the horses had been securely hobbled. What was the major trying to do? Was it part of a plan to meet his accomplices?

There was nothing to do but feign innocence, as if he suspected nothing. But the business was coming to a head. And he'd learned long ago, as a soldier, and then again with the Indians, that the only way to deal with a danger was to face it.

If only the danger had a face.

What if it was his man Pernier?

He'd pulled Pernier off the St. Louis docks, taken him into his home, and paid the doctor with his own money when the man was sick. Pernier professed to be grateful. But there was much that was mysterious about John Pernier, things the man said that did not ring true, as if he reinvented his story with every passing day. Worse, now he owed Pernier back wages, because he'd had to scrape together all he could put his hands on to make the Washington trip. Pernier had seemed satisfied. But lately he'd appeared restless, almost shifty. What if . . . ?

Then there was the woman. She said she was alone here, with her children, but how could he be certain? What if the general had sent a rider, paid off her husband? What if the husband was waiting in the woods, had his rifle leveled at this very moment?

The man wiped his forehead with an arm. The fever was coming back. He was getting the sweats. God, how could he fight this battle if he was going to be sick?

A sound on the trail caught his attention and he put his hand on one of the pistols in his belt.

Who . . . ?

The bushes parted and a pair of riders emerged. Which way had they come from? Why hadn't he noticed?

He rose, swaying, and drew both pieces.

The men took one look at him, turned their mounts, and spurred away.

"Is something wrong?" the woman called from behind him.

"No, madam." He stuck the pistols back into his belt and sat down again. "There's nothing wrong."

"Do you want some supper?"

He didn't answer and a few minutes later she handed him a plate with some corn gruel. He looked down at it.

What if she's poisoned it? It would be so easy to put something in it.

Don't be insane: You drank her spirits.

Maybe you were lucky. Don't take another chance.

He set the gruel aside.

"Someone else is coming," she said from behind him.

He looked up, reached for his pistols, and kept his hands on their butts as the sound of riders echoed across the clearing.

It was Pernier and Neelly's servant.

He stood up unsteadily and watched the men plod toward the house.

"Are you alone?" he hailed.

"Yes, sir," Pernier replied. "The major hasn't come."

"Do you have powder?" he asked, thinking it would be as well to be prepared.

"Yes, sir." Pernier looked perplexed.

The woman came forward and directed the young Negro boy to take the horses.

"They can stay in the stable," she said, and the traveler nodded. Safer for him to be alone. People had been shot in their beds.

Then he had second thoughts: If the woman was a part of it, she could be trying to isolate him.

But he was tired. His eyes were closing and he was already trembling from the fever. What could he do?

He followed her into the single room of the cabin.

"I'll fix your bed," she offered.

"Madam, I'm used to the floor," he said, nodding at the split-board flooring. "Have my man bring my bearskin."

Pernier handed in the skin.

"Governor Lewis, do you want me to stay with you?"

"No, sir, I do not."

"Governor—"

"Good night to you."

He closed the door, spread his bearskin, put his pistols on the floor beside him, and lay down.

God, how he craved sleep, and yet his mind would not be still. Instead, the speech he had so carefully prepared for the Secretary of War raced through his thoughts. He got up. Maybe if he paced a bit, practiced the speech, it would fatigue him enough to make him sleep.

He rose and began to articulate the words he'd prepared.

"Mr. Secretary, if my ruination were able to save the nation I would gladly give all that I own. But you must know that there is a grave danger . . ."

"Sir, are you well?"

It was the woman's voice, calling from outside the door. With a start he realized he'd been enunciating the speech aloud.

"I am well, madam."

He lay down again and this time, when the door opened slowly in the early hours of the chill morning, he was asleep.

The man Pernier awoke with a start: A gun had been fired outside. As he rose from his blanket another shot exploded nearby. He threw on his trousers, grabbed his pistol, and ran out into the chill mist. The woman was screaming now and there was a sound of struggle near the cabin where the governor was staying. When Pernier reached the cabin the door burst open and two men fell out onto the ground, their bodies locked together. One rose, a dagger in his hand, but Pernier knocked it away. The man swore, pulled a small pistol from his waistband, but Pernier fired at the man's head. The man coughed and fell onto the ground, writhing, his face a mass of blood and torn flesh.

Pernier looked down at the man's victim. Even in the grayness he could make out the face of Governor Lewis.

He leaned down, put his ear over the governor's mouth, and felt Lewis's breath. Ragged but present. The governor was still alive. But he was badly wounded, his head a mass of blood.

The woman came up then, holding a candle.

"In the name of God, what is it?" she cried, holding her shawl closed with a trembling hand.

Pernier seized the candle and held it near the dead man's face.

A stranger.

"Do you know him?" he demanded.

"No."

"Madam, do not lie."

"I swear by the Almighty."

"Then he was sent here."

"By whom?"

"Never mind. Madam, this is what we must do: We must undress this man and put his clothes on the man who still lives."

"Are you insane?"

But Pernier was already dragging the dead man around the end of the cabin.

A rush of footsteps announced Neelly's Negro servant, but Pernier blocked the man with his body.

"There has been a tragedy. You must ride back along the trail and find Major Neelly."

"A tragedy? But what?"

Pernier pointed at the fallen Lewis. *"The governor is dead."*

"Good Lord."

"Go!" Pernier commanded, and only when the man had saddled and ridden away did he turn back to the trembling Mrs. Grinder.

"Now listen to me. What I am telling you must be between us and your husband. The life of a great man depends on it."

The Grinder children and the Negro slave boy and girl were staring from the door of the other cabin now, and Pernier lifted Lewis under the shoulders and carried him to a spot away from their gaze.

"Help me change their clothes."

"But this makes no sense. The law—"

"I will represent the law. I promise you, madam, that I answer to people who can do you infinite good or harm. The man on the ground before you is the governor of the Upper Louisiana Territory. I was sent to protect him and I have failed. But I swear to God I shall not fail again. Where is your man?"

"On Swan River, twenty miles off. He sleeps there during harvest."

"Send the black boy for him. In the meantime, you and the girl must take this man to a safe place in the woods. When your husband comes, tell him what happened. Tell him that the government will pay a reward for his attentions. But this man must not die, nor must it be known that he has survived, else other assassins will be sent after him—and you."

"Before God, sir—"

"Madam, do as I say."

They unclothed both men and then dressed each in the other's garments. When they were done, Pernier asked for a shovel and, in a clearing a hundred yards from the cabins, dug a shallow grave.

It all hinged on Neelly, of course. The man was a drunkard and a coward. He had clearly dawdled in recovering the lost horses because he didn't want to be here when the deed was done.

It was on his cowardice that Pernier placed all his hopes. Now all Pernier could do was wait.

Neelly came just after dawn, unsteady in his saddle, leading the two pack animals, with his servant chattering away excitedly as they entered the clearing. Pernier got up and went to meet them.

"Pernier, what the devil's happened?" Neelly asked, slurring his words slightly.

Pernier assumed his servant's attitude.

"A terrible tragedy, Major, sir. The governor is dead."

"Dead? By God, man, how did it happen?"

There was a bit too much bluster in Neelly's tone, but Pernier could tell that it masked fear, and that was good.

"From all I can tell, sir, he destroyed himself."

"What?" The idea seemed to hit Neelly like a cannonball. "You mean . . . ?"

"I heard a terrible row, and shots, and we found the governor dying on the ground. His pistols had been discharged. He begged us to put an end to his pain."

"And he did this to himself?"

"It would appear so."

Neelly swayed and for an instant Pernier thought he was about to topple from the saddle.

"Did the woman see this?"

"Yes, sir. She says that he was talking to himself, that he all but admitted it after the shots, as he lay wounded."

"Where is she now?"

"Gone for her husband."

Neelly looked over at his own servant, but the man only shrugged.

"Where is the body?" the major asked.

"Buried," Pernier declared. "It seemed indecent to leave him exposed. I can show you the grave."

He walked ahead of Neelly's horse to the place where he'd dug the shallow grave and, reaching down, began to scrape away the dirt and stones with his hands.

Dear God, let him be too drunk to care. Let him be afraid. Let him be anything but a conscientious man . . .

His hands came to the body's clothing and he cleared away enough dirt to expose the leather coat the governor had been wearing, but which was now on the body of the man who had tried to kill him.

"Shall I go further?" he asked, and began to clear away the neck area, and then the head. The face, with its awful, disfiguring wound, had just been uncovered when Neelly cried out from his horse, "Stop. Enough. Cover him back up."

They returned to the cabins and Neelly dismounted, wavering in the morning sun.

"I'll have to make a report. I am the representative of the government here. Suicide, eh?"

Pernier went into the cookhouse, now deserted by the Grinder children, who had been herded away by their mother, and found a jug. He brought it out to the major.

"Something to drink, sir?"

Neelly grunted and yanked it out of the other man's hand.

It was easy to tell what he was thinking: The governor had been acting in a deranged fashion, had even talked about killing himself, so suicide would be a believable verdict. If the real murderer had gotten away, so much the better. There would be no outcry, no demand to punish the guilty. Yes, this would work out very well, and Neelly would collect his fee.

By midmorning Neelly was gone, on the way to Nashville with the news, and the woman had returned with her husband, a rough-looking man with a scowl.

"Keep the governor out of sight," Pernier ordered. "You will be paid. When he has recovered, an escort will be sent for him."

"And his things?" the man asked.

"The major took them on the packhorses. His personal belongings are to stay with him. I know of nothing of any importance."

"There's some land I'm looking to buy," the man Grinder said.

"Handle this and you'll buy it," Pernier promised. "But mind you this: When the inquest is held, you are to swear to the story I told you. The man in the grave is Governor Lewis. Show him to the justice of the peace, and then rebury him. But there must be no hint that Lewis lives."

Grinder, who did not look like a man who would be bothered by false swearing, nodded.

"I'll take him to the Chickasaws when he gets better. He was awake when I stopped to look at him."

"But saying crazy things," the woman said. "His head wound is terrible. I'm afraid it may have knocked all the sense out of him."

"Then take care of him until he regains it," Pernier said. "But I have a journey to complete."

And more mountains and forests and rivers to traverse, until he came to the hills of Virginia and the great white hall of Monticello and the man who waited inside for his report. He wondered what that man would say.

▰ EPILOGUE

It was the next day and I'd insisted on leaving the hospital. I was stiff, and there was a gauze bandage on my left arm where I'd been singed, but I was on the mend and it was fall, my favorite season, when the nip in the air made me feel alive and even young.

Pepper and I had driven over to Désirée and climbed the mound to stand by the old tombs. Nick DeLage had drawn in his claws and, I heard, was sulking in his office, now that it seemed likely that his aunt would have her ancestral property restored. Kech had backed off in the face of a potential embarrassment and was saying nothing, though I had already received what I considered an unconscionably large bill from Dogbite. Marvin Ghecko had come to visit me in the hospital and actually brought me a box of candy. Even La Bombast seemed reasonably mollified, though she made it clear that murders and near murders were no excuse for not meeting Corps deadlines.

I gazed down at the disheveled old brick crypts and the names that had started it all: *Charles Franklin Hardin, John Clay Hardin, Sarah Elizabeth Hardin, Louis* . . .

"You think Pernier was really working for Jefferson, then," she said.

"It's one scenario," I told her. "It could have happened a lot of ways. I just think Lewis survived Grinder's Stand and was hidden with the Indians, whoever arranged things."

"But Jefferson would have known."

"Probably."

"And he never did anything. Why?"

"For the same reason he protected Wilkinson," I said. "It would have opened a can of worms. Jefferson was a politician. He decided to let sleeping dogs lie. The country was on the verge of another war with England, Spain was hovering in the west . . . He opted for the lesser evil."

"What a terrible decision to have to make. But why would Lewis have left the Chickasaws?"

"We can't know. Maybe he was found out and somebody else tried to kill him. Remember the story about Pernier killing himself?"

She nodded.

"Maybe they chased down Pernier and killed him and then did some digging into the facts around the case and decided to make sure Lewis was really dead."

"Or maybe Jefferson started the rumor about Pernier's dying to help him disappear and get away from them," she suggested.

"Could be." I looked out at the brown waters. "I like to think Lewis, even with amnesia, had some kind of memory of the documents he buried at Pickering and set out to get them."

"And lost his way?"

"Something like that. Or he may have fallen in with a crowd that left him in Natchez, instead of his taking the trail north to Pickering. The important thing is he ended up on the river and, eventually, in it. Maybe courtesy of another one of Wilkinson's friends."

"Alan . . ." There was alarm on her face. "What if he wasn't amnesic at all?"

"You mean what if he and Pernier cooked up the whole business?"

"Yes. What if it was a way to protect Lewis until he could escape from his enemies? What if, when he realized Jefferson wasn't going to help him, he just gave up?"

I nodded. It was the one scenario I'd tried to put out of my mind.

"He belongs here," I said. "It's where he ended up spending most of his life. But I guess there'll be a push to disinter him now."

"Not exactly," Pepper said.

"What do you mean?"

"We did some preliminary examinations yesterday—myself, David, and Marvin Ghecko—just to see what we could see . . ."

"And?"

"There aren't any bones in there."

"What?"

She shrugged. "You know how these old tombs are. The bricks fall out, the concrete crumbles, and animals go to work."

"An animal got the remains?"

"Or someone else took them."

"Like Flowers?"

Another shrug. "I don't know. I just know they aren't there."

"Jesus. And that means the only way to really prove it would be to disinter the remains at the national monument in Tennessee, and the Park Service isn't about to allow that."

"No. They have a vested interest in ignorance."

I sighed. "That's a hell of a thing."

"A hell of a thing," she repeated. "Alan . . ."

She half turned to face me, but I was still staring at the broken bricks.

"Hey, do you know what day this is?" I asked.

"It's Saturday."

"The tenth of October," I said. "The day he came to Grinder's. A hundred and eighty-nine years ago exactly." ·

"Alan . . ."

Her hand found mine and squeezed and I raised my head to look into her eyes.

"There's something I have to say."

A little chill ran through me. It had been too good to be true.

"I'm listening."

"Alan, sometimes people hurt other people when they aren't honest. But they aren't honest sometimes because they don't want to hurt people. Does that make sense to you?"

"What are you trying to say?"

"Like Shelby: He told us somebody ran him off the road on the way to Tennessee. But he admitted to Esme yesterday that he really *had* been drinking. The first time since he went on the wagon. It was because he was scared of seeing Dorcas again. He felt too much for Esme and yet he didn't know what seeing Dorcas would bring back. So unconsciously he figured a way to keep from having to see her. And lied because he didn't want to hurt anybody that cared about him.''

"I wondered about that," I said. "But he seems okay now."

"That's not what I'm trying to say. Alan, I haven't been completely honest with you about something, either."

She'd waited for me to get out of the hospital to lower the boom . . .

"Pepper . . ."

She put a hand on my arm. "I blew you off when you asked how I found you at Rosemary's. I thought maybe I could keep from having to answer. But if I lied it would just complicate things."

I nodded. "So how did you come to find me there?"

"I followed you. I woke up and you weren't there. Then I heard you downstairs, so I slipped on my jeans. By that time you were already leaving. Something about the way you pulled out of the driveway made me decide I'd better follow. And when I saw you go inside that house I knew it must be something important. I kind of blundered in because I was scared for you."

"I'm glad you did."

"But that's not why I followed you. I followed because you seemed so furtive. It was like you were running away, and I was scared. I've been left before."

"Your brother and your father," I said and she nodded. Suddenly she seemed very vulnerable, not at all like the self-assured women I'd met a year before.

She stopped and removed her sunglasses.

"I've got some hangups, Alan. I tried not to get close to you because I didn't know how it would work. I still don't know. But if you want to try . . ."

I pulled her to me then and we kissed for a very long time. When we finished, I took her hand and led her down the mound and away from the tombs.

▰Author's Note

The unexplained death of Governor Meriwether Lewis, as recounted in this novel, is a fact, as is the treason of General James Wilkinson. The Jefferson cipher is also a part of history. A number of explanations have been offered for Lewis's demise, ranging from suicide to murder, and there is still no scholarly consensus. Recently, a second inquest was held and a plea was made to disinter Lewis's body. Perhaps by the time this book is published this will have been done. In the meantime, the truth will remain buried at Grinder's Stand.

Malcolm K. Shuman